Romancing the Dog

Romancing the Dog

Everyone Loves Zelda
Love Between the Vines
Love on the Links

Three romance novellas
by
Marjorie Pinkerton Miller

SUNACUMEN
PRESS
PALM SPRINGS, CA

Cover art by vanda_g/istock.com
Cover design, interior formatting by Sunacumen Press

ISBN: 978-1-7345643-5-8
Printed in the United States of America

Contents

To Chrissy Meyer, the world's best beta-reader

Everyone Loves Zelda

One

THE DAY SHE LEFT PARIS, Julie thought she had the rest of her life figured out.

André would follow her to Seattle as soon as his boss hired his replacement, and they would get married. She would take over her parents' wine shop in the market. She would get Zelda back, and the big dog would live a long and happy life with them.

Some of that worked out. Some of it didn't.

Sitting at their favorite patisserie the morning before her flight, Julie and André kept to the routine they'd developed over the past fourteen months. They held hands, drank espressos, and split a buttery croissant. The only change was the suitcase that sat under their table.

"What time is your flight?" André asked for the tenth time.

Julie rolled her eyes but smiled. "A little after eleven. I need to leave soon."

"I can drive you."

"No. That's silly. Driving in Paris is an exercise in attempted suicide."

"You are not accustomed. Parisians are not so afraid."

"Still, I'll take a cab. You need to get to work. Aren't you working the lunch shift?"

"Yes." André squeezed her hand and paused. His eyes sought hers. "I'll miss you, Julie."

"I'll miss you too, André." She looked at her watch again. "Do you have any news about when you'll be able to come over?"

"I'll get there as soon as I get a visa and they find someone at the restaurant to replace me."

Julie nodded. His answer was always the same.

She stood and threw the long strap of her purse over her head and across her chest. "I should go. I'll text when I get there. It will be too late here to call."

André walked to the door and held it open for her. At the curb, he hailed a taxi and put her bag on the seat next to her. As she ducked in, he leaned forward for a quick kiss.

"*Je t'aime.*"

"I love you too."

TWELVE HOURS LATER, JULIE WALKED out under the long overhang of the arrivals curb at Seatac and shivered. She'd forgotten about the rain. How could she? She'd lived in Seattle her entire life. She knew it rained from September through June, and yet this dreary drizzle caught her by surprise, and then she felt a wave of nostalgia.

"Yes," she whispered. "This is home."

She took note of the number over the terminal door she'd just exited and texted it to her brother. Just minutes later, he pulled up at the curb in his ancient SUV and jumped out, grinning effusively.

"Hi, big sis! How'd it go? Can we keep you down on

the farm now that you've seen Paree?"

Julie laughed. Of course, he'd say that.

"I'm back, aren't I?" She leaned in for a kiss on the cheek and let Cary put her suitcase in the back for her.

"Did you like it there?" he asked as he pulled out into the traffic lane. "Mom said you got a boyfriend."

"Well, I did meet someone. We're talking about getting married, but he has to come to the U.S. first."

Cary glanced over with his eyebrows pinched.

"But you won't go back, will you?"

"After getting stuck there with the pandemic, I think it will be a while before I want to go overseas again. I got a little homesick."

Taciturn as ever, Cary just nodded and drove north toward the interstate in silence. The rain on the windshield was just heavy enough to require intermittent wiping, and the rhythm lulled Julie into a daze. She shook her head to wake up. She was tired, but it was only two o'clock, and she needed to force herself back onto Pacific time.

"How are things with you, Care Bear?" she asked Cary. "Are you working?"

"I started a new job two weeks ago. So far, so good." He looked at Julie and winked. "But you know that doesn't mean much," he said. Julie nodded. They both knew that it was probably only a matter of time before it wouldn't be "so good."

"Where?"

"An Amazon warehouse in Redmond."

Julie nodded appreciatively. "Good benefits. But hard work, isn't it?"

"Hard work is never my problem. My problem is stupid bosses. So far, this woman seems okay. If she stays out of my face, we'll get along fine."

"But isn't that what bosses do? Get in your face?"

Cary chuckled and nodded. He sped up to pass a truck

that was spraying a cloud of mist at them. "Yeah, that's why I have trouble dealing with them."

"Well, good luck with this one. I know it would make Mom feel a lot better if you stick with it."

"So, what are your plans, sis?"

"First, I'm going to get Zelda from whoever is fostering her. Then, the store. I've got to get back into the swing of things before Mom and Dad retire in a couple of months. And I'll need to hire someone. I can't do it all myself."

"Good luck to you too. I couldn't work for Dad if my life depended on it."

Julie knew that was true. She got along with her father fine. She let him remind her he was boss because he seemed to need to, and she didn't fight it. But for Cary, it had always been a test of wills.

"Well, then, it's a good thing that you haven't had to," she said.

"Was that some kind of a shot?"

As much as he made fun over his inability to hold a job or suffer authority, Cary bristled when others did. She reached over and put her hand on his arm.

"No, little brother. It wasn't. It's not easy to work for your parents. Not for anyone. But probably easier for me than it would be for you. And I love the wine business."

"For that, I'm jealous. You've always known what you wanted to do," Cary said with a wag of his head. "Must be nice."

Julie looked out the window at the familiar passing scenery and wondered if she always knew what she wanted to do, or if she'd always been told. "I'm not so sure about that. But it's a place to start."

JULIE LEFT HER SUITCASE INSIDE the door of her apartment without opening it.

"First things first," she told herself.

She pulled her cellphone out of her purse and pulled down her contact list and then her veterinarian's name.

"I'm back!" she announced when Glenda answered.

"Hey, Julie! How was it? Was Paris everything it's supposed to be?"

"Well," Julie paused. How much did she want to reveal about André before he showed up in Seattle? If he never showed up, how embarrassed would she be?

"It was great. I didn't intend to stay so long, but you know what happened."

The noise in Glenda's clinic reminded Julie how busy the place was, so she got to the point.

"I'm ready to pick up Zelda. Can you tell me who is fostering her for me?"

Glenda retrieved the name and number for Julie and read them to her.

"Thanks, Glenda. I appreciate it."

"We should get together so you can tell me all about your trip."

Julie was surprised. "Sure. Maybe we can meet for a cocktail some evening, once I get settled again and figure out how to manage the store."

Julie knew that it was unlikely. She'd taken Zelda to Glenda since she first adopted the big dog, but she and the veterinarian had never become friends.

Immediately after they hung up, Julie dialed the number she got from Glenda. An answering machine picked up, and Julie left a message.

"Hi, Jon. My name is Julie. I got your name and number from Glenda, my vet. She said you are fostering Zelda, my dog. I'm back from France, and I'd like to pick her up sometime soon. Please give me a call. Thanks! Oh, and thanks for taking care of her while I was gone. I hope she wasn't too much trouble."

Two

JULIE HUNG UP THE WRINKLED dress from her suitcase and threw the rest of the clothes she had unpacked into a laundry basket. If she washed the wrinkles out, she could avoid a bunch of ironing.

She closed the empty suitcase and put it in the deepest corner of the closet. She hoped she wouldn't be needing it again for a while. It was good to be home.

Her cellphone buzzed, its tone muted by the comforter on the bed where she'd laid it. The caller ID showed it was the number she had called earlier, looking for Zelda.

"Hello?"

"Hi, this is Jon, the guy who adopted Zelda. I'm returning your call—"

"Oh, thanks for calling back," Julie interrupted. She couldn't contain her excitement over seeing Zelda soon. "Thanks so much for taking care of Zelda. Can I come and get her?"

"As I was trying to say, I'm returning your call as a courtesy. But I can't let you have Zelda. She's my dog now."

Julie twirled and sat down on the bed hard. She shook her head.

"No. She's my dog," she said, trying to keep her voice calm. "The vet asked you to foster her, not adopt her."

"But you've been gone more than a year. What did you expect?"

"I didn't expect to be gone so long."

"Well, you were. Zelda's been with me too long now," he said, his voice stern. "You have to let her go."

Julie took a deep breath, her heart pounding. This couldn't be happening!

"Look. I'm sorry. I expected to be gone only a few months."

"So, what happened?"

Julie hesitated. Did she have to explain herself to this man intent on stealing her dog? If that's what it took, she decided, she would.

"Well, I took an apprenticeship with a sommelier in Paris to learn French wines. My parents own a wine store here, and I expect to take it over soon. They thought it would be great experience for me to go overseas and see if I could pick up some wine smarts. I was only going to be gone for six months."

"So why the year?"

"And when the pandemic hit, I couldn't come home. So I ended up hanging out longer."

Jon made a dismissive snort. "I hope you had a great time. But Zelda is mine now. I can't give her up."

"But you agreed to foster." Julie heard the whine in her voice and lowered it. "That means you give up the dog when the owner returns."

Jon paused; perhaps he was considering her logic.

"Yes, I was going to foster," he said instead. "But hear

me out. My dog died from cancer just two months after he and I got back from Iraq. We had been there together for four years. I missed Milo so much I was afraid to give my heart to another dog. My vet—Glenda, I guess you know her—asked if I'd foster Zelda. I didn't know how attached we were going to get. And Glenda said it would only be a few months. But it was more than a year."

The story disarmed Julie. "Uh, well ... thanks for your service. I think military dogs are so great. But I love Zelda. I've missed her so much. And she's mine. I didn't plan the pandemic."

Jon chuckled. "No one did. But if I remember right, people have been coming back from Europe all the time."

Julie tried to rein in her anger. She was getting impatient with this conversation. There was no question. Zelda was hers; always was and always would be.

"Yes, I suppose some people found a way to come back. But I had another reason to stay."

"What was that?"

"It's really none of your business."

"Not much of an argument."

"Okay." Julie exhaled with exasperation. Who was this Jon and why did he think he had the right to hear her explanation? Whether she had one or not didn't change the fact that Zelda was her dog. "His name is André."

Now Jon laughed. "What? Who's André?"

"The man I fell in love with."

"Ohhhhhh." His tone was condescending. "Oh, now it's making sense. And where is André now?"

"Back in France. He's waiting to get a visa so he can come here. We plan to get married."

"Oh. Then I think you should wait till André gets here and you guys can go and get another dog. The way I see it, you traded Zelda for André. And now you're not happy with the bargain."

10

Julie was getting frantic. She didn't expect any debate, and this argument was going on far too long. Perhaps if she pretended to compromise, she could get Zelda back.

"Please. You have to at least let me see her. You'll see how much she loves me."

Jon was stern again. "I don't think so."

"Why not?"

"It will just confuse her."

"Oh, come on. Dogs don't register 'confused.'"

"Shows how little you know about dogs. Or Zelda."

"Please." She switched to pathetic pleading. "I had Zelda for three years before you got her. You've only had her for a year."

"Fourteen months."

"Whatever. Please!"

Jon hesitated for a moment, and Julie started to hope he'd relent.

"I'm sorry, but this conversation is over," he said instead. "And don't you try to stalk us. I'll call the police."

The line disconnected. Julie stared at the phone in disbelief and lay back on her bed, her face in her hands.

"Wow. What a jerk!"

JULIE ACCEPTED HER MOTHER'S INVITATION to dinner that evening. She hadn't had a chance to stock up on groceries, and she was too distraught over Zelda to sit in a public restaurant.

She found her mother in the kitchen of her childhood home and gave her a big hug.

"I'm so happy you're finally home," her mother cried, her arms around Julie. "Did you feel trapped?"

"I had my moments, my panic attacks, but André helped. If it hadn't been for him, I would probably have figured out a way to get back sooner."

"Well, your dad and I wished you had."

"Yes, but André and I wouldn't be engaged if I'd come home right away." Julie thought her reasoning was sound until she said it out loud. Her mother reached over and grabbed Julie's left hand and lifted it into the air for inspection.

"Engaged, huh?" Her mother sniffed. "I don't see a ring. Or don't they do that over there?"

Julie pulled her hand back. "We decided to get married right before I left. He didn't have time. Anyway, rings, diamonds. Whatever. You don't need them to get engaged."

"You'll have plenty on your mind for the next few weeks as your dad and I retire and head for Alaska." Her mother gave a dismissive wave and turned back to the loaf of bread she was slicing. "So, if it takes André a while to get here, that might be for the best. You should go say hi to your dad. He's in the TV room with Cary."

A few minutes later, Julie rejoined her mother in the kitchen to help her bring the food to the dining room table. As they set the dishes down, Cary and her father pulled out their chairs and sat.

Such an American scene, Julie thought. She'd missed these family dinners, even though at one time, she'd been impatient with their routine. She picked up the wine bottle from the buffet and filled their glasses before sitting down.

"Have you gone to get Zelda yet?" her mother asked as she started passing the dishes around. "You could have brought her here, you know. We've missed her so much."

Julie fought back a sudden rush of tears—tears that she'd held back all afternoon, nurturing her anger with the man who held Zelda captive instead.

"I don't know what to do." She sniffed and stood up to grab a Kleenex off the dining room bureau. "The guy who fostered her won't tell me where he lives, and he won't give her back. He says she's his now."

Cary threw up his hands theatrically. "But wasn't he

12

just supposed to foster her until you came back?"

"Yes! I called him but he said he won't give her up," Julie said. "He said I was gone too long."

"Did you explain the situation?" her mother asked.

Exasperated at the obvious answer, Julie retorted a bit more strongly than she intended. "Yes, of course I did. But he said he had lost his dog and didn't think he wanted a new one right away. He didn't think he'd ever love another dog. But you know, everyone loves Zelda."

"Just go get a new dog," her father said. He appeared more focused on choosing just the right pieces of chicken off the platter than on the conversation. "There's lots of them in the pound who need homes. That's where you found Zelda."

Julie, her mother, and Cary all stopped what they were doing and looked at him with disbelief. Had he just suggested group suicide, it would have shocked them no more. Her father felt the tension and looked up.

"What? What did I say?" he asked, looking from one to the other. He received three disgusted looks but no answer.

Julie's mother shook her head. "Pay no attention to him. He's never understood dogs. Why don't I ask my sister if there isn't some law?"

"Mom, I can't afford to bring a lawyer into this. I'll figure this out—"

Cary cut her off. "I'll steal her for you. I'll figure out where he lives, and I'll case the joint and when he's not there, I'll grab her."

Their mother pointed her fork menacingly at him.

"Cary, you're not going to risk another misdemeanor over this. I thought you'd turned over a new leaf."

Cary looked sheepish. "I'm just trying to help." He held up his glass of wine, as if in atonement. "By the way, Mom, this is pretty good. Is it Willamette Valley pinot?"

"Yes. Good guess." His mother seemed pleased.

"It's not a guess, Mom. I have a pretty good palate, thanks to you." He tipped his glass at her.

"Ha! Look at you. So sophisticated all the sudden," Julie said, laughing and slugging him in the shoulder.

"Mom made me do all the wine tastings while you were gone," Cary explained. "I guess she thought I was handsome enough to pull it off."

He leaned over to Julie and pretended to share something confidential. "And, I'll tell you. It was a pretty good gig. Lots of really nice young women come to wine tastings."

"Fun, fun, fun," his father mocked. "That's all you think about, Cary. The wine business isn't about pretty young women."

He turned to Julie. "Forget the dog, dear. You need to concentrate now on catching up at the store. Your mom and I expect to retire in three weeks."

"I will, Dad, but I love Zelda, and I have to get her back first."

Cary interjected. "My offer remains."

"Shut up, dummy," Julie said. "We're not going to commit a felony together. I'll figure something out."

"Back to the store," her father said. "Are you coming in tomorrow?"

Three

"Three Maison Bleue Frontiere Syrah, 2017," Julie called out from where she kneeled in front of the bottom shelf of a rack of wine. "And one Graviere Syrah, also 2017."

Her mother checked the bottles off on the list. She held the clipboard in one hand and a pen in the other and let her arms fall to the side. She shook her shoulders to loosen the strain from the second full day of taking inventory.

"Boy, this is tiring," she said, exhaling a big breath. "I don't remember it ever being this hard."

"Well, it is the first time you're doing inventory at age 65," Julie said. There was no compassion in her voice.

"I did it at 64."

"So now you're a year older. Let's start on cabs."

Julie's mother stared at her daughter and shook her head. "No, let's take a break."

Julie hoisted herself up on one of the stools they kept behind the checkout counter and pouted while her mother went into the back to get a cup of coffee and returned.

"What's with you today? I used to count on a little enthusiasm from you. I may be cranky because I'm old and tired, but you don't have an excuse."

Julie shrugged and didn't answer. She stared into the distance, out the big store windows to the street. The rain had stopped, but it was still a dreary mid-50s, one of those June days that seemed to portend that summer would never come.

"Chin up, girl," her mother said, pulling herself onto the stool next to Julie. "You seem so sad. No luck with Zelda yet?"

Julie shook her head. "I haven't figured anything out yet. I called Glenda back and she said she'd talk to Jon."

"Who?"

"The guy who has Zelda. And meanwhile, I've been too busy trying to get my new phone and cable set up and restarting mail and stuff. But I plan to do nothing this weekend but work on getting her back."

"Aren't you going to work on Saturday?"

"Mom, I really have to do something. If I had any inkling I had lost Zelda, I'm not sure I would have come back."

"Did Glenda have any ideas?" Her mother sipped her coffee noisily, adding to Julie's irritation.

"No, and she wouldn't give me Jon's address. She said it violated privacy rules." Julie leaned forward on her elbows and hid her face in her hands.

"You weren't planning to take Cary up on his offer to steal her, were you?"

"No, but I thought if I could stop by he would see how much Zelda loves me, maybe it would change things. And I tried texting him, but he hasn't responded."

"Well, perhaps your dad is right. Maybe you should just find another Zelda. You can't be such a sad sack when André gets here or he'll wonder why he came."

16

Julie's phone rang, and she glanced at the caller ID. Her face brightened.

"I'm going to go in the back to get this. It's André. I've been calling and texting him, but I couldn't get through."

"Sure, dear."

Julie pushed through the swinging door to the warehouse and office space in back of the store.

"André!"

"*Mi amor*! I see your text. Is everything good there? Your flight was okay?"

"Yes, but I miss you André. I can't wait for you to get here. Do you have any idea when you can come?"

"You must be patient, *mi amor*. Jacque is looking for a new sous chef to replace me. As soon as he finds one, I'll get my ticket and come." André was calling from Paris, but the reception was so clear it made Julie's heart ache. He sounded like he was next door.

"So you got your visa?" she asked.

"Turns out, I don't need a visa yet. I just have to pack and get my ticket."

"But you can do that now, right?"

"But no hurry. I'll do it as soon as I know when I can leave."

"You are coming, aren't you?"

Julie knew she sounded desperate. Her apartment felt empty and sullen with the constant drizzle and the absence of Zelda.

"*Oui, petite*! I will call you as soon as I make plans. How are your parents?"

"Fine. They want to meet you. I hope you get here before they leave on their sailboat."

"And I want to meet them. But I must go now. Jacque has me closing the restaurant tonight, but I wanted to catch you while I could."

"I'm so glad you called—"

"*Bientot!*" he said, not waiting for her to finish. "*Ciao!*" The line disconnected.

Julie let the hand that held the phone drop to her side and walked back into the front of the store.

"You don't look happy, my dear," her mother said.

"Sometimes I wonder if André is really coming. He doesn't seem to be in much of a hurry."

"It's a big change, honey. Give him some time. Maybe he has things to work out before he leaves. Now, we need to get to work. If we're going to sign this store over to you, we need to get this inventory done and finish the rest of the paperwork. Your father's eager to get on the boat. You know he's been wanting to sail to Alaska forever."

"Alaska's not going anywhere, Mom."

"Yes, but we can't go if we aren't out of here by the end of June. We can't sail in the winter, you know."

Julie sighed. "Yes, let's get back to it." Julie locked her fingers behind her back and stretched her arms out, her chest thrust forward. "The sooner we finish this miserable task, the happier we'll both be."

JULIE MET ANDRÉ AT THE restaurant in Paris where she was studying under the sommelier in the dining room and he was working in the kitchen as a sous chef.

At first, she barely noticed him—just another young, pretty French man in tight pants and a stark, asymmetrical haircut that looked like it was meant to communicate edginess and trendy-restaurant *savoir faire*. She actually snorted to herself derisively the first time she saw him across the serving counter.

"What's that mean?" the sommalier asked.

Julie was embarrassed that he had overheard her.

"*Rien*," she said, shaking her head. "Just a little sinus problem."

"*Vraiment?*" he asked, smiling as if he agreed with her

assessment. He nodded at André. "He might be a bit of a dandy, but he's going places. Chef thinks he'll be famous one day."

Working until close at a restaurant is a recipe for tryst-building in Paris, as it is anywhere, Julie soon learned. The staff sat on the high stainless-steel tables in the kitchen into the early morning, draining bottles of Champagne and fine wine, munching on leftovers from the evening's specials. Only the most dedicated bachelors and single women and a few married employees avoided some kind of entanglement for long.

At first, Julie was able to keep her romance with André hidden, but another truism of the restaurant business is how hard it is to keep secrets. Everyone knew everyone else's business, whether financial, romantic, or familial.

When her six-month stay was extended by the pandemic, their affair was just starting to heat up. The virus and the difficulty of travel gave her an excuse to postpone her return again and again. But eventually, the excuses wore out, as did her patience with all things French. She was homesick and she missed Zelda.

Just before she left for Seattle, André's indifference to their seperation suddenly morphed into a sorrow he could not abide. He proposed marriage. Surprised, Julie took a few days to try to figure out what had happened between them, examine his motives, and to consider the idea. But, enchanted by the idea of bringing home a successful, good-looking fiancé, she shed her suspicions and said yes.

JULIE STEPPED OFF THE BUS and turned to walk up the hill. It was only a couple of blocks to her apartment building, but in her mood, the incline felt like Mount Everest. Head down, she wondered how much of her exhaustion was due to jet lag and how much was due to everything that had gone wrong since she got back.

She had tried to talk her parents into digitizing their inventory and computerizing their business systems for the past two years, but they weren't interested. Now they were trudging through their usual two weeks of annual inventory with pencil and paper, and she had another two weeks of entering the information onto an old Excel spreadsheet that was her mother's idea of modern bookkeeping. André seemed to be stalling when it came to following her to Seattle, and so far, she'd had no luck in getting Jon to pay attention to her pleas for Zelda.

Looking up before crossing the street, she noticed a man walking ahead of her, heading up the same hill, with a dog that looked just like Zelda—a big brown, black, and white Australian Shepherd mix. Was she going crazy? Was every dog going to look to her like Zelda from now on?

She ran ahead, gaining on them until she was sure it wasn't an illusion. It was Zelda. It had to be.

"Zelda!" she yelled. "Is that you, Zelda?!"

The dog stopped and turned. In less than a second, Zelda recognized Julie and started barking. She pulled on her leash and yanked it out of the man's hand.

Too late, he turned to catch Zelda, but she was too fast. Julie put down her grocery bag and purse and knelt down, anticipating all 80 pounds of Zelda crashing into her. She knew how easy it was for Zelda to knock a person over.

"Oh my god, Zelda!" Julie cried as the dog nuzzled her and pranced in her hug. "I was so worried. I thought I'd never see you again!" Tears ran down her face, and Zelda lapped them up with her big tongue.

The man walked back toward them and stood a few paces away. Julie looked up at him with Zelda still wiggling in her embrace.

"You must be Jon. See? See how much she loves me?"

Jon stood and watched for a long minute. Finally, as Zelda started to settle down, he called, "Zelda! Come here!"

Zelda waddled over to him, still dancing from happiness, and Jon picked up the end of her leash. Julie stood, brushed off the knees of her jeans, and picked up her purse and groceries.

"Don't tell me," he said, a snarl in his voice. "You are Julie. You're stalking me. I told you I'd call—"

Julie held out her free hand. "No! I wasn't stalking you. I was walking home." She pointed to her apartment building a hundred yards ahead. "I live right there!"

"Where?" he said, spinning around to see where she was pointing. "In my building?"

"I don't know what building is yours. Honest. I'm not stalking you! I live in 1256. Do you?" She wiped her face with the back of her hand, but the tears still fell.

Jon turned back to her, his frown gone. Replacing it was a sheepish grin. "Yeah. I do. I guess we're neighbors."

Zelda pulled Jon back toward Julie, still wiggling with excitement. It would have taken a zombie, Julie thought, to not see how much Zelda loved her. The dog nuzzled her head between Julie's knees, and Julie bent down to scratch her head with her free hand.

"Oh, Zelda," she said through her tears. "I missed you so much! Will you ever forgive me?"

"Well, this is unfortunate," Jon said. He didn't seem as oblivious to Julie and Zelda's happiness as he was irritated by it.

"Why would you say that? I think it's serendipity!"

Jon shook his head and looked away.

"We have to talk," Julie said, finally gaining control over the waterworks on her face. "Look, it's clear that Zelda missed me. If you really love her like you say, you wouldn't want her to be hurt, would you?"

Jon turned back to face her. "Why? You say you love her and you left. That probably hurt her."

"Come on, Jon. We have to talk about this seriously.

Let's pick some neutral territory and figure this out. I don't want to have to call a lawyer or something."

Jon laughed at that with an exuberance that confused Julie. Why would that be so funny?

"A lawyer, huh?" he said.

"Oh, please, don't make me do it that way. We don't need to make this a supreme court case, do we? Can't I at least see her some until we get this worked out?"

Jon's laughter stopped and for the first time, he seemed to take a good look at Julie. She wiped the last of her tears away and returned his stare. He was handsome in a boyish kind of way. She had trouble placing his age, but his full lips, freckles, and long red curls probably made him look much younger than he was.

His steady gaze didn't bother her. Julie knew she was pretty. Even if her mascara and eyeliner were now smudged or streaming down her cheeks, she had a face like the girls next door of the 1950s movies. She knew it disarmed men, and she tried not to take advantage of it when it wasn't necessary.

Now it seemed necessary, and she smiled at him charmingly and reached up to fluff the curls of her long, brunette hair. An involuntary smile crept across his face, and he turned away, as if to make it stop.

"Okay. I can see how much you mean to her. Maybe we can go for a walk with her sometime. We can talk this over."

"Great. That's great." Julie wanted to sound grateful, but Zelda was her dog, and she shouldn't need to beg for a chance to see her. Still, this was progress.

"How about in the park around the corner? Tomorrow morning?" he asked.

Julie didn't want to sound pushy, but she needed to nail down his commitment before he disappeared behind his apartment door with Zelda. "How about tonight? Why not now?"

Jon shook his head. "I'm sorry I have company for dinner tonight. A nice woman who I'm happy to say likes Zelda very much."

Horror swept across Julie's face.

"You're not considering another mom for Zelda, are you? That's just—"

Jon chuckled at her desperation. "Well, I haven't proposed or anything. We just met two weeks ago."

"Well, good," Julie said, relieved. "I could watch Zelda while you guys have dinner tonight."

Jon shook his head and turned to continue up the walk.

"She *is* my dog, you know," Julie called after him.

"I'm not so sure. Isn't possession nine-tenths of the law?"

"Not when it comes to kids and dogs."

Jon turned again, smiling broadly at that. "You just made that up."

"No." She tried to look serious, but his smile was contagious. "Yes. But okay. Park tomorrow morning. How about six?"

"Most nights I work until two. Two a.m., that is. Six isn't in my wheelhouse. Can we do it later?"

Julie scrambled. She needed to make her case as soon as possible. What if Jon moved away? Or his new girlfriend took Zelda to keep her from Julie.

"Well, I've got to go to work at nine. But, how about noon? I'll try to get away from the store for an hour."

Jon nodded. Clearly, she wasn't going to give up. "Okay. Noon it is. We'll see you there. Say goodbye, Zelda."

He turned again to walk away, and Julie laughed and caught up with them.

"I'm walking with you, you know. We live in the same building. You can't get away from me that easy."

Four

THE NEXT NOON, JULIE WALKED to the park from the bus stop, her arm hooked through her brother's. Cary spotted Jon and Zelda first and pulled them in the right direction. Julie waved and Zelda turned toward them, wiggling with excitement.

As they drew near, Cary stuck out a hand to shake.

"Hi, I'm Cary."

Jon looked confused and stood back. "Another boy-friend? Didn't she trust me?"

He turned to Julie. "And what does André think of this?"

"No," Julie said, surprised that he remembered André's name. "Cary's my brother. Moral support. The boyfriend is in France, remember?"

Jon looked Cary over as if he were evaluating him for a job. He smiled, perhaps having decided Cary was a suitable uncle for Zelda.

"Yeah, well, nice to meet you," Jon said, finally accepting the handshake.

"Cary misses Zelda, too," Julie said. "He wanted to come along."

"What do you do, Cary, that you have noon hours free?"

"Amazon," Cary said simply.

"Oh, what department? I know some folks there."

"Warehouse. Night shift."

"Oh." Jon looked embarrassed, as if he'd expected an entirely different answer. "Let's walk, shall we? I usually take Zelda for a long one in the morning and again before I head off for work. But I made an exception for today."

Jon turned to walk down the path, and Julie fell in step. "And where do you work?" she asked, reaching over for Zelda's leash. Jon relinquished it without resistance.

"Bin 409. Bartender. And you?"

"I'm taking over my parents' wine store in a month. I'm usually working from nine to five. No lunch. But Mom's covering for me today."

They came to a fork in the path, and Zelda led them down the narrow choice on the left. Apparently, it was her new routine. Julie and Zelda stepped ahead, and Cary and Jon walked behind them.

"So, you're a bartender," Cary said.

"Well, yes. For now."

"Maybe it's something I should get into. How long have you been doing it? Forever?"

Jon laughed. "I'm not that old."

Julie turned to judge for herself. Until then, she hadn't focused on Jon's relative age. He looked older than she did, but not by much.

"I've been bartending since I got back from Iraq," Jon elaborated. "I'm in law school during the day—mostly online classes now. From home. I want to practice family law."

"You were in Iraq?" Cary sounded impressed. "Wow,

remind me never to introduce you to my parents. They already think I'm a slacker. They'll meet you and probably want to adopt you."

Julie heard the awe in Cary's voice. Was this emergent bromance going to turn her brother against her? Would he now argue that Jon should get Zelda?

Jon laughed at Cary's ebullience. "Well, I doubt that. So are you here to convince me to give up Zelda?"

Julie turned to see how Cary would respond.

He was shaking his head. "Like Julie said, 'moral support.' And you don't realize how much our family loves Zelda. I wanted to see her again too."

Jon's face turned sour. "Of course. But Zelda is mine now. I've had her for more than a year. I lost my dog—"

"Yes, Julie told us," Cary interrupted. "Your dog had cancer. I'm sorry."

That tamped down the camaraderie a bit, and they all walked in silence. Julie pulled Zelda to a stop at a point where the trail tracked close to the edge of a cliff overlooking Puget Sound. She squatted down and put her arm around her big dog. Zelda wiggled closer, snuggling her back.

"Look at that," Cary said, pointing at them. "How can you—"

"... break them up?" Jon completed his thought. "It was her decision. She's the one who left."

Julie's eyes started to burn with developing tears. "I didn't…" She wanted to argue, but her throat tightened, and she couldn't get another word out.

Cary came to her rescue. "Can I make a suggestion?"

"Sure," Jon said. "As long as it doesn't mean I give up Zelda."

Julie stood and frowned at Cary. Was he going to sabotage her?

"You work at night, right?" Cary asked Jon. "And you

study at home in the day. You go to work at what, six? Seven?"

"Six." Jon sounded as skeptical as Julie felt.

But Cary continued. "And when you work at night you don't get home until when? Two?"

"Yes. About that."

Cary nodded. "And you take Zelda out that late?"

"When I'm not too tired."

Cary shook his head, as if disgusted. "And if you are too tired?"

"She has to wait until morning," Jon admitted, grimacing.

Cary turned to Julie. "And you work all day at the store. Right?"

She nodded.

Cary clasped his hands in front of him, like he'd figured it all out. "So, how about this?"

He paused, and Julie kicked him lightly in the shin. "Get on with it, brother," she urged.

"Jon will keep Zelda during the day while he's home studying. One or both of you can walk her at five. Jon hands her off to Julie before he goes to work. Zelda stays with Jules overnight. Next morning, Jules can drop her off at Jon's place after their walk and before she leaves for work. You split vet bills, license fees. Everything."

Julie stared at Cary. She wasn't sure she loved the idea. But she had to give him credit: it made sense.

Cary held out his hands to his sides and looked back and forth at them. "No brainer, don't you think?"

Julie looked at Jon. Was he going to budge first or was she?

"Come on. You live in the same building. Easy peasy!" Cary exclaimed.

"But is she mine or Jon's, Cary?" Julie asked.

Cary raised his arms higher. "Does a dog really belong

27

to anyone? A dog isn't a thing. It isn't a possession. A dog is love. And you both love her. It actually solves a problem for both of you. Do you know how much doggie day-care costs?"

Julie shook her head in wonder. How did Cary get so smart? Why was he pretending to be such a slacker when he clearly had talents?

She turned to Jon. "What do you think? At least in the short term, it seems like an idea. Then once you get your law degree, I guess you can figure out the legal answer."

Jon studied Julie's face, as if he were noticing for the first time how much he liked it. He looked away and shrugged. "Okay. Let's give it a try. How about three months. See if it works."

Quickly, Julie stuck out her hand to seal the deal. Jon smiled, as if in spite of himself, and shook his head. He clasped her hand and held it. He looked over at Cary. "Remind me when I get a job as a lawyer to hire you as a negotiator. You're a natural."

Cary grinned. "Years of having to talk my way out of trouble."

Zelda stood up and shook herself, perhaps sensing something had been settled and it was time to go back to Jon's apartment for a nap. The humans turned around and Julie handed Jon the leash.

"Your turn," she said, winking at him. She slipped back to walk beside Cary and patted him on the back.

"You're really too smart to be working in a warehouse, you know."

"I know," he said. "Maybe someday I'll turn things around. Don't give up on me."

A WEEK LATER, JULIE STOOD at the front of the elevator, impatient for the door to open. She was late again. As the doors opened and she ran down the hallway toward Jon's apartment, she saw Jon hooking up Zelda's leash outside his apartment door. He stood up, leash in hand.

"Julie, this is the third time this week that you've been late," he scolded her. "This new plan isn't going to work if you don't do your part. You have to get here on time."

Julie had run from the bus to the apartment building, and now she was breathless.

"I swear … Jon … it will get better." She huffed, trying to catch her breath. "Once I get Mom and Dad out of the picture and can hire some help, I won't have to run like this."

Jon didn't look convinced.

"I'm sorry, really I am," she insisted.

Jon shook his head in disgust, and together they walked to the elevator and waited in silence, Julie still catching her breath.

The elevator opened and they stepped inside.

"I know this might be a bad time to talk about this, but …" Julie started, then stopped. She looked over at Jon, who stared straight ahead. A "bad time" might have been an understatement, she realized.

"You know, there's something about the way people say 'but … ,'" he said.

Julie faked a little laugh. Humor him, she thought.

"Yes, I know what you mean. But I've been meaning to ask you what you feed Zelda. I think we should agree on a diet for her."

Jon raised his eyebrows and finally met her eye.

"A diet? You think she's fat?"

Julie shook her head. "I don't mean *diet* diet. I mean we should agree on what kind of food she should eat and when. And yes, she is a little overweight. Big dogs have enough problems with their joints. They don't need to carry extra weight."

The elevator door opened, and they walked out onto

the street, Julie still carrying the purse she took to work.

"So what do you recommend?" Jon asked, snarkily. "I suppose you have some high-end, gourmet, available-only-at-the-vet brand in mind."

Julie didn't like his tone. "Look. If keeping Zelda half-time is above your budget, just let me know. I'll be glad to take over full-time."

"Oh, so this is another ploy to try to steal her from me."

This conversation wasn't going well. Perhaps the day she came home late wasn't the time to raise the issue. But it wasn't her fault. With her parents focused on retiring and getting out of town, she was shouldering more and more of the responsibility at the store, and so far she hadn't found an employee to help.

Still, Jon's attitude pissed her off. "Steal her? You stole her from me, remember?"

"Might I remind you, that is an unsettled debate," Jon said, setting a quick pace down the park path with Zelda leading. "Let's get back to the diet thing."

"Well, cost shouldn't be an issue," Julie said. "If you were feeding her before, and now you only have to buy half as much food, you should be able to pay for something better than that low-grade chow you've been feeding her."

Jon took a deep breath, indicating that he, too, was trying to keep his cool. He was nearly grimacing, and Julie wondered what had gone poorly for him that day. He looked uncomfortable and impatient.

"Let's cut to the chase, Julie. What do you want me to feed her?" He sounded like he couldn't wait to get to work and end this exchange.

"How about if I buy the food, and I'll just let you know what half of the bill is," Julie offered. "You can pay me as we go along."

"Fine. End of discussion, okay?"

Julie signed audibly and involuntarily.

"What? What was that all about?" Jon said, laughing. Somehow he seemed to have recovered his sense of humor.

"It was so much easier when it was just me and Zellie."

Jon looked over and smiled. "But back then, you weren't taking over a wine store. Look," he said, "I think Cary was right. I think if we can get this figured out, it will be best for all of us. Especially Zelda."

Julie met his eyes. He was a decent guy, she realized. Maybe she was lucky that it was Jon who had fostered Zelda. Maybe everything would work out for the best.

Five

Julie scrambled out of the elevator and ran down the hall, looking at her watch. Late again.

Jon had not been happy the day before, and she had promised to get to the apartment on time. He was going to be furious.

She knocked on the door and held her breath. Would he threaten to take Zelda away from her again? She waited. No answer. She knocked again. Finally, she gave up and took the stairs up one flight to her own floor. As she unlocked her door, she glanced at her phone to see a text from Jon:

> We couldn't wait any longer. Perhaps you should reconsider your commitment.

She groaned. Obviously, Jon didn't understand the pressure she was under trying to get her parents out of the store and off on their retirement. Every time she thought things were copacetic and they were ready, her mother came up with more issues they needed to settle; more reorganization that needed done. And some days, her mother was late showing up for the short evening shift because she was tied up with packing and getting the house ready to rent out.

Inside her apartment, Julie laid her purse down and reached in the refrigerator for a bottle of wine she'd opened the night before. If things kept going this way, her self-medicating with wine would put ten pounds on her petite frame.

Before she finished extracting the cork she'd wedged into the bottle, she heard the knock on the door. No mystery who that was.

Jon stood outside with Zelda on her leash. Zelda pushed past them both and ran into the living room to find an old chew toy. She settled down, clearly unconcerned with Julie's tardiness. Before Jon could complain, Julie apologized.

"I know I was late. It's just getting really hard to get out of the store. Mom is covering evenings, but I can't leave until she gets there."

"We had a nice walk. Thanks for asking." Jon's smile was more of a smirk than a grin.

"I promise things will be better once Mom and Dad are out of there and I can hire someone."

"Sure," Jon said, turning away. "I've got to get to work. I can see you're busy."

"But you can't take her away from me," Julie said, expecting an argument. "I'll work this out."

Jon turned back and held up a palm. "Calm down, Julie. I'm not going to take her away from you. I've got to go now, but we can talk tomorrow."

"Okay. I'll be here on time. I promise."

Jon leaned past her and waved at Zelda. "Bye, girl. See you, Julie."

Zelda hopped up and joined Julie at the door. They watched Jon walk down the hallway toward the elevator. As the bell dinged and the door opened, he turned to look back at them. Julie ducked inside and closed her door.

"We don't want him to think we were mooning over him, do we?" she asked Zelda. Julie laughed as the dog shook vigorously as if agreeing and returned to her chew toy.

THE NEXT EVENING AT THE store, Julie's mom came rushing in, and Julie greeted her, relieved. "Thanks for coming in early, Mom."

"What's the urgency?" her mother asked as she put her purse away and checked her hair in the mirror behind the counter. "Big plans tonight?"

"No, I've just been late for the walk with Zelda and Jon twice this week. I'm afraid he's going to use this as proof that I don't have time for her."

"I don't think he's going to do that," her mother said, strangely confident.

"How do you know?"

"From what Cary says, he doesn't seem like that kind of guy."

Julie folded up the rag she was using as a dust cloth and stuck it under the counter. "Cary?" she asked. "Cary hates everyone. You mean he said he likes Jon?"

"Well, not romantic likes. He said he seemed reasonable."

"Cary likes reasonable? Boy, he has changed! I was only gone a year!"

"Well, he hasn't changed that much. But he liked the fact that Jon had been in Iraq."

"Which is odd, too," Julie said, gathering her purse and her keys for a quick exit. "Cary's never had much affinity for the military."

"Ah, Cary the enigma. Who knows what he's seen on TV lately? Anyway, you go ahead. Meet with Jon. Figure something out. You need to get things cleared up before your dad and I leave for Alaska."

It was misting at five o'clock when Jon and Julie walked Zelda to the park. Zelda was wrapped tightly in a doggie raincoat—one Julie had never seen before.

"Where'd you get the raincoat?" she asked.

"The pet store down the street by Whole Foods."

"Does she like it?"

"She seems indifferent to it once we start walking, but she always argues a bit when I put it on her."

Glad to put off a discussion of her tardiness, Julie told him about the time she tried to get Zelda to wear booties. "It had rained about 90 days straight, and I was trying to keep the floors cleaner, you know. But once I got them on her—that wasn't easy!—she wouldn't walk. She just stood there trying to figure out how to get all four feet off the ground at one time. It was pretty funny. I decided it wasn't worth the angst it was causing her."

Jon said nothing. He didn't even chuckle.

Uh-oh, Julie thought. Here it comes. The "talk."

"Any trouble getting off early today?" he asked.

Julie took a deep breath before she answered. "No. But I can't ask Mom to come in early every day. They're trying to wrap things up here and get ready to head to Alaska on their boat."

"So what are we going to do? I have to be at the bar five days a week at six. I can't wait for you."

Julie frowned. "Yeah, I understand. And it's likely to get harder for me to leave when I get a new employee. I'll probably need to be there until we close at seven every night."

"Right, so I've been thinking," Jon said. His tone was more conciliatory than she expected. "Why don't I walk her at four or five every afternoon, and then leave her in your apartment? She'll be here when you get home and you can walk her before bedtime. Of course, you'd have to trust me with a key to your place."

Julie was surprised. She had expected this problem would lead to more of an argument about who was best situated to keep Zelda—full-time. Instead, he was offering an easy and reasonable compromise.

"Well, it's not like I don't know where to find you," she said, trying not to sound too eager. "I guess that would be okay. It would take the stress out of trying to coordinate our schedules every day."

Jon looked over at her, his eyes smiling like he read right through her nonchalance. "So, it's a deal?"

Julie nodded. "Yes, I'll go to the hardware store tonight. I'll drop the key off at your apartment later. I can put it under the door."

"No, tonight's my night off. I'll keep Zelda until then. Just come by when you get it, and you can take her home then."

Julie skipped a little step and then tried to drag her feet. Why was she so afraid of admitting she was coming to like Jon so much? Not only was he reasonable and sympathetic, he was good looking, ambitious, and smart. But while he had shown a willingness to work with her to solve the Zelda problem, he hadn't indicated anything more than a platonic interest in her as Zelda's mom.

Which was for the best, Julie admitted to herself as they walked the rest of the park circuit in silence. André was likely to show up on her doorstep soon, and her fascination with Jon would recede.

Six

Two hours later, Jon opened his apartment door and stepped aside to admit Julie. Zelda got up and sauntered over for an ear scratch. Clearly she was comfortable here.

Jon's apartment was clean and neat. No groceries on the kitchen counter or dirty dishes in the sink. The tile floors shone, reflecting the ceiling lights. Beyond the kitchen, the walls were bare, devoid of artwork or posters. A large desk piled high with law books sat in the far end of the living room, and a couple of La-Z-Boys, a small end table, and a tiny TV on a hand-me-down table filled out the space.

"I guess you can see I haven't had much time to decorate," Jon said apologetically.

"It's *so* clean though," she said. "Where's the dog hair? I have dog hair everywhere!"

Jon laughed and grinned shyly. "Yeah, you caught me. I just vacuumed. Didn't want you to think I don't know how to house a dog."

Julie handed him the little envelope with the apartment key she had just had made at the Ace. "Here's the key. The lock is a bit sticky, just so you know. You have to jiggle it a bit."

"Good to know," Jon said, accepting it and putting it immediately in a drawer by the door. Julie stood where she was for a moment, awkwardly, wanting to stay and talk but having no reason to.

"I guess Zelda and I should—"

"Uh, do you want a drink?" Jon interrupted. "A glass of wine? My nights off are the only time I can imbibe. I'm on my best behavior behind the bar."

Relieved, Julie nodded, accepting the offer. "I don't know if I could go five nights a week without wine. Good for you."

"Well, I am more of a beer kind of guy anyway."

"But, yeah, I'll take that glass," she said. "I guess it would be good for us to get to know each other a little better, now that we share Zelda."

Jon waved his arm at the reclining chairs. "Make yourself at home. Is pinot noir okay?"

"Perfect."

Jon slipped around her to get into the kitchen. Julie sat down on one of the La-Z-Boys and pushed back to lift the footrest. Zelda followed her and flopped down. Julie heard the cork pop and the friendly, welcome gurgle of wine. Jon walked back into the living room with a glass for her and a beer for himself.

"I was thinking, under this new arrangement, since we won't be walking together in the afternoon, maybe we could walk Zelda together on Sundays. Once in a while?" he said, lifting his glass for a clink with hers.

"Sure," Julie said. "That would be fun. To be honest, I don't have many friends here anymore. With college at UC-Davis, work at the store, and now a year in France,

38

everyone sort of disappeared from my life."

Jon sat down in the other recliner and kicked his footrest up. "Same here. I came back after four years away and now I know no one. Only it was Iraq, not California and France."

Julie took a sip, letting the wine sit on her tongue for a moment. It was fine. Perhaps a French Burgundy, not an Oregon pinot, but fine just the same.

"Yeah, it turns out Cary's probably my best friend now. Imagine that. My little brother turns out to be my best friend."

Jon gestured toward her with his beer. "And right now, you and Zelda are mine."

A little embarrassed by his warmth, Julie hid her smile by leaning over and scratching Zelda's head. "She certainly seems comfortable here."

"I was worried at first that she'd smell Milo and there'd be a problem."

"Milo?"

"My dog. The one I got in Iraq," Jon said, his voice suddenly sad. "He was here for a couple of months."

Julie looked up. "Oh, right. I don't know how I forgot about Milo."

She took another sip and paused. "So, I have to ask: How did a guy who wants to be family lawyer end up in Iraq? They haven't reinstated the draft, have they?"

"No. No. It's a long story. Or, really the story's not so long. It just started a long time ago." He paused, as if uncertain he should continue.

"And ... ," Julie said to encourage him.

"Okay. If you really want to know." He took a long draw on his beer. "My dad was a lifer in the Marines. When I was just a kid he asked that I consider doing a stint in one of the services. He didn't make me promise I'd do it, but just that I'd think about it. So when I finished my undergraduate degree, I thought about it. And decided not to do it."

"But you did."

"Yeah. This is the hard part." He paused again, and Julie wondered if it was mean of her to insist on hearing the story.

Jon continued. "I was a semester through law school, and I got the news. Dad was hit by an IED in Afghanistan. Died right there."

"Oh, I'm so sorry. That's awful."

"Yeah. It was. Still is. But it made me reconsider. I signed up and ended up in Iraq. Stayed for four years."

"My god. I've never had to do anything so hard," she said.

"But what made it bearable was Milo," he said, his voice now wavering as if it were getting hard to hold back tears. "Milo got me through it."

Julie felt tears well up on her lids. "What kind of a dog was he?" she said, struggling to get the words out.

Jon pushed his footrest down and stood up to retrieve a photo album from his desk. He handed it to Julie.

Tentatively, she accepted it and let it fall open to the first photo. It was a picture of Milo with Jon in his fatigues in a desert setting, apparently Iraq. Milo looked like a shepherd of some sort—perhaps part German, perhaps Belgian. She looked through the pages of photos, unable to hold back the stream of tears they triggered. She closed the book, sniffling and wiping her eyes with the back of her hand.

Jon stood again and brought a box of Kleenex back to the end table and placed it between them.

"I'm sorry. I don't know why I'm ... ." She couldn't finish the sentence. She gulped, grabbed a tissue, and blew her nose. She tried again. "He was beautiful."

Jon pulled a tissue and wiped his eyes.

"I'm really sorry," he said. "I didn't mean to upset you. I shouldn't have shown you that." He reached for the book.

Julie handed it back. "No, I'm glad you did. Like I said, we should get to know each other better. I understand so much more now. And now, I can see why you bonded with Zelda. And she with you."

Jon nodded, looking like he was struggling to talk. They looked away from each other and sipped their drinks.

After a couple of minutes, Julie broke the silence. "You know, this is kind of out of left field, but what do you think about going out to eat next week. On your night off?"

Jon laughed. "A date? I thought you were engaged."

Julie shook her head. "No, not a date. Of course not. But I'd like to take you out for dinner to thank you for taking such good care of Zelda for me. What do you think?"

Jon looked skeptical. "Does it have to be somewhere fancy?"

"Whatever you like. But I'd prefer not fancy."

Jon nodded in agreement. "How about Ivar's? Fish and chips?"

"I think I owe you more than fish and chips," Julie argued.

"You said whatever I like. I like fish and chips."

Julie laughed, the tension gone. "Okay. Okay. You'll get no argument from me. How about you meet me at the waterfront Ivar's at 7:15? On Wednesday. I'll text if I'm late."

Jon reached over and offered his hand. "Deal," he said. Julie accepted his gesture, and he held her hand longer than necessary.

Jon finally relinquished her fingers. "Too bad we can't bring Zelda."

Seven

Julie looked out across Puget Sound toward West Seattle from the picnic table outside of Ivar's and threw a couple of French fries as far as she could. Two gulls swept down, anticipating the spuds' flight and swooped them up just as they hit the water.

"You know, we're not supposed to feed the gulls. It only encourages them," said Jon, laughter in his voice.

"I know," said Julie. "But it's so much fun."

Jon shook his head and grinned broadly. "And you're a lot of fun, Julie." They smiled at each other over their paper bowls of fried fish and chips and dove back in.

"Thanks," she said, holding up a French fry as a toast.

Sitting side by side on the bench so they could both look out over the water, they munched for a few minutes, saying nothing. Julie wiped her greasy fingers on her napkin and reached for a fresh one. She loved fish and chips, but it was good that she didn't indulge in them too often.

"I'm sorry I gave you such a hard time when you came back," Jon said. "I was so afraid of losing Zelda."

Julie blinked in accord. "I understand. When I thought I'd lost her, it was the worst day of my life."

Jon tipped his head and looked out across the water with her. "Pretty easy life, huh?"

"I guess. So far," Julie said, recognizing the truth. She'd never lost a dog to cancer. Never gone into a battlefield. Never lost a father. "Not like yours."

"No. Not like mine," said Jon, soberly. "I've seen some pretty awful stuff." He paused. "Atrocities. Lost some good friends. Human ones. And of course, Milo." He pulled his eyes off the water and looked at Julie. "But I feel like I'm being rewarded now."

"How's that?" Julie stuffed a couple of fries in her mouth, ignoring the greedy, accusatory looks from the gulls sitting on the railing next to them.

"Well, getting to finish law school without debt. Getting to share Zelda. You."

Julie felt herself blush and looked away. "I know about your dad. Where is your mom?" she asked.

"She lives in Denver now. We don't talk much. After we lost Dad, she tried to talk me out of going to Iraq. She didn't want to lose me too. She hasn't forgiven me for scaring her like that."

Julie let that sink it. She did have it good, and she didn't mind Jon reminding her of that. Her parents were still together. They were entering retirement, well situated financially. She was set to inherit the wine store, a secure job already in place and a fiancé on his way across the Atlantic.

"I'm sorry. I am so lucky to still have my parents. They give me so much strength."

Jon bumped her on the shoulder. "I think you're pretty strong on your own."

"You're so nice to me, Jon," she said. "I don't think I've

ever dated a guy who was more thoughtful."

"But this isn't a date, remember?" he answered, teasing.

Julie looked down, embarrassed at her slip. "No, no. Of course not. I just meant all the guys I dated ... uh. I mean, of all the guys ... Oh, never mind."

She looked up at him bashfully. "Can I just ... kinda ... just slide out of this somehow?"

Jon laughed and threw his arm around her and pulled her to his side. "You do tend to get tangled up in your words sometimes."

Julie laughed with him. "Only around you. It only happens when I'm with you."

"Is that a good thing?"

"It's a thing. I'm not sure if it's good or bad."

Jon crumpled up his napkin and threw it in his empty paper bowl. "It's getting kind of deep here, don't you think? Maybe we should get back. Zelda needs her bedtime walk."

Julie wound her legs out from behind the seat and stood. They dumped their waste in a trash bin and Jon turned to her and swallowed her shoulders in a hug.

"Thanks for dinner, Julie. You sure know how to make a guy happy."

They stayed in the hug for a long moment before breaking apart and heading toward the bus stop.

AT THE NEIGHBORHOOD PARK THE next Saturday, the week's drizzle continued, a little more robust than usual. Although the Seattle "wetness"—as residents called it—rarely required one, Jon and Julie shared an umbrella. Zelda walked ahead on a long leash, wrapped tightly in her raincoat.

Julie had the day off, as her mom and dad had decided to spend the day alone in the store, sort of a last-time, nostalgic tour of duty. It sounded almost romantic, Julie had said, and she was happy to give them the opportunity.

"I was thinking we should take Zelda out somewhere different sometime," Jon suggested. "Even dogs crave a change of scenery, don't you think? Maybe take her out to one of those dog beaches on the islands?"

"Yeah, maybe," Julie said. She'd been preoccupied all morning, and her tone was sullen.

"Oh, come on." Jon bumped against her. "I thought you'd like that." He watched her for a moment. "Is something wrong?"

"No," Julie said unconvincingly. She shrugged. "Well, yeah."

"Want to talk about it?"

"Not really." They walked a few more steps in silence. "Well, okay," she said. "I'm starting to wonder if André is really coming."

Jon didn't jump right in, and Julie wondered if he was considering whether that was good news or bad. Finally, he responded, "Why do you say that?"

"Well, he never calls me. When I text him, he doesn't text back. The only time we talk, I call him. And he's making no progress on getting here. It's the same story every time. Waiting for the chef to hire his replacement."

"Well, maybe it's just because it's a big move. Immigration isn't as easy as it used to be. Could be scary for a guy."

Julie nodded. They stopped to let Zelda pee and continued down the path.

"Yeah, I know," she said. She knew she sounded less than convinced.

"Give him some time," Jon added. "I'm sure he is still planning to come. It would be hard for any guy to stay away from you."

Julie smiled to herself. She wasn't the only one finding their relationship more than she had expected it to be. She turned toward him. "What? What did you say?"

Jon looked away. "I mean, you are engaged, right? It'd

be hard to turn your back on that, right?"

Julie laughed. She didn't want to embarrass him, even though she thought it was time for both of them to admit how close they had grown. She had a reason to hold back. Did he?

"Yeah. That's it," she said. "We are engaged. But thanks for the compliment."

Eight

JULIE LEAFED THROUGH THE PILE of résumés that had come via email and in the mail at the store, trying to find one that impressed her. But nothing jumped out at her as saying, "I'm the one!" The amount of typos and misspellings was depressing enough. Adding to that was the fact that nearly all the applicants lacked any qualifications as a wine expert.

Her mother sat nearby, leafing through invoices and sorting them for payment.

"I have looked at so many résumés, the type is blurring," Julie whined.

Her mother looked up. "I don't know why you're having such a hard time finding the right person. The unemployment rate is so high. There's got to be lots of people looking for a retail job."

"Yeah, but I need someone who knows something about wine. Do you know every cover letter I've received from candidates talks about how much they love wine, but none of them have experience with anything but drinking it?"

"Well, maybe you'll just have to teach them," her mother said. "I had to teach you, you know."

Julie's eyes held fast on the résumé in front of her, but her mind wandered back to the after-school hours and Saturdays in the shop that had soaked up her teenage years. At first, all the wine descriptions and names of grape varieties just bounced off her as she wiped the dust from the shelves and bottles and listened to her mother's lectures. But by the time she was in high school, she had unconsciously absorbed much of it. She knew how the taste notes of an Oregon pinot noir differed from those in a French Burgundy, even though the grape was supposedly the same; she knew that Beaujolais was made with the gamay grape; and the Sancerre from the Loire was not only acidic but was forever linked to the French resistance in World War II. Her friends were out riding their bikes down the steep alleys of First Hill and hanging out in the market, smoking cigarettes with the cool art school students. But she was perfectly happy to be flying over the high, dry mesas of the Rioja region in her imagination, as her father described his travels in Franco's Spain, dodging fascist spies who trailed him through vineyards and villages as if he knew anything that might be of interest to them.

She shook herself out of her reverie.

"Yes, I learned it all, but it took years," she said. "And the easy part of this job is holding down the sales floor showing wine, helping people choose a bottle for dinner and for a party. But that can't be learned overnight, and I need to be back in the office, doing the hard stuff. The books, the ordering, the marketing, the website, the shipping ... ."

Her mother laughed. She had been in a better mood

lately, now that her retirement was fast approaching. "You're making the job I did all my life sound awful, Julie. I liked it."

"No. I don't mean to. I just mean we need someone up front who knows what they're talking about."

"Keep looking. That person is out there."

Julie hoped her mother was right. She had no idea how she was going to take care of the store all by herself in two weeks when her mom and dad took off.

"What do you hear from André?" her mother asked, standing up to pour herself another cup of coffee.

Julie sighed and leaned forward on the counter, her head in her hands.

"Same old. Same story. Still waiting for the chef to replace him."

"You think there's a problem?"

"I don't know," Julie said, her thoughts suddenly across the ocean with André. "I just don't know. And the problem is, there's no one who can help me figure it out. Jon thinks there's nothing to worry about, but I don't know."

"Didn't you still have some friends over there who knew him? Can't you ask someone in Paris?"

"My mentor at the restaurant knows him. He introduced us. But if I call him, he'll tell André, and I don't want to make a big deal out of this." She paused and tried to pull her focus back to the résumés. "Maybe there is no problem, and I'll just spook André if he thinks I'm checking up on him."

Julie looked at her mom and shrugged. Her mother smiled reassuringly. "I understand. Maybe just give him a little more time. You've got plenty to do here."

The front door chimes rang, and they looked up to see Cary walking in. He stopped at a new end-cap display Julie had just constructed to feature wines of Washington's Columbia Gorge.

"What are you doing here?" their mother asked.

Cary looked up at her, a bit of sneer on his face. It was a look Julie knew usually meant he had something to hide or something he needed to confess that he'd prefer to keep a secret.

"What? Can't I stop by?" He sounded just as defensive as Julie had expected. "You were happy to see me when you needed me. Before your darling Julie got back."

Julie and her mother exchanged knowing glances.

"No, I mean, don't you have to work today?"

"No. Not today," Cary said.

"Did you quit? Again?"

Julie stayed out of the exchange. Her mother was a bit harder on Cary than Julie liked, but she had to admit that Cary deserved much of the criticism he got.

"Not exactly," Cary said, walking away from her, down one of the aisles, picking up a bottle here and there, stalling.

"Then, what, exactly?"

"Got fired."

Her mother snickered. "Well, color me surprised. What did you do?"

Cary looked at Julie. Did he expect her to intervene? She had a number of times over their lifetime in their parents' house, but it had never done much to soften her mother's disappointment in her son. Julie shook her head. She couldn't help.

"It doesn't matter," Cary said. He replaced the bottle he'd been studying and shoved his hands in his jeans pockets. "It was time for me to go. I couldn't do it much longer. It was like a prison. Pay was good. Benefits great. But I couldn't stand the clock, the ticking clock. The supervisors. The quotas. It just wasn't right for me."

Julie's mother shook her head. "Well, Cary, life can't be a wine tasting party all the time. You're going to have to find something that's right for you pretty soon."

"I know. I just thought I should come and tell you before you found out from someone else."

He waved at Julie. "Hey, sis," he said. "How's Zelda? And Jon?"

"Fine," Julie said, happy to help him change the subject. "We're going to the dog beach on Sunday. Want to come along?"

"Nah." Cary shook his head. "I'm playing golf with Ted."

He turned back to their mother. "Tell Dad about the job for me, will you? I don't think I can face him right now."

He exaggerated a sigh. Cary continued down the aisle and out the door without another word.

"Can't either of my kids ever be happy?" Mother asked, shaking her head at Julie.

"I'm not so sure Cary isn't happy," Julie answered. "He's just lost for the moment."

"Well, it's been one very long moment."

Nine

THE MORNING THAT JON AND Julie drove to the ferry terminal, rode the Tokitae across to Whidbey Island, and followed the meandering, narrow roads to the leash-free Double Bluff Beach, it was low tide, and the dark sand stretched 300 yards from the bluff to the foamy water of Puget Sound.

The chilly breeze off the water didn't faze Zelda. She darted straight for the edge of the water with abandon and high-stepped through the surf, grinning like only dog owners know a dog can. Julie pulled her down jacket tight around her chest and shivered.

"Let's walk," she said. "Zelda won't let us out of her sight. As much as she may dream of running away when she's on a leash, she's really a mommy's girl."

"You think so?" Jon's voice was teasing. "Maybe she's really a daddy's girl."

Julie laughed. "I suppose she could be both."

They walked along the hard-packed sand near the water and watched Zelda stop and sniff, run ahead, turn around to sniff something she just about missed, and then leap ahead again. The girl was having a blast and suddenly Julie felt guilty for not taking her to the beach more often. There was a dog beach in Seattle too, along the west side of Lake Washington, but it was always crowded, and as gregarious as Zelda was with people, she tended to be shy around dogs she didn't know. Whenever Julie took her there, Zelda hung around the picnic table where Julie sat, often hiding under her knees. She didn't look like she was having a good time.

Zelda stopped ahead and looked straight out across the water.

"Perhaps she can see Russia from there," Jon joked. "Do you think she's thinking of swimming there?"

"Not Russia. But maybe Vancouver. After I adopted her from the rescue agency, I always thought she might be part Canadian," Julie said.

"Why?"

They fell into an easy pace that suited both Julie's long strides and Jon's long legs.

"I was taking French lessons before I went to France," Julie answered, "and she seemed to understand French better than English."

"Hmmm." Jon nodded. "I think they respond to your tone of voice. You were probably being more expressive in French. You know, trying to learn intonation."

Julie wondered why she hadn't thought of that. She knew how faithfully Zelda responded to different pitches of her voice.

"It scares me how smart you are," Julie said.

"That's odd coming from you. I have thought you might be much smarter than me. What was your degree in?"

Julie felt herself blush at the compliment, the heat in her cheeks welcome, even as she hoped Jon wouldn't look over to notice. "Double major. French literature and viticulture. And yours?"

"Interesting combination. Renaissance-like. Mine was history, of course."

"Ah, yes," Julie said. "Makes sense as a pre-law degree, right?"

Their conversation shifted from family and schools to old friends and former pets as they continued down the beach, following Zelda. They bumped into each other every few steps, the lumpy sand making walking a perfectly straight line difficult.

Zelda stopped to sniff something at the water's edge in front of them. "Don't you dare roll in that!" Julie yelled into the breeze, as she watched. With her eyes on Zelda, she tripped on a piece of driftwood, and Jon caught her by the elbow. He slipped her arm under his and pulled it in close.

Julie's heart skipped. What did this mean? Was this simply a kind gesture by Jon to make sure she didn't fall or was there more meaning to it than that? She waited for her heartbeat to return to normal and decided she wouldn't read too much into it. It felt good, whatever his intention.

Despite the brisk breeze, Julie started to warm up. Was it the walk or the proximity to Zelda's new dad? She wasn't sure, but she slowly realized she was smiling. Broadly. Unabashedly. It had been a while since she had felt this kind of unforced happiness. She had been happy with André too, but it had always been something she had felt separate from—outside of, actually—imagining how other women would see her and consider her lucky, or how someday she'd look back at her time with him in Paris with nostalgia.

"Hey, a perfect bench," Jon said, pointing to a large log sitting parallel to the water and Zelda's trajectory. "Think if we sit, Zelda will hang close?"

"Sure," Julie said. "She's not going far whether she's a mommy's girl or a daddy's girl."

Julie picked out a flat spot on the wood and sat, glad she'd worn a pair of old jeans that wouldn't show a little salt or sap stain. Jon sat next to her, close enough that he could pull her arm back through his again. They sat, watching Zelda play in the wet sand, entertaining herself like the only child she was.

"She's going to be a mess after this," Julie said, shaking her head to get her wind-blown hair out of her face. "I think she should go home with you."

"Ha!" Jon laughed. "Nope. I just vacuumed, remember?"

"That was a week ago Wednesday! You mean you haven't vacuumed since then?"

"Okay, when was the last time you did?"

Julie faked a sniff. "I have an excuse. I'm trying to keep the store running, find an assistant and plan a retirement party for my parents."

Jon looked over and pushed a wind-blown lock of her long bangs out of her eyes. It was an intimate gesture, one that Julie couldn't ignore as easily as she had dismissed the way he held her arm.

"When's the party?" Jon asked.

Julie fought to keep her voice calm as heat rose again to her face. "Just a few days. It's a Wednesday night, so I was hoping you could come and bring Zelda by. Lots of our customers know her."

"Sure," Jon said, still looking intently at her face. His voice sounded cool, not sexy or romantic, but his body language was communicating something else. "Sounds like fun. She won't knock the bottles off the shelves with her tail?"

"It'll be your job to make sure she doesn't," Julie said. "And she's really good in the shop, even with all those bottles." Her words were neutral and platonic, but she realized how much she had lowered her voice. Was she flirting?

They sat in silence for a few minutes, Julie relieved that

Jon's focus had returned to Zelda's antics. Her blush faded, and she concentrated on breathing slowly and deeply. Finally, feeling like she had regained control of her voice again, she spoke.

"I think this thing is really working out for Zelda." She paused, uncertain if she should continue. "And for us. What do you think?"

Jon turned to her and held her eyes. "It's working out very well for me," he said, his voice low now too. He leaned closer and looked down at her lips. For a moment, neither of them did anything. Then he slipped his hand behind her neck, and Julie closed her eyes, waiting for his kiss. Had she known this was going to happen? How long had she known?

Whoosh!

Just before their lips touched, eighty pounds of wet, sandy dog plowed into them, dumping them backwards onto the beach.

"Zelda!" they yelled in unison, arms and legs flying as they fell. They pulled themselves up on their elbows and laughed.

Julie struggled to her knees and stood up, brushing as much wet sand as she could off her clothes and out of her hair. Jon still lay on the ground with Zelda prancing around him, barking as if she'd discovered a new game. Jon was laughing too hard to get up. Julie reached down and offered him a hand. He pulled upright, and she started to work on the crusty sand that covered his backside.

"Well, that was a shocker," Julie said.

"You think she knew what we were about to do?" Jon asked. He stopped and looked at Julie, a different question in his eyes.

"I'm not sure I did," Julie said. She shook her head and looked away. "Do you mind if we … ? I really need to forget that just about happened. I'm en—," she started to say, but she couldn't get the word out.

"Yes, I know you're engaged. I'm sorry." Jon looked as remorseful as he sounded. He took her hands and met her eyes, an apology written on his face.

"Do you mind?" she repeated, afraid he'd try to kiss her again.

Jon paused for a moment, holding her hands between then, before letting go with a sad shrug.

"No," he said. He pulled Zelda's leash out of his coat pocket. "I think it's time we headed back."

Ten

RETIREMENT PARTIES WERE NEVER JULIE'S thing. She had to attend dozens of them with her parents over the past few years, as their friends had all reached their own magic number—55 or 60 or 65—the age at which they had promised themselves they would hang up the spurs and walk hand in hand into the sunset.

As generous as she tried to be with her time, sympathies, and kindliness, the parties always left her drained of every ounce of congeniality and impossible to be around for the following days.

This one had to be different. It was for her own parents. It was their swan song. She owed them so much for providing her with a career, a job, a business—all things that her classmates and friends had to struggle and beg for from unrelated, disinterested employers and bankers. It was all so easy for her.

Easy, if she didn't consider the after-school hours and

weekends she was committed to working for Mom and Dad from the time she was about fourteen. Yes, she had it made now, but she'd given up a lot of what it meant to be a kid to earn it.

Was that why Julie had such a soft spot for Cary? Why she didn't write him off the way her parents seemed inclined to? She recognized he was, in many ways, more normal than she was. It was normal to search for an identity, to rebel, to struggle to figure out what you wanted to do "when you grew up." If Cary had problems keeping a job, if he jumped from one thing to another, it was only because he hadn't yet matched a profession or a position to his personality. It would come to him, Julie was convinced. He was smart, good-hearted, and gregarious. And he was still young. Plenty of time, she told her parents. "Quit riding him."

As she slipped around and between the well-wishers who had shown up at the "Going Sailing" party she was throwing for her parents, Julie realized how many of their faces she recognized and names she knew. Would it be the same in forty years when it came time for her to get on the sailboat—or the jet plane or the highway—and disappear into happy retirement? Would she have regular customers, friends and neighbors among the shops up and down their street? Or would retail stores be a thing of the past, replaced by fast, overnight delivery and online wine stores that wouldn't require customers to leave their houses and find a parking spot just to get a bottle of bubbly for an anniversary dinner at home?

Maybe her future wasn't so certain after all.

Setting a tray of cheese and charcuterie on the table where Cary was serving wine, she waited for him to finish what he was doing.

"Let me know what you think of this mourvèdre," he was saying to Christine Mayer, one of the shopkeepers in the neighborhood who had retired in the past year.

"Thanks, I will," Christine said, winking at Cary. Julie smiled. Her brother was handsome, and even if he was as worthless as her mother thought, the women at the party seemed to approve of him. Even those twice his age.

"You're getting really good at this, Cary," she said as Christine rejoined her husband in a small knot of friends. "Maybe you should look into getting a job in a wine-tasting room in the Columbia Valley."

Cary rewarded her compliment with a quick frown. "I don't know anyone there," he said curtly.

"Didn't you meet some of the distributors when you were covering for me here last year?"

"Yes, distributors. But their wine tastings are in supermarkets. I can't think of anything worse than standing all day in a supermarket."

Julie pulled the plastic wrap off the tray she was delivering and adjusted its placement. She accepted an empty tray from Cary. "What's wrong with supermarkets?"

Cary shrugged and avoided her eye. What was his problem today? Usually they got along wonderfully. "They're sterile, I guess."

"Well, once I get done with this party, I'll make a few calls for you. I know marketing people in the Tri-Cities."

"Well, don't you worry about me," he snarled.

"Hey, what's wrong?" Julie asked. "Did I say something?"

"Never mind." He dismissed her and smiled up at a tall man who had just approached the table with an empty glass. "What can I get for you? The same or do you want to try something different?"

Julie shook her head and walked away. She stopped next to her mother, who was momentarily standing alone, watching the partygoers mingle.

"What's wrong with Cary?" Julie asked.

Her mother looked surprised. "Nothing, as far as I know. He really likes these wine-tastings. And he's good at it. He knows his wine. He helped us a lot this past year when you were gone."

Julie watched Cary interact with a couple more guests before she headed back to the office to refill the tray.

Just as she let the door close behind her, she heard her mother shout. "Zelda! Come here sweetie!"

Julie put the empty tray down and opened the door to watch Zelda run toward her mother, Jon trailing behind her, holding her leash. Her mother leaned down to give the shaggy dog a hug and accepted a quick lick on the face from Zelda's big tongue. Julie let the door swing closed again and stood with her ear close, listening.

"You must be Jon," her mom said. "I'm Ellie, Julie's mom. She's told us all about you. You're an angel for helping her take care of Zelda."

"Well, it's my pleasure. I think of Zelda as mine, too. Fifty percent responsible for her."

"That's great. Here, let me take her for a minute," Julie's mom said. "She needs to say hi to some old friends of ours. You go get a glass of wine."

"Is Julie here?" Jon asked.

"Sure. She just went into the back."

Julie scrambled away from the door and got busy arranging another tray of cheeses and meats. When Jon walked in, she looked up, pretending to be surprised.

"Hey." She tried to sound calm, but her mind's eye kept seeing their near kiss on the beach a few days before. She wasn't sure how Jon was going to treat her now. She'd kept her distance the past four days, letting Jon come and go to retrieve and return Zelda, making sure she wouldn't be there when he did.

"Yeah, hey," Jon responded. He stood by the door, his hands in his jeans pockets.

"Did you bring Zelda?" It was disingenuous. Julie knew the answer, but it seemed like the safest topic.

"Yes, your mother took her from me. Seems everyone loves Zelda."

"So you met my mom."

"Yeah. She said you'd told her a lot about me."

"Well, Cary and I both." Julie blushed. "Some. Don't get a big head about it." She continued unwrapping tubes of sausage and arranging the slices on the tray. She didn't look, but she could sense Jon fidgeting.

"What is it?" she asked. "Something bothering you?"

"I think we should talk about what happened on the beach on Sunday," he said quietly. Exactly what she was afraid he'd say.

"I know you are engaged," he continued. "And I know you are still expecting André to come. But I'd like to know about us. Do you think there something here? Do you have any feelings for me?"

Julie was surprised he spoke so bluntly. She would have beat around the bush, if it had been her desire to talk about it. She put the sausage down and wiped her hands on her apron. She turned to him soberly.

"Jon," she said. "I'm sorry. It was just the beach. Walking Zelda. The fresh air. The surf. Whatever. I didn't think anything about it. You shouldn't think anything about it, either."

Jon shuffled his feet and looked away. Julie started to load wine glasses on another tray, wiping them off with a cloth, setting them upside down on a layer of napkins.

"It was just the moment, huh? Nothing else?"

Julie looked up. "You said it yourself. I'm engaged. I'm not going to obsess about what almost happened but didn't." She picked up the tray and handed it to him. The glasses rattled against each other, betraying her shaking hands.

"Here. Can you take those out to Cary for me?"

Jon nodded sadly and turned to the door. He pushed it open with a hip and slipped through with the tray, like a professional waiter. André couldn't have done it better.

Julie watched him go before turning around and burying her face in her hands. She took a deep breath.

"André," she whispered. "Get your butt over here soon. Before I do something stupid."

The crowd had thinned to just a handful of couples by the time the party reached its advertised duration. No one was pushing the stragglers out the door. If her parents' best friends hung out for another hour, that was fine.

Jon had left just fifteen minutes after he dropped off Zelda, and Cary had disappeared. Zelda was zonked out on her doggie bed, and Julie was mellowing out with a glass of a fine Rhone wine she wouldn't have bought for herself. Up until Saturday, July 1, the store profit and loss was her parents' problem, not hers.

A half hour later, the crowd was gone, and Julie and her mother gathered up unused napkins and paper plates, and tossed out the used ones.

"I liked Jon a lot," her mother said. "So did your father. Is there anything going on there, Jules? Between the two of you?"

Julie rolled her eyes. "Mom. I'm engaged." She looked away, worried her eyes would then betray her. "There is nothing going on with Jon except Zelda."

"Well, I saw the way he looked at you. There's something there, dear, at least for him. Are you sure you don't like him?"

Julie sighed loudly. "Of course, I like him. He's smart and ambitious and he loves Zelda. What's not to like?"

"And yet, you're still waiting on André. This mysterious André." Julie wasn't sure, but it sounded like her mother clucked her tongue.

She stopped working and threw her hands on her hips. "Mother. André is not mysterious. I'm sure he's coming any day now."

"Has he said so?"

Julie gestured at the remains of the party fixings. "In case you haven't noticed, I've been a bit busy here over the past couple of weeks." She changed the subject. "By the way, what happened to Cary?"

"He left a half hour ago. Seemed in one of his moods. I thanked him for taking care of the bar."

"I talked to him about finding a job in the wine industry," Julie said. "Maybe over in the Tri-Cities or Walla Walla."

"And what did he say?"

Julie shook her head. "He kind of blew me off. He said he doesn't know anyone there. But I'll make a few calls next week. See if anything is available. He's a good-looking guy. Personable … most of the time."

Julie's father walked around the end of the aisle and put his arm over Julie's shoulder. He kissed her on the forehead. "Jules, you put on quite the soirée." He put his other arm around her mother's shoulder and pulled her close. "We can't thank you enough."

"You can thank me by finding me an assistant before you leave. You guys are still hoping to leave end of next week, right?"

Her father nodded. He understood the situation. "Maybe Cary can help out until you find someone. He did some of that when you were in France."

"But, can I depend on him?" Julie asked. "You know I love him, but he doesn't do reliable very well."

"Yes, you're right," her father said. "Well, it was just a thought." He picked up an empty charcuterie plate and a plastic tub of dirty wine glasses. "I'll take these back for you."

Eleven

THE NEXT DAY, JULIE WALKED into her apartment after work, and was greeted excitedly—as usual—by Zelda. She put her purse down on the table, and saw a note, a small bag of doggie treats, and a small box of Seattle chocolates.

She picked up the note and opened it.

> I thought you and Zelda needed some Treats. Thanks for inviting me to the party the other night. Your parents are cool. XO Jon PS: Sorry about obsessing over the other day. I'm over it.

"Hmmm," Julie murmured. "I hope I can get over it too."

She opened the bag of dog treats.

"Sit!" she ordered Zelda, who complied as she always did. "That's from your buddy, Jon."

Julie had called him "daddy" at the beach the other day, but after their near-kiss, that seemed too dangerous.

She opened the little box of chocolates, chose one, walked over to the chair by the window, sat and looked out, nibbling on the chocolate. When she finished, she reached for her phone and texted:

Thanks for the chocolates and the treats. If not for Andre maybe things would be different.

That was as close as she wanted to come to admitting the truth. She stopped to think and then backspaced over the second sentence before hitting "send."

IT WAS ONLY EIGHT DAYS before her parents planned to leave "forever"—at least until winter weather on the west coast of Canada and Alaska made sailing treacherous—and Julie was still looking for an assistant. Late morning, she stood behind the counter at the store, looking over three piles of résumés: "definitely not," "maybe," and the shortest pile, "call."

She wasn't eager to start making those calls, knowing how hard it was to get much of a feel for people over the phone. Instead, she picked up her phone and dialed. Jon answered quickly.

"Hey," she said. "I wondered if you can drop Zelda off here on your way to work. I'm going to be working really late tonight."

"Sure," he said. All the awkwardness between them seemed to have dissipated, to Julie's relief. "Is something wrong there?"

"No, nothing's wrong. I'm just trying to get through these calls to assistant candidates. And I had to let Mom off the hook tonight. She needs to finish packing for their big adventure."

"Right," Jon said. "I'll be there about five."

Julie hung up but she stood for a few minutes, staring out the window, distracted by her thoughts.

A few hours later, Julie had lined up three in-person interviews with candidates from her "call" pile. She stood in the French Burgundy section, listening as a customer described her recent Backroads bike tour of the region.

"And the food," the woman said, dramatically clasping her stomach with both hands. "The food! It was incredible."

"Yes, it is hard to miss with those wine tours," Julie responded, patiently. She knew the type—the customers who wanted to talk and impress, and only rarely bought. They wanted exactly the same wine they'd had that night on the Loire, when … blah, blah, blah, but the wineries visited by the American-run tours weren't usually the ones that exported wine to the U.S. Even less likely were they to distribute on America's West Coast. "And so what are you thinking you'd like to try today? Making dinner tonight?"

The customer shifted her big shopping tote on her shoulder and picked up a random bottle, turning it over to look at the tasting notes. "I'm not sure," she mumbled. "Maybe I'll see something that trips my trigger."

"I'll be happy to help if you have any questions," Julie said, retreating back to the counter to wait. This customer, she knew, would be "just looking" for a couple more minutes to ensure that Julie thought she had been worth her time, and then she'd slip out the door.

As she sat back down on her stool behind the counter, Julie's cellphone buzzed. She looked at the incoming text:

WHAT'S YOUR PARENTS NUMBER?

Oh, André! It had been four days since she'd heard from him. He always used all caps, as if he were Donald

Trump. But why was he asking for the address? Did he plan to ship them some wine?

She typed in the address, adding "Why?"

She waited. No answer.

The customer slipped out, setting off the door chime, and Julie called out, "Thanks for coming by. Let me know if I can ever help you find something." She returned to her phone screen, waiting for André's response. The door chime rang again. Julie looked up and nearly dropped her phone.

"André! Is it really you?"

Her dark, handsome fiancé was walking toward her, his arms outstretched and a huge smile on his face. Julie ran out from behind the counter into his arms and let him envelop her in a long, tight hug. She pulled back and tipped her head up for his kiss.

"So this is why you needed the address," she said. She pretended to pout. "And here I thought you were sending us some great French vintage."

"Oh, disappointed, are you?" he said, laughing. "Maybe I should go back and—" she interrupted him, locking her lips on his again. It felt like she was back in Paris, her heart pounding, her love soaring.

Finally, they separated, and André followed her back to the stools behind the counter. "Sorry I didn't call," he explained. "I only thought to text for the exact address when I was in the neighborhood."

"Oh, no need to apologize!" she assured him. "But such a surprise? Why no warning?" She leaned forward toward him and put her hands on his knees.

"I'm sorry, I didn't think you needed one. Chef found someone and he let me go right away. So here am I!" André got up and sauntered down one of the aisles of wine stacks. "So, this is the shop I heard so much about."

Julie watched him walk slowly down a row of Washington wines, pick up a bottle here and there, and study the labels. "Do Americans always list the varietals on their labels?" he asked.

"Not always. Not usually with typical Bordeaux blends, but often with the Rhones, sometimes with the Spanish and Italian varietals," she said. As she watched him move around the store, she was struck by how he was dressed. He looked so French, something she'd first noticed in Paris but had forgotten. He wore skin-tight jeans and a silk scarf, a tight-fitting sweater and low leather boots. The gay men of Seattle would pick him out of a crowd in an instant, she thought.

Finally, he'd exhausted his interest in the wine and returned to her side. "*Puis, comment ça va?* When are you going to start being the boss? Have your parents traveled?"

"No, they're leaving this weekend for Alaska. I'm still trying to find an assistant. So I'm afraid the next few weeks are going to be kind of hectic."

André scooted close and parted her knees. He slipped his legs between hers and held her head with both hands. He pulled her eyes close to his. "You are making an excuse to not see me?" he whispered.

Julie felt a crooked smile cross her face. Maybe she was. But why? In the ten minutes André had been in the shop, her initial elation at seeing him had dulled. Was it now a mild revulsion?

What was so French about him thrilled her in Paris. Now she wondered if he could ever seem at home in Seattle.

"Hey, I know! While you're looking for a job, you could come and help me out," she said to cover her ambivalence.

André shook his head. "I don't think I can do that. I don't know about wine."

"It won't matter. People will hear you talk. and they'll think, 'Ah, he's French. He must know his wine.'"

André laughed and leaned in to peck her on the lips.

"Let's close up the shop and go celebrate," he said. "I can't believe I'm finally here with you."

Julie slipped off the stool and shuffled the résumés. She didn't want to brush him off, but she was confused. Why had she so quickly lost her enthusiasm for this man she'd waited so long to see?

"Hey, *cherie*," André said. "What's wrong? Not glad to see me?"

Julie fought the urge to say yes. "Oh, no, André. I'm thrilled that you're here. It's just that I have a lot to do tonight. I have three interviews with possible assistants tomorrow."

André moved in behind her and wrapped his arms around her from the back. Just then, the door chime rang, and Julie turned to see Jon walking in with Zelda, his focus on keeping the leash from tangling in the door. Julie caught her breath, and Jon looked up.

"Oh!" he exclaimed. He looked startled and deflated at the same time. There was no chance he didn't know who this man standing behind her was. He looked the part. He was acting the part.

Julie shook herself loose from André's arms and darted around the counter to take Zelda's leash.

"Uh, J-J-Jon," she said, nearly tripping over his name. Was she embarrassed at being discovered in her fiancé's arms? She gestured at André. "This is André. André, this is Jon. Jon and I are sharing custody of Zelda."

Julie leaned down and let her hand roll down Zelda's back as he headed back behind the counter toward André.

Jon forced a smile and nodded toward André, extending his hand over the counter. "Nice to meet you, André. I've heard much about you."

André ignored the hand, looking sideways at Jon. "*Ami o frere?*" he asked.

"Uh, Jon doesn't speak French, André," Julie interjected.

"*Ami,*" Jon answered. "*Buen ami.*"

"Oh! *Excusez moi!*" Julie laughed nervously. "I didn't know."

She stood back and looked back and forth between them. Her eyes stuck on Jon's and she gave him an embarrassed shrug.

"We met because of Zelda," Jon said with not a bit of uncertainty. "I'm sure Julie will tell you all about it." He saluted Julie and backed down the aisle. "But I have to get to work. Welcome to the U.S., André. I hope you like it here."

Jon turned and left quickly, and Zelda whined after him. André watched him leave, narrowed his eyes just for a second, as if understanding something, and turned to smile at Julie.

"He seems nice. And you two...?"

Julie picked up the résumés again and tapped them against the counter to straighten the pile.

"Oh, nothing. No. I didn't even know he spoke French. He kept Zelda while I was in France, and now we share her so we can both work."

André seemed to accept that without concern. "Oh, and where does Jon work?"

"He's a bartender at a restaurant downtown. A very nice restaurant."

"Maybe he can put in a word for me with the chef," André said.

"I'll ask him, but he doesn't do much with the kitchen."

Zelda leaned against Julie's leg, begging for some attention. Julie leaned down and hugged her as André watched. Clearly, he wasn't charmed.

"I should get myself settled, and you should get your work done so we can start spending our time together," he said, giving Zelda and Julie wide berth as he headed toward the door.

"Where are you staying?"

"I've lodged myself at the Kimpton. Is it nice?"

"Yes." Julie nodded. "I think you'll be comfortable there. It has a kind of Euro vibe. I'd come by tonight. but you probably need some sleep. Jet lag and all. And I need to take Zelda home. So, how about I call you tomorrow and we'll see ..." She stopped. What questions could there be?

André's eyes reflected her confusion. "See what?"

Julie scrambled to explain. "Uh, see how we can help find you a job," she ad-libbed.

André stepped toward her again and put his hands on her hips. He raised her face to his with a finger.

"I am very happy to see you, Julie." He leaned in for a kiss, and Julie let him brush his lips against hers, her eyes open, looking across the room and out the door.

Twelve

Out on Zelda's morning walk the next day, Julie pulled her cellphone from her pocket and called André's cellphone. His answering service declared his voice mailbox full. She looked the number up for the Kimpton, stored it in her contacts, and dialed it.

The receptionist transferred her call to André's room. An answering machine demanded in a smarmy monotone, "Leave a message for … [André's voice] André Lebover … then hang up or press pound for more options."

Julie waited for the beep.

"Hi, André. I hope you slept well," she dictated. "Why don't you come by the shop today about noon. I'll order out for sandwiches. Okay? Okay. *Bientot*."

She hung up and dropped the phone back into her coat pocket.

"Oh, what are we going to do, Zelda? What are we going to do?"

Zelda looked up at her, and Julie was struck again, like she had been hundreds of times, how clearly the dog understood exactly what she meant. The dog shook a bit of water off her raincoat and plodded forward through the puddles as if to say, "All we can do, Mom, is keep moving."

"That's right," Julie answered. "We'll just shake it off. Get back with the program." They splashed through another dozen steps. "André it is."

AT NOON, SHE AND ANDRÉ were eating cream cheese and prosciutto sandwiches at the counter in the store, and Julie had started to feel less conflicted about his presence. Perhaps her earlier anxiety had more to do with worries about the store than concern about her relationship with her fiancé. And it looked like everything was working out.

"I think I may have found an assistant," she said. "I interviewed someone this morning who seems like she's great for the job. She obviously knows her wine and she's worked in retail."

"Great. Then you won't be so busy." André looked pleased. He reached over and put his hand on hers. "You can pay more attention to me, now that I'm here. I will not be alone."

Yes, Julie thought, suddenly feeling like her sanguinity had taken a step backward. Of course, he would think only in terms of what this meant for him.

"What do you mean?" she asked, forcing herself to stay pleasant when she really wanted to ask, "Why is everything always about you?"

"You don't feel the same here, Julie. You seem distant."

Again, she chose not to argue. "It's work. It's just tough now until I get some help. I'll be fine. Really I will."

André, however, must have caught something in her tone. He pushed his dark eyebrows so close together they almost touched in the middle, above his long, Latin nose.

"You still want to get married ... ?" He lifted her chin with a finger, forcing her to look into his eyes. It wasn't a question and it wasn't a statement. Something in between.

"Of course," Julie answered quickly, shaking her head loose. "Of course. Once you get a job and get settled, we can talk about it."

"Just talk? Or actually get married?"

"Plan," she said. "Yes, plan to get married."

André's eyebrows relaxed and he smiled broadly. "Good. I know how you Americans go for your big weddings. I'm looking forward to seeing ours!"

Julie couldn't help smiling back. His grin had always cheered her, even on dreary days in Paris, when she'd wondered if she'd ever get back home.

"Yes, me too," she said, mainly to close the topic. It wasn't necessarily true. She couldn't imagine summoning up the excitement to plan one of those multi-thousand-dollar weddings that some of her old classmates had staged in the past few years. She wasn't close to any of these women anymore, but she guessed they got some return on their investment, if only more stuff from their Amazon.com gift registration.

"Hey, do you think you could talk to Jon about his restaurant?" André asked. "Maybe they need a chef? Or maybe he knows some other kitchens, can ask around?"

Julie hated this topic too. She didn't feel like asking Jon to help André find a job, given the way she knew Jon felt about him. Or really, about her with him. But she couldn't admit that to André.

"Sure, I'll ask him. He isn't too involved with the restaurant scene. He's actually in law school. Doesn't have much time to socialize."

"Law school?" André jerked his head toward her, surprised. "He's going to be an attorney? I thought he was a bartender. A barrister? That's impressive."

Julie laughed. "Well, attorneys … not so much in the U.S. There are already too many lawyers."

Her phone buzzed, and she picked it up off the counter and checked the caller ID.

"Hi, Jon," she said in the most neutral voice she could manage.

"Hey, Julie," he said. "Hey, I hate to ask, knowing you are probably busy now with André, but could you keep Zelda this weekend? I mean, no back and forth?"

"Oh," she said. "Something come up?"

"Yeah," he said. He sounded like he was trying to be cheerful, not like he really was. "I have to go out of town. I'll be back in time for online classes on Monday. I can watch her as usual during the day."

"Okay, sure. That's fine," she said. "Zelda and I can find something to do on our own this weekend. No problem."

Jon lowered his voice. "Is André there? I mean, with you now?"

"Yes, he's here." Julie looked up and nodded at her fiancé. André bumped her elbow and held up a finger.

"Just a moment," she said into the phone, and covered the speaker.

"*Qué?*" she asked.

André whispered, "Ask him about jobs. About the kitchen. Maybe he can ask the chef to talk to me."

Julie fought the urge to roll her eyes but nodded and turned back to the phone.

"Sorry. I'm back."

"What was that about?"

"Well, he wants to know if you can introduce him to the chef there."

"Uh … ." Jon paused. "I really don't think so. It's not my place to … ." He stopped. Julie looked up at André's anxious face.

"Okay. Sure," she said, as if he'd really had an answer for

her. "Well, have a nice trip. Zelda will miss you."

Julie hung up and André grabbed her arm. "What did he say?"

"He said he'd ask." Julie put down the phone and looked away, hiding what probably looked like a guilty face.

"Maybe I should talk to Jon. Tell him my credentials."

"Sure, but that will have to wait. He called to tell me he's going out of town for the weekend. We usually walk Zelda together on Sundays. He had to let me know he can't do it this weekend."

André leaned back and knit his eyebrows again. "You are close, *n'est-ce pas*? Closer than you tell me?"

"No," Julie said. She shook her head. "It's just Zelda. We only spend time together with Zelda."

"Okay. I will walk with you and Zelda Sunday. Where do we go?"

"Yes. That's good. You can meet me in the morning tomorrow too, if you want to walk. We get out about six."

"It is not dark?"

Julie stood up and started to gather up their sandwich wrappers and napkins. "This is Seattle. It's light by 4:30."

André looked shocked, and Julie laughed. "Didn't you see that this morning?"

"Uh, *non*. I was sleeping until 10."

"So, *oui ou non*? You coming?"

Thirteen

If André wanted to reignite Julie's romantic feelings toward him, joining her and Zelda on a morning walk didn't accomplish it.

They stepped into the park in what Julie thought was a pleasant mist. Having lived in Seattle all of her life except for the fourteen months in Paris, she considered a misty day "wet" but not "rainy." Rainy was rare in Seattle, but from September through June "wet" was kind of usual. It felt nice, cool even. Sweet on the skin. Better than the harsh sun she experienced on a vacation trip to Palm Springs one winter.

"Do you have an umbrella?" André asked.

Julie looked askance. "For this?" she asked, holding out her hand to show how little moisture was falling. "This stuff comes up about as much as it comes down. An umbrella doesn't help. You should get a 60/40 coat."

"What's that?"

"Like this," she said, pulling on the front of her rain parka. "It sheds moisture, but it also breathes."

"Breathes?"

"Lets your body moisture out, you know?"

André frowned and pulled his suede jacket closer around his slim torso.

"Not very smart."

Julie shook her head. "Smart? Oh, you mean like fashionable. Well, leather really doesn't work in rain."

Zelda scampered ahead quickly, stepped to the side of the walk, and started turning a tight circle.

André pointed at her. "What's she doing?"

"That means she is going to poop," Julie said. She stopped while the dog hunched her back and took care of her business. Once she was finished, Zelda hopped away and stood, waiting.

Julie pulled a plastic bag over her hand and leaned down to pick up Zelda's pile.

"What are you doing?" André jumped back, disgusted.

"Cleaning up after her," Julie said, turning the bag inside out and tying it closed.

"You do that every time?"

"Of course. You can't just leave it there for someone to step in."

Julie handed André the leash and stepped over to a trash can and deposited Zelda's contribution. She looked back at André.

"You're not much of a dog person, are you?"

"I like dogs," he said, unconvincingly. He sounded like even he didn't believe it.

Julie retrieved the leash, and they returned to the path and headed toward the cliff overlooking the sound.

"How long do you have her?" André asked.

"Well, I wish it were forever. But she's a big dog. She'll probably only be with me another ten years."

"*Années?*"

"*Ouí. Années. Est-ce-que un problem?*"

"No. No," André said, hesitantly. "But when we go to France?"

"You mean to visit? I'm sure Jon will be happy to keep her."

Zelda pulled up to the spot on the cliff overlooking the water where they usually paused to take in the scenery and sat.

"Yes, to visit," André said, holding back a ways from the edge of the cliff. "But maybe later to live?"

Julie spun around. "You want to live there?"

"After a while. Don't you? I think you love France."

"Yeah, but not until Zelda is gone for sure." She shook her head. "We have a lot to talk about, André."

André grabbed her free hand and pulled her back to him. "Yes! We do," he said. "So much to talk about!" He leaned forward to kiss her, but Julie moved back toward Zelda. She squatted down and put her arm around her big dog.

"Don't listen to him, sweetie," she said, her mouth close to Zelda's ear. "I'm not leaving you again."

MONDAY MORNING, JULIE LED HER new assistant up and down the aisles in the wine store, pointing out its organization. "And here are our imports, organized by country. I've thought from time to time that perhaps we should organize them by varietal or by region. Most Americans choose wine by their preference for the grape or region, not by country."

"Oh, I agree," said Sara, a bit too enthusiastically. "It makes no sense by country. People don't come in and ask for a 'French wine,' do they? They say, I'm looking for a Burgundy."

Julie let Sara's sycophancy slide. She was undoubtedly trying to make a good impression as an agreeable and faithful employee from the start.

"Exactly," she said. "That's exactly what I'm saying. Or sometimes they'll say I want a mourvèdre, not knowing that a monastrell from Spain is the same grape but maybe just a different style."

They were interrupted by chimes at the door. Julie peered around the end of the aisle.

"André! What a surprise!" Julie sounded elated, she realized, but in fact, it was the surprise of seeing him that raised her voice.

Sara walked up behind her, and Julie turned sideways to introduce her.

"*Je suis enchante!*" André said, grasping Sara's hand and bending down to kiss it. "I am certain you will sell much wine for *ma cherie*."

Julie caught herself rolling her eyes and stopped before André noticed. "Perhaps you can tell that André is from Paris," she said to Sara. "We met last summer when I was apprenticing there."

Sara, apparently enchanted as well, smiled sweetly, revealing deep dimples that transfixed her look from grown-up to cherublike.

"*Enchantee, aussi,*" she answered André.

Perhaps she'd do well with male customers, Julie thought, watching her. Julie herself had always preferred to help women choose wine. She had less patience with the flirtations of men.

She turned to André. "Why the surprise visit?"

André bounced on his toes, excited about something. "I know how much you like to plan ahead. I made a reservation for tomorrow night at Jon's restaurant. Will that be okay?"

"Ah, sure," Julie said. "I'll have to figure out what to do with Zelda. But that will be nice. I've never been to Bin 409."

"Why not?" he asked. "Is it not good?"

"No. It's supposed to be great. I just have never had a reason to go there. It's a little above my pay grade."

Sara jumped in. "It's great. I've been there a couple of times. Great wine list."

André winked at her but turned back to Julie. "So, it's a date?"

"Sure. I hope it is after seven. I don't close the store until then."

"Of course not. Earlier than eight *est barbare*. I can pick you up, no?"

"Sure. I just have to see if Jon can look after Zelda."

André frowned at the dog's name. "Oh, yes. Zelda. Yes, of course. Okay. I will leave you to work." He leaned forward for a kiss, and this time Julie let him meet her lips. He waved and skipped out the door.

"He seems genuinely infatuated with you," Sara said as they watched him turn down the sidewalk. "But I sense a bit of tension there?"

"You are very perceptive. I appreciate that. Perhaps I'll explain later." Julie shook her head sadly. "When I figure it out for myself."

THAT AFTERNOON, AFTER SPENDING A few hours showing Sara the store, demonstrating the point-of-sale system, and going over store policies, Julie excused herself and slipped into the back room to get some bookkeeping done. As she sat in front of her computer, she pushed the speaker on her landline and dialed Jon.

"Hello?"

"Hi, Jon."

"Julie? What is this number?"

"It's the store. I'm in the back, working on updating the website, so I've got the phone on speaker."

"Oh."

Julie waited for Jon to continue, but he said nothing. Why the cold shoulder? she wondered.

"Are you there?" she asked.

"Yes. You called me. What do you want?"

Julie frowned. "Is something wrong?"

"I'm studying, Julie. What is it?"

Julie paused, wondering if it was a bad idea to call, but she continued. "I wanted to know if you're working tomorrow night."

"I always work Tuesday nights. Why?"

"I apparently need someone to watch Zelda, so I was just thinking if your schedule had changed…"

"You know it hasn't changed. I would have told you if it had. But is this going to be a habit with you now that André is here?"

"What do you mean?"

Jon snorted. "Well, I suppose you will be busy now. No time for Zelda."

"That's not true. It's just one night. One dinner. It won't be a habit. I can't afford it to be a habit."

"Perhaps André doesn't have the same restrictions."

Julie considered taking on the argument that Jon seemed interested in starting. But they had become such good friends. This change in his attitude was distressing.

"Yes, maybe not," she answered instead. "Well, sorry to bother you. How was your trip?"

"I'm sorry, Julie, but I've got to go." And with that, the phone went dead and the dial tone came back.

Julie stared at the phone for a minute before punching in another number.

"Hey, Jules," Cary answered. "What's up? I heard you found an assistant. Just in time."

"Yeah, I think Mom and Dad left this morning."

"They did. I took them to the marina. I've never seen them so excited."

"That's great."
"So, you called?"

Fourteen

CARY'S LONG LEGS STRETCHED ALL the way across the narrow deck that flanked the south side of the houseboat he rented on Lake Union. His eyes were closed, his hands relaxed and folded on his stomach as he soaked up the late-day sun on an old wooden bench that perfectly matched the gray siding behind him.

As Julie and Zelda stepped down the boardwalk toward him, Zelda pulled, anxious to greet her uncle, and Julie stopped to unhook his leash. The dog leapt forward, ran down the walk, and jumped up to hit the dreamy Cary on the chest.

"Whoa!" Cary jerked awake and fought to keep his balance on the bench. "What the ... ." He sat up and shook off his surprise.

"Ah, how are you girl?" he said, wrapping his arms around the big dog.

"Hey," Julie said, catching up to Zelda.

"My god, she's not losing any weight, is she?" Cary asked.

"Not with two of us to spoil her." Julie sat down beside her brother.

"So, I hear André finally made it. When do I get to meet the lover boy?" Cary prodded.

"Yeah, well, we'll have to figure that out. Thanks for keeping Zelda. Can I pick her up in the morning? Our dinner reservation isn't until eight, so I'm guessing it will be dark down here by the time we're done."

"Sure," Cary said. Zelda quieted down and flopped onto his feet.

Julie sat closed-eyed, her face tipped up to the sun, frowning. She could feel Cary's eyes on her.

"Anything wrong, Julie? I thought I'd see you happy as a clam."

Julie blinked her eyes open and forced a smile. "Who says I'm not?"

Cary said nothing; his stare communicated his concern for her.

"Okay, you could always see right through me," she said. "But I'm not really sure what it is. I just feel a little confused right now."

She stood up and handed him Zelda's leash.

"Could it be—" Cary started, but Julie held out her palm.

"Please. Let's not talk about it now. I've got to get home and change. André is picking me up in a half hour." Julie saw Cary shaking his head, but she turned to leave, hurrying up the boardwalk, back to her car.

Cary called after her: "I think I have a pretty good idea what the problem is." Before she stepped off the walk, she heard him say to Zelda, "And I'll bet you do too."

As the limousine pulled up to the restaurant, Julie's

mood darkened. The prospect of Jon watching her and André together from his post at the bar saddened her more than it made her nervous. She didn't expect Jon to make a scene—or show any reaction at all. But she did worry that André might misbehave. Would he walk right up to Jon and beg for an audience with the chef?

The driver hopped out before Julie could find the door handle, and her passenger door popped open. He reached in to offer her his hand. André followed her out and up to the big door of Bin 409.

"Is there a problem, Julie?" André asked, reacting to her gloomy face.

"I'm not sure it's a good idea to come here," she said. "Jon knows you're interested in a job. Doesn't it look too obvious?"

André opened the door and took her arm, steering her inside. "What do you mean? Wouldn't you want to check out a restaurant where you might work? I need to see the menu, and see how things are prepared. I need to know something about the cuisine."

Julie nodded at his logic, but she couldn't force a smile. How miserable would the next couple of hours be?

The host greeted them and checked off their reservation on his tablet. He pulled two menus and a wine list off his desk. "This way, please."

He led them to the middle of the restaurant, and Julie avoided looking toward the bar. André pulled out the chair, and she tried to wave him off.

"Oh, that's not necessary," she said.

"Of course it is. Chivalry is not dead," he said, helping her pull the seat up to the table.

Julie sat and stole a glance around. Jon stood at the bar, but he was looking in the other direction and she breathed a sigh of relief. Perhaps he hadn't seen them come in. Maybe he'd not notice them at all as long as he stayed busy and

André did nothing to call attention to them.

"May I offer you a cocktail, madam?" The waiter interrupted her thoughts.

"Ah, sure. How about a glass of Prosecco?" she said, looking up into his fawning face.

"Oh, no, no, no!" André nearly shouted. "It must be Champagne. Give me a moment with the wine list, monsieur?"

Julie watched the waiter's expression change from obsequious to charmed. Apparently, he was impressed with André's accent. He bowed slightly and backed away to give André time to consider what bottle to order.

Julie looked over her menu as André perused the wine list. The waiter returned and André pointed. "A fine selection," the waiter said. They always say that, Julie thought.

"I hope you are not spending too much, André," she said. "I don't need to be spoiled, and you need to find a job. And chefs aren't paid here in Seattle like they are in New York."

"This is not your concern, *mi amor*. This is a special night."

"Our first date in this country?"

André smiled smugly. "Yes! That's it!" he said, leaving Julie with the impression that it wasn't it at all.

A GOOD NINETY MINUTES LATER, the waiter was removing their entrée plates, and Julie tried to stifle a yawn.

"Another bottle of the Champagne, *s'il vous plait?*" André looked up at the waiter.

"Oh, no, André," Julie pleaded. "I work tomorrow."

André spoke to the waiter. "Do not mind the lady. I insist."

"In no more than a moment," the waiter responded, walking away with his hands full of dishes.

Julie was beaten. There was no way she could convince

a man who was accustomed to occupying a dinner table until well after midnight that 10 p.m. was a respectable time to retire. She would have to try to catch up on sleep over the weekend.

"This has been an incredible night, André," she said, and in many ways, she meant it. André had behaved himself, leaving Jon alone at the bar. Her lamb chops were perfectly broiled and deliciously seasoned. The Champagne was the best she'd ever tasted on U.S. soil. "I haven't been so pampered since that night before I left Paris."

"Aw, but the night is not over!" André exclaimed, pointing to the waiter with a flourish of his arms.

The waiter approached with two ramekins of creme brulé. Immediately behind him, the sommelier arrived with an open bottle of Champagne and filled their glasses.

As the flurry continued in front of her, Julie looked up and saw Jon watching from the now-quiet bar. She had avoided meeting his eye all night. But now, her heart jumped at the sight of his placid expression. He saw them, but it appeared that he didn't care.

"I propose a toast to us," André said, raising his flute to get Julie's attention. "To our future."

She lifted her glass to his, but instead of drinking, André stood up and swiveled down to a knee beside her. Julie was confused for only a moment before it dawned on her. He was going to propose. Officially.

He pulled the little velvet box from his jacket pocket, opened it and held it out for Julie's inspection. It was, of course, a ring. She glanced at it and then back up at the bar. Jon was still watching, his face still blank, and she looked away.

"I am sorry I wasn't able to give you this before you left France," André was saying. "But this gives me a chance to ask you again. Julie DuChamps Bouvier, will you be my wife?"

Julie shot a glance at the bar. Jon wasn't there, and she turned back to André's expectant eyes. She hesitated, but she knew this wasn't the time nor the place to change her mind.

"Of course I will, André," she whispered. "Of course I will."

Fifteen

As Julie approached Cary's houseboat the next morning, he and Zelda were sitting in the same place she had found him the day before, enjoying second-day-in-a-row sunshine. This time, Cary was sipping from a large mug, and Zelda was the one snoozing.

As Julie's steps vibrated the planks of the houseboat deck, Zelda shook herself awake and sauntered over to greet her.

"Well, that's an unenthusiastic greeting," she reprimanded her dog. "What, you've decided that Cary's your favorite now?"

Cary grinned. "You seem chipper this morning," he said. "Want some coffee?"

"No, I have to get Zelda home and get to work," she said. She walked up to the bench and held out her left hand, showing off her new diamond.

Cary looked at it solemnly.

"Aren't you happy for me, Care Bear?" she asked, pulling her hand back.

Cary shook his head. "Are you sure?" he asked.

"Why wouldn't I be?"

Cary paused, looking as if he were parsing his words in his head before he spoke them. "Well, for one thing, he isn't particularly fond of Zelda. You told me that yourself."

"Maybe he just needs some time to get used to her. She can win anyone over. Everybody loves Zelda."

Cary patted the seat next to him.

"Sit down, Jules," he said.

Julie hesitated. She didn't want her positive attitude that morning—the first she'd had about André since he arrived—to be squelched by her brother. What? Was he jealous?

"Okay, out with it," she said. "What's your problem?"

"I saw what had happened between you and Jon," he answered quietly, sounding afraid to state anything too vociferously.

"Nothing was happening—"

Cary held up his hand to stop her. "No, hear me out."

Julie sat back and looked out over the lake. She'd better let him have his say now or something unresolved would sit between them.

"I've never seen you get that close to someone so quickly," Jon continued. "It was only a month and you were finishing each other's sentences. Your face lit up when he was around. You have to admit it. You feel something for him. A whole lot of something."

"What do you know about this?" Julie didn't want to think about Jon. It was time for her to move forward with her life, and her plan for months had been to do that with André.

"Well, I'm a guy," Cary said, chuckling at his own obvious observation, "and this much I can tell you. I've never seen a guy more smitten than Jon."

Julie closed her eyes and breathed deep. "Thank you very much for that information, brother. But I'm sorry. André came all the way to the U.S. to be with me. Jon just happened to live next door. You don't really fall in love with the boy next door except in the movies."

"Oh, but you *do* fall in love with the gorgeous Frenchman who swept you off your feet in Paris?" Cary laughed. "That sounds like a movie script to me."

Julie lifted her left hand and waved it in front of Cary again. "This says 'yes,'" she said. "André wouldn't have given this to me if he weren't 'smitten' with me too."

Cary paused and looked away. "Well, then I guess you're a very lucky girl," he said. "You get to choose between two smitten beaus."

"I already have. And as far as I know, Jon isn't even a choice."

"And what if he is?"

Julie signed deeply. "Care Bear. This isn't your problem. Wait until you meet André. You'll see how charming he is. Then you'll understand."

"I can't wait," Cary deadpanned.

Julie sat for a long minute, saying nothing. She didn't want to hear this. Thinking about Jon would only delay and complicate things. There was nothing wrong with marrying André, and nothing to gain from a relationship with Jon.

"I've got to get going, Jules," her brother interrupted her thoughts. "I've got a couple of interviews in Yakima with wineries. Thanks for making those contacts." He stood up and handed Julie Zelda's leash.

"Well, don't go mad," she said, standing up and leaning in to hug him.

"I'm not mad," Cary said unconvincingly. "I just need to get going." He scratched Zelda on the head and turned to walk into the houseboat.

"Come on, Zellie," Julie said, hooking up Zelda's leash to her collar. "I've got to get to work and you have to go visit your uncle Jon."

COMING IN THE FRONT OF the apartment building from work that evening, Julie scrounged in her purse for her keys and nearly ran into into Jon.

"Oh, hey!" she said. "Sorry. I should look where I'm going."

"Hello, Julie," Jon muttered. "I hear you're now formally engaged."

"Did you hear or see that?" she asked, eyeing him suspiciously. Had he seen André get down on his knee before disappearing from the bar the night before.

"See what? I have no idea what you're talking about. I talked with Cary today. He told me."

Julie held up her hand. "Yes. We are formally engaged," she said. "Now I have a wedding to plan at the same time I'm trying to train a new employee."

Jon smirked. "Yeah. Well, life is rough. But, hey. I just let Zelda in your apartment. We finished our walk. I've got to get to work."

"But it's Wednesday, your day off."

"I picked up an extra shift. Something to soak up my free time." He stepped around her.

Julie grabbed his arm as he passed. "Jon. I still want to be friends," she said, pleading. "Can't we? We still share Zelda. And we're neighbors. Can't we still walk Zelda together sometimes? Like we used to?"

Jon looked away, down the street, avoiding her eyes.

"Sure. Sure. Sure, we can. I'll give you a call sometime." He pulled away and strode out the door and down the sidewalk. Julie watched him go. Why was he making her so sad?

"Damn him," she said, unlocking her apartment door. "He has no right to try to ruin my happiness. Him or Cary."

A WEEK LATER, JULIE HAD found no time to think about a wedding. Teaching Sara what she needed to know, doing the bookkeeping, and managing the store took up every minute of her day; and making dinner and walking Zelda with André soaked up her evenings and the weekend. She was glad they hadn't set a date yet, as she didn't need the added pressure of a wedding deadline.

Updating her inventory on the computer on the counter, Julie heard the door chime and looked up to see André rushing in. Sara stepped aside as he scooted past her in the aisle.

"Julie! Julie!" he shouted. "You won't believe this." He stopped, breathless, and put his palms on the counter before her. She looked quizzically at him, and before she could ask him what was so exciting, he spat out his news. "I just got a call from Chef Luke Guillot in New York. Isn't that great? Can you believe it?"

"Who's that?" she asked, knowing her question risked his disdain.

André huffed, as she expected he would. "Only the best French chef in *Etas-Unis! Proprietaire de L'Escargot*! I can't believe you have not known of him!"

Julie smiled apologetically. "I'm kind of a West Coast girl, André. What goes on in New York is fairly peripheral to us here."

"But New York is not *secondaire*! In your country it is the capital of cuisine!" He waved his hands with enthusiasm.

"Well, I think there are those who would argue the point," Julie said softly. She saw Sara smile with amusement. "But what did Chef Guillot want?"

"He wants me to come to New York to interview for a position in his restaurant!"

Julie stared at André. Was he serious? He had just arrived in Seattle, and now he was heading to New York?

"Sara, if you need something we'll be in the back," Julie said. She motioned to André. "André, *avec moi.*"

As soon as he followed her into the back room, Julie turned and confronted him. "What are you talking about? We were going to get married. And now you want to move to New York?"

André grinned. Clearly, he wasn't reading her right. "You will come with me," he said. He was so excited he was bouncing on his toes. "We will get married there. All the best of America is in New York City!"

Julie took a deep breath to keep her temper from was flaring. "I don't know why you think that, but I certainly don't."

André finally picked up on her mood. "Please, Julie," he pleaded. "You must come with me to see. Let's see if there's a place for us there. This is the chance I want! The very best French restaurant in *le monde nouveau!*"

He stepped forward to grasp her shoulders, but she moved back.

"I don't know," she said. "My life is here. This is my store now. I'd have to leave Zelda behind. This makes no sense to me, André."

He lowered his voice and looked at her sweetly. "It makes sense because we are to be married," he said. He stepped toward her again and pulled her toward him. He kissed her lightly on the forehead. Julie turned away, folded her hands, and put her knuckles to her lips.

"André," she said. "The other day you told me you want to move back to France some day and you want me to come with you. Today you tell me we should move to New York so you can follow your dream. When were you going to ask me what I want?"

"But we want the same thing, Julie," he insisted. "To be married. You said yes. You said you wanted to be married, *oui?*"

"I do want to marry you, André."

She hesitated before continuing, wondering if that was still true. He'd slipped the ring on her finger only a few days before, and she hadn't slept well since. Backing out of an engagement would be one thing—hard enough—but moving all the way to New York and then deciding it was a mistake would be far worse. "I need some time to figure this out. To think it through. Can I have a couple of days?"

André walked around to face her and waved a long blue envelope in front of her face. "I thought you might need some time. So, these are for Thursday."

"What is that?"

"Airplane tickets. Two days from now. How is that?"

"So much for giving me time," she said sardonically. He just smiled at her brightly.

This was not going well, she thought. Not going well at all.

Sixteen

JULIE CRADLED THE PHONE ON her shoulder as she bent over her suitcase and pulled on the sticky zipper.

"I'm glad you still have reception, Mom," she said. "How far up the coast have you sailed?"

"Oh, not far," her mom said. "We're taking our time. This is the first time in our lives we don't have to hurry. No deadlines! Can you imagine?"

"That's great. But, there's something I need to talk with you about."

"You're getting married."

Julie grabbed the phone in her hand and sat down on her bed. "So, who told you? Cary?"

"Yes, he called us a couple of days ago. I'm so sorry we didn't get to meet André before we left. But you're not in a hurry, are you? You won't get married before we get back."

"Of course not."

"Are you excited?"

"Well, something else has come up," Julie said. She paused before divulging the news of her trip to New York.

"But you're not planning to move there, are you?" Her mother's voice rose, and she didn't sound happy.

"Oh, no," Julie said. She planned to put off that decision as long as possible, and she didn't want to raise the issue until she had to.

"So, anyway, Cary is going to move into my apartment while I'm in New York so he can help Jon take care of Zelda. I guess things in Yakima didn't work out. He didn't get either of those jobs. The other thing is that Sara is leaving as soon as I get back. I liked her a lot, but she got a better offer. Cary's going to help her in the store too."

"Wow, you're depending a lot of that little brother of yours."

"I know," Julie said with a little chuckle. "Who would have guessed that would ever happen."

"Well, he's growing up," her mother said. "Finally."

"So, I'll be back in a week, and I'll start the search for an assistant all over again."

A loud knock on the door triggered Zelda's even louder barking.

"That's André at the door, Mom. He got a car to take us to the airport. Apparently, Chef Guillot is sparing no expense to get him there. I have to run."

"Okay, honey. Be careful. I love you. Dad too."

"I love you too," Julie said, pulling her suitcase off the bed. "Give Dad a kiss."

Julie hung up and pulled the bag to the door and out to the foyer.

"Quiet!" she ordered Zelda and opened the door. André stepped in and kissed her on the cheek. Zelda walked away, not waiting for a greeting from him. She plopped down at the other end of the living room and put her head down to pout.

"Could you wait right here for a minute?" Julie asked André. "I've got to take Zelda down to Jon's apartment. I'll be right back."

She picked up the leash, and Zelda jumped up and ran to her.

"Why didn't you do that earlier?" André asked.

"I wanted to spend as much time with her as I could." Julie ignored André's disapproving head shake. He plopped down on a chair and looked at his watch.

"Please hurry. The car is waiting."

JULIE SAT ON THE SQUARED-OFF chair in the first-class Alaska Airlines' lounge, pulled her roller bag close, and sank into the uncomfortable foam cushion. The fabric was scratchy on her legs, and she wondered if she should have worn pants instead of shorts. Airplanes could be over-cooled, especially in first class, where there were fewer bodies packed into the space. She hadn't flown on a domestic flight for so long, she didn't even know if the airlines supplied blankets anymore.

André had sat at one of the long counters provided as work spaces for passengers and pulled out his laptop as soon as they came in. Julie sat and watched planes taxi back and forth out on the tarmac. Why did they have to get here so early? she'd asked André when he was checking his big bag, but he shrugged her off. He seemed anxious—perhaps he was worried about the upcoming interview with Chef Guillot.

She left him alone after that, but it still bugged her to be separated from Zelda before she had to be, just so she could sit in this uncomfortable chair for the next two hours and watch André scroll through his Twitter account and emails.

She rose to check out the fruit buffet along the wall just as André's phone buzzed. He pulled it out of his pocket and glanced at the screen. "It's the chef. Could you watch my computer?" He pointed to the wall of windows overlooking the runways. "I'm going over there to get better reception."

With his phone to the ear, André sang a French greeting and walked away. Julie sat down at André's laptop. Already she felt like his lackey, his assistant. In the two weeks since he had arrived in Seattle, he seemed like an entirely different man than she'd known in Paris. There, he'd been fun and entertaining, eager to show off his hometown, and happy to spend lazy days with her at outdoor cafés and benches along the banks of the river, while she read classic 18th-century French writers who had never interested her before.

She glanced down as the screen of the laptop. André had been in the middle of a response to an email from Guillot's secretary:

> There will be no problem with the green card.
> I get married soon and we have no problem
> with immigration. Plan is to

The email was unfinished. Reading it, Julie frowned. She looked up at André, standing with his nose practically touching the window pane, his back to her. She scrolled down to read the email that Guillot's secretary had sent to him.

> We are very excited to talk with you about the
> position of sous chef here this week. However-
> er, we are concerned that you do not have a
> stable immigration status. Immigration is get-
> ting a lot stickier these days. Do you have
> plans to get a green card. How are your mar-
> riage plans coming? As we talked last week,
> marriage would solve the problem. Or are you

applying for citizenship? Please get back to us asap. I'll send a limo to Newark for you. Bientot! Marie for Chef Guillot.

Julie looked away, perplexed. André had proposed marriage just before she left for Seattle. Was this his plan all along? To use her to cement his immigration status in the U.S.? Was she just convenient? She thought back to her time in Paris, remembering what she had tried so long to forget. For nearly a year, he had insisted their relationship wasn't exclusive, until, all of the sudden, just before she left France, it was. She'd wondered at the time what triggered his change of heart, but she put it out of her mind, believing his love simply had grown—and thinking she was lucky he had come to realize just in time that he didn't want to lose her.

Instead, she wondered now, had he realized just in time that she could be his ticket to New York?

As André put his phone back into his pocket and walked back to her, Julie stood up.

"I've been thinking, André," she said. "What if I move to New York, but we don't get married right away? You should be sure your job is going to work out before we take any more big steps, don't you think? Perhaps I should stay in Seattle until—"

"What?" André interrupted. "No, I just talked to the chef about this. We must get married. I cannot stay in Les Etas-Unis unless we get married."

Julie nodded and put her hand over her eyes. She took a deep breath before facing him again.

"Is that what this is about?" she asked, pointing to his laptop.

André cringed.

Julie held up her hand, holding the engagement ring right in front of his eyes. "This ring is all about you getting to stay in the United States? All about your plan?"

André stepped closer and put his hands on her shoulders. Julie noticed people had turned to watch them. She must have been talking too loud. Now they had an audience.

"No, no! I love you, Julie. I want to marry you because I love you," André insisted. Julie saw a woman directly behind him shake her head and roll her eyes. Apparently she wasn't convinced.

"You're wrong, André," she said, lowering her voice. "You want to get married because it's part of your plan. It's not about me. Everything we did back in Paris was just a setup, wasn't it?"

Julie's knees felt weak, and she turned to sit down on her uncomfortable chair. Tears stung in her eyes.

André flipped the lid down on his laptop and stood over her.

"I'm sorry you saw that email, Julie. It doesn't take away from the fact that I love you. I would want to marry you even if we weren't in *Etas-Unis*."

Julie blinked down the first stream of tears. She looked up at him angrily. "Can't you say 'United States?' Why is it always '**Etas-Unis**?'" She knew her complaint was vapid. She wasn't one of those people who insisted that immigrants spoke English. She was tolerant, knowing how hard it was for her to learn a foreign language. But suddenly everything André had done over the past two weeks bugged her.

"I'm sorry. But what does—"

"André, it's just part of our problem," she interrupted. "I didn't realize until you got here that we are so different. In Paris, I was happy to fit into your life. I ate what you ate. I dressed the way your mother dressed. I spoke French. It was lovely. But here, you don't want to live like I do. You don't want to know Zelda. You don't want to stay in Seattle.

You haven't even asked to meet my brother, my best friend in the world."

André raised his eyebrows. "I thought I was your best friend."

"For a while, I did too," she said in a harsh whisper. "But I was wrong." She pulled the ring from her finger and held it out to him. He looked at it, and when it appeared she was about to drop it, he put his hand under it and caught it.

"This makes things so much more difficult," he said. He sighed deeply and looked away as his eyes reddened.

"For you, maybe," Julie said. "But I have a feeling you'll do just fine. You'll figure things out."

She stood up, extracted the rollerbag handle, and threw her purse over her shoulder.

"Goodbye, André," she said, wiping the last of her tears off her face. "And good luck. Now, I have to go see a man about a dog."

Seventeen

Settling into the back seat of a cab minutes later, Julie took her cellphone out of her purse and pulled up her speed dial. She punched in a number. Cary answered.

"Hi, it's me," she responded. "I'll be at the store in about a half hour."

Cary said nothing, and Julie could sense his confusion from miles away.

"Look, I'll explain when I get there," she said. "You're at the store, right?"

"Uh, yes. Me and Sara are here."

Julie stopped herself from correcting his grammar. This was no time to pull her big sister act. "And, Cary, when I get there, I'd like to talk with you."

"About what?"

Julie paused. She really wanted to wait until she could look him in the eye. But she plunged ahead.

"Would you consider coming to work at the store with

me? Permanently? Not as my assistant, but as a partner?"

Cary laughed so loud she had to pull the phone away from her ear. "What took you so long? I've been wait—"

"I know, I know," she butted in. "I don't know what took me so long to figure it out. But it makes sense, doesn't it?"

JULIE WAS MORE NERVOUS KNOCKING on Jon's door than she had been talking to Cary. She had screwed a lot of things up the past year and a half, and it was intimidating to try to fix them all at once. Especially when so much had changed in just the past hour.

Zelda barked inside, and Julie heard Jon admonish her, unconvincingly. So, he was far more of a pushover and far less of a disciplinarian than he tried to project, she thought, smiling.

The door opened, and Jon stood frozen for a couple of seconds, his eyes wide.

"Didn't you just leave?" he asked. "Won't you miss your flight?"

Julie squatted and petted Zelda. "Can I come in?"

Not waiting for an answer, she stepped into his apartment, Zelda by her side.

Jon closed the door behind her. "What are you doing here?"

Julie walked into his living room before turning around to face him. "Look, I'm sorry. I know I'm not the brightest person in this room—"

"No, Zelda is," he quipped.

Julie laughed, relieved. If Jon were really fed up with her, he wouldn't be making a joke.

"Yes, she probably is," she agreed. "But what I want to say is sometimes I don't see things that are right in front of my eyes."

Jon slipped past her and bent down to save something

on his laptop. "Like what?" he asked, standing up and facing her.

"Well. Like, I should have offered Cary the job at the store a long time ago."

Jon looked at her sideways. "You missed your flight to tell me this?"

"And especially …," Julie shook her head and paused. "Especially like I never really wanted to marry André. I fell in love with France, not with a particular Frenchman, and all it took for me to understand that was to see André here. He isn't part of my life here."

Jon stood, his expression blank as if he wasn't yet impressed with her epiphany.

"And I'm not who he thought I was either," Julie continued. "I'm not his rootless American girl, willing to move across the country and then across the ocean with him so he can live his dreams. I'm Julie from Seattle, owner of a wine store, mommy of Zelda."

She paused again, for a moment uncertain whether to go on. He nodded, and she breathed deep before continuing. "A woman who is in love with a man from Seattle. A man who is a daddy to Zelda."

Slowly, a smile grew across Jon's face. It tipped up on one side. "And who is this 'daddy to Zelda?'"

Julie stepped close and took hold of his shirt collar with both hands. Jon looked down into her eyes and put his hands on her waist. "You are sure about this?"

"Yes. I am absolutely sure."

Jon paused, his eyes searching hers. For what? Sincerity? Finally, he seemed to find what he was looking for and leaned forward, his lips meeting hers. Julie caught her breath. His lips seemed to be searching as hard as his eyes had for an answer. She tried to help him find it.

Their kiss was too much for Zelda. She ran out of patience, barking and bouncing on her front paws. Their lips parted and they reached down together to scratch her ears.

"Oh, Zelda, we love you too," Julie said.

"Yup. Everybody loves Zelda," Jon added.

Well, maybe not everybody, Julie thought. But everybody who matters.

She looked up, Jon looked down, and they picked up where they left off.

Love Between the Vines

One

THE HOST INSIDE THE RESTAURANT entrance greeted Thomas like an old friend.

"Your regular table, Thomas?"

Sofia was surprised. Regular table?

"Thanks, Tyler," said Thomas. "That will be fine."

"How often do you come here?" Sofia asked quietly as she stepped around the host stand to follow Tyler into the hushed bowels of the restaurant.

"About once a week," Thomas whispered.

Tyler led them through the labyrinth of tables, past well-dressed and coifed patrons, to a table for two in a dark corner at the back of the restaurant. No one looked up as they passed.

The host pulled out a chair for Sofia and bent slightly toward her. "I don't believe we've met."

Although he didn't extend a hand to shake, Sofia took the cue and introduced herself. "Sofia Michaelis."

"Well, any friend of Thomas's is a friend of mine." He nodded, smiled politely, and handed Thomas the wine list.

"Actually, I'm his fiancée," Sofia said.

The host paused a beat.

"Of course," he responded with an apologetic glance toward Thomas. "I should have remembered." He handed Thomas a large, heavy leather menu.

Thomas opened what Sofia assumed was the wine list. "Could you send the sommelier?" he asked without looking up at either of them.

"Immediately." The host retreated.

"You're here once a week?" Sofia continued to pursue her question.

"We have most our business lunches here," Thomas explained, keeping his voice low. "We have an account."

"Why didn't I know this?"

Thomas flashed his patronizing, crooked smile—one that he had only recently begun using whenever he didn't want to discuss something she wanted to talk about.

"It's not important," he said, his voice as condescending as his smile.

"So, you have business meetings back here at a table for two once a week?" Sofia asked as soon as the host was out of earshot. "It seems a bit cozy. What if there are three of you?"

Thomas studied the wine list, ignoring her question. Sofia stared at him, but he refused to take her bait. Lately, he'd left a lot of questions unanswered, and she had come to feel there was a lot she didn't understand about Thomas's advertising firm.

As her eyes adjusted to the dark interior, Sofia glanced around. In the corner, a pianist touched his keys so lightly it took her a moment to identify the song he was playing over the clink of forks on china and hushed conversations. The crowd little resembled the patrons she was accustomed to dining with here in Seattle. Most of the men wore suits, even though ties and top buttons had been loosened to accommodate the evening. The women's suits and dresses were not ones Sofia had seen on the sale racks at Nordstrom, where she shopped. Designer, she guessed.

Thomas wore his usual Seattle business attire—khaki pants and a blue blazer, no tie. His thick thatch of blond hair masked his age, but Sofia had noticed over the past six months how all those business lunches had softened his once-trim physique.

She wore her best dress—a red knit with a pinched waist that showed off her slim figure. But it was modest compared with the fine couture that surrounded them. She fingered the modest diamond pendant at her nick. It was certainly the least expensive piece of jewelry in the room.

The sudden, silent approach of the sommelier surprised her. Thomas looked up.

"We'll have a bottle of Dom Perignon, 1990." The man nodded appreciatively and turned away.

"That's really not necessary, Thomas," Sofia said. "We can drink all the free bubbly we want next week when we're on vacation."

"Yes, I know." Thomas shook his head. "But that would be Walla Walla bubbly. I wanted this anniversary dinner to be special."

"It's already special," she said. "You know this is the first relationship I've ever had that lasted three years?"

Thomas continued to stare at the wine menu. Sofia reached across the table and put her hand on his.

"I'm really looking forward to getting away next week, aren't you?" she said. "It's the first time I think we've ever had my parents' place to ourselves."

A waiter slid up and gently laid dinner menus in front of them, making Sofia jump. The extremely muted nature of the room was getting on her nerves. Was she going to cringe each time someone approached their table? This kind of fine dining wasn't in her budget, and she realized she was glad it wasn't.

Thomas laid the wine menu down and picked up the dinner menu, still without meeting her eye. "Can we order first? I am famished."

Resigned to his cold shoulder, Sofia picked up her menu. "What do you think you'll have?"

AN HOUR LATER, THEIR PLATES clean, Sofia sat back with her last half of a glass of red wine. She had ordered the sockeye salmon and would have preferred a white wine with dinner, but Thomas ordered a cabernet without consulting her.

It hadn't been much of an anniversary dinner, in Sofia's estimation. Thomas had grunted out a few responses to her questions about his work and his progress toward getting the promotion he wanted, but he'd asked her nothing. It seemed odd. He used to have plenty of advice for her about the marketing she managed for a local microbrewery. Since they both worked in marketing, they once had much to talk about and share. Over time, though, he'd withdrawn, and at first, Sofia had chalked it up to the stress over work. But lately when they did talk about work, he shrewdly intimated his were the loftier concerns of a marketing executive, not a low-level practitioner.

Thomas caught the attention of their waiter and crooked his finger at him. The waiter hurried over.

"Can we have the check, please?" he asked. It was the first "please" Sofia had heard him utter all night.

"Can't we sit here for a few minutes?" she protested. "I still have quite a bit of wine left." Sofia picked up her glass and swirled the liquid to demonstrate.

"I'm sorry. I just remembered I have an early meeting tomorrow," he said with a forced smile.

"With your new marketing director?"

"What? Why would you ask that?"

Thomas pressed his eyebrows together.

"Well, you've just been working with her a lot lately. I guess it's a lot of work to break in a new employee."

"Well, yes, it is. But what was that inuendo?"

Sofia had intended none, but she tilted her head apologetically.

"I'm sorry. I didn't mean to suggest anything. I know it's crazy at work for you right now. I know you want that promotion. It will be nice to be away—"

Thomas interrupted. "About that. I am not sure I can make it after all."

Sofia put her glass down hard; the wine came close to sloshing over the edge. "What do you mean? We've been planning this trip for two months!"

Thomas grimaced. "I know. And I was really looking forward to it. But we have this new marketing team in Denver, and I have to go out there and get them started. It's only for a few days."

"But—"

"You know how important work is to me. I'm working my butt off to get that promotion. If I get this team off to a good start, I have a good chance at executive VP."

Sofia pouted. "But this is important for us, too. We haven't been away from work forever. We haven't gone out of town together since last May. That was more than a year ago!"

"I know." Thomas reached over and placed his hand on hers. "I'll make it up to you, I promise. But you should go anyway. You need some vineyard time. I know how much you love the wine country. It's in your blood. And you can spend some time touching up your golf game."

He pulled his hand away and reached in his jacket pocket for his wallet. "Besides, you promised your parents you'd take care of Rufus while they're on vacation. And

Rufus isn't very fond of me. Go without me."

Sofia looked away, blinking at the sting of tears. The waiter arrived and lay the leather American Express portfolio next to Thomas's hand. Thomas put his credit card on top of it and handed it back.

"Let's split this," Sofia said, pulling her purse off the back of her chair.

"No, I insist," he said. "It's my anniversary present. And it's not often I have the chance to dine with the prettiest girl in Seattle."

"It would be a lot more often if you gave me the time." Sofia forced a smile, but she couldn't alter the bitterness in her voice. She knew she was pretty—always had been. His compliment meant little to her, and she guessed it meant little to him as well.

Thomas met her eyes. "I know, but really, Sofia, you should go to Walla Walla. You've been working so hard, and you deserve this time off. Go."

Sofia looked away again and considered. "Maybe I will. But you'll call me from Denver, okay? That will make it seem like you're with me. A little."

Two

Sofia held her phone on her shoulder with a tilt of her head while she pulled the packaging off a frozen dinner. Diet, of course, but not cheap.

"Yes, Mom," she said into the phone. "I know. But he has to go to Denver for a meeting with the new marketing team there. Otherwise, I'm sure he'd come with me."

She could envision her mother in her kitchen in Walla Walla, her bobbed hair held perfect with just the right amount of spray, her make-up expertly applied even though only Sofia's father was likely to see her all day.

"Honey, I hate to remind you. But this is what happened when you planned to go to Palm Springs last year," her mother said. "Does he ever follow through? Does he ever commit to anything? And speaking of commitment, when is he going to put that ring on your finger?"

"Mother, I'm not in as much of a hurry for a ring as you are," Sofia answered. "And I'm not sure it would change his behavior. He's all about work right now. That promotion he wants, you know."

"Well, perhaps you shouldn't marry him, anyway."

Sofia rolled her eyes and opened the microwave, nearly losing the phone off her shoulder. She caught it, stuck it back under her ear, and punched in the frozen dinner settings. The microwave started to whir.

"I don't know what you're saying, Mom. One minute you ask when we're getting married and the next you say maybe we shouldn't. I know you've ever really liked Thomas. Maybe if you spent more time—"

Her mother interrupted. "I don't know how we can spend more time with him when he doesn't even have time for you. He has refused to come back here since that first year you were dating. I think he doesn't care for us."

"I think it's probably more that he doesn't care for Walla Walla. He keeps telling me he's a big city guy. I expect at some point he will have his eye on a job in New York City."

Sofia set out a plate and fork on the kitchen bar and pulled a sheet off the roll of paper towels for a napkin while she listened to her mother describe her only trip to the Big Apple a year ago. Sofia had heard it a dozen times. "I have never been so happy to see the Walla Walla wheat fields in my life as I was when we got back," her mother concluded.

"I know, Mom. I've heard it before."

The microwave dinged.

"Is that the microwave?" her mother asked. "Are you eating that junk food again?"

"It's not junk food, Mom. It's a high-end frozen dinner."

"Oxymoron if I've ever heard one," her mother quipped.

Sofia laughed, switched her phone to speaker mode, and set down the plastic dish. She pulled off the hot plastic wrap and tossed it in the sink.

"So, I guess I'm going to come anyway," she said before

she sat down to eat. "I want to see Rufus and chill for a while. I might even bring my golf clubs."

"Oh, honey, you should. The courses here are in the best shape I've seen in years."

"And you and Dad have a great time in Sun Valley. I know how much you love it there in the summer. That's where I met Thomas, remember?"

"Yes, I do remember," her mother answered. "Oh, one minor complication. Your brother arranged to have a friend of his stay at our house for a couple of weeks to study winery marketing. He'll get here on Friday, the day after you come."

"What? Who is it? Do I know this guy?"

"His name is Enzo, and he met your brother in Mendoza a couple of months ago. He is going to visit some tasting rooms and talk with some wineries about how to do wine tours. I guess his family owns a winery. It's hard to believe, but your brother says that Walla Walla is ahead of Argentina when it comes to wine tourism."

Sofia put her fork down, cancelled speaker mode, and put the phone back to her ear. "But Mom! I don't know this guy! How can I share the house with him? What if he's a creep?"

"Michael says he's a really great guy. And this is a very large house, Sofia. You know that. You grew up here. We'll put him in the west wing. You can have your old room. You won't even see him much. And if you want to set some house rules, go ahead."

Sofia shook her head. First Thomas cancelled on her, and now this. "Maybe I should come another time," she said. "This guy ... what's his name?"

"Enzo."

"Wow, how exotic," Sofia said as sarcastically as she could. "Enzo. Maybe he can take care of Rufus for you. I'll come another time."

"No one can take care of Rufus like you, Sofia. I think you should still come. Rufus misses you."

It didn't take much imagination for Sofia to see her mother bend down to scratch Rufus's ears as she cooed, "He's such a good boy!"

"You're not trying to set me up with some stranger because you don't like Thomas, are you, Mother?" Sofia put the phone back on speaker and took a bite of chicken.

"Of course not. I had nothing to do with inviting this young man. I've never met him. We're just helping a friend of Michael's. You know how much it costs to stay in a hotel for two weeks."

Sofia choked and grabbed her water to clear her throat. "Two full weeks? Are you serious? So, he'll be there the entire time I'm there?"

"Sofia! This is not about you. Come on, I'd think you'd be happy to have company now that Thomas isn't coming. I understand he plays a little golf. Maybe you two—"

"Mother! I am not playing golf with him or entertaining him or taking him around town. Nothing. Okay? This is my vacation. I need some peace and quiet. I want to come, but I need him to leave me alone."

"Just tell him that, dear. I'm sure he speaks fine English."

Sofia wasn't going to win this argument. "Okay. I'll be there Thursday. But I am in no mood to put up with some Latin playboy. I hope he's on his best behavior. Remember Julio? He was from Argentina, too."

Her mother laughed. "Yes, I remember Julio, dear. But that was a long, long time ago. And you're the one who's always telling me not to judge someone by where they come from."

Three

Nothing in the Walla Walla airport had changed that Sofia could see, but it bustled with summer tourists. It had been a year since she'd been home—the May before last when she and Thomas cancelled their vacation to Palm Springs, and she took a solo trip back to the vineyards instead.

She waited in line at the rental car agency, collected her rollerbag and her golf clubs from the baggage carousels, and stepped outside into the bright sunshine. The sun hurt her eyes. It was July, but it was still raining in Seattle, and she wasn't used to the bright light. She took a deep breath of dry air, pulled her sunglasses down from the top of her head, and headed for the car lot.

The wine tasting rooms in the business park just east of the airport tempted her, but Sofia looked at her watch and decided noon was too early to start drinking. And it was better to let someone else drive if she decided to visit some of her favorite wineries. Anyway, she wanted to be sure to get settled in the house and establish her territory before Enzo showed up.

Instead of turning onto the highway to head directly to her parents' house west of town, though, she drove the three miles to downtown. Already, wine tourists were sauntering down the street and filling the sidewalk cafés. Sofia remembered when Walla Walla was still a sleepy farm town, and it was more common to see tractors and combines on main street than Lexus's and Mercedes. Wine had transformed her hometown during her junior high and high school years, and it appeared the transformation wasn't slowing down.

Sofia drove slowly, turning her head from side to side, noting the new tasting rooms and bistros that had sprung up in just the past year. Her curiosity sated, she turned north on Second Avenue, glancing at the Maison Bleue Winery storefront, happy to see it was still in business. She'd spent many afternoons in high school working in store room, helping with shipping. She pulled onto the highway and headed west, passing the Wine Valley Golf Club sign before turning off and winding her way around, over the creek, and finally up a steep hill to home.

From the top of the driveway, rows of grapevines ran down the hill where apple orchards once dominated the landscape. Sofia sat in the car for a minute, taking in the familiar sights. Far down below, the Waterbrook Winery's pond shone in the mid-day sun.

She rolled down the window and took a deep breath. The hot dry earth smelled like home. How long, she wondered, would she have to be gone before coming back here felt unfamiliar, like some distant past?

Shaking herself out of her reverie, she picked up her purse and headed up the path to the stately house her parents had built atop their vineyards more than a dozen years ago. Ten years later, they retired from viticulture and sold the vineyards, but they'd held onto the big house, unable to part with the quiet of the countryside and the views.

Out of the corner of her eye, Sofia spotted a big, furry mass bouncing toward her. She dropped her purse and leaned down to give Rufus the welcome he expected. Rufus rammed his big head into her knees, nearly knocking her off her feet.

Laughing and scratching his ears, Sofia gave the Bernese Mountain Dog a big hug and let his big tongue lap her face before she pushed him away. She picked up her purse, headed toward the front door, and pulled the house key from her bag. She turned it in the slot, but the door wasn't locked. Had her parents left the house open? That certainly didn't seem like something her father would do. Suddenly, the door flew open and Sofia was nearly run over by a tall, dark-haired man.

Sofia screamed and fell back, tripping over Rufus. The man reached out and caught her by the elbow before she hit the ground.

Regaining her balance, Sofia glanced up at a tanned, handsome face framed by a surfeit of thick, dark hair. His dark eyes danced with amusement.

"You must be Enzo," she said, shaking loose of his hand and sticking hers out for a shake. "At least I hope you are. I thought you were coming tomorrow."

The stranger ignored her hand, grabbed her shoulders, and leaned in to kiss her on both cheeks. Rufus bounced excitedly between them, forcing them apart.

"Yes, I am Enzo. And you must be the lovely Sofia." The first words out of Enzo's mouth sounded so familiar, and Sofia was transported back to the summer before her senior year in high school when Julio was staying with her family. His accent was exactly the same.

Enzo backed up and looked Sofia up and down, finally

settling his eyes on hers. "And you are much better looking than your brother said."

Sofia felt herself blush and tried to cover it with a frown. Somehow when Thomas said things like that these days, it didn't affect her. But Enzo's compliment certainly did.

"You got here early," she said. Her throat was tight, and Sofia forced her voice to drop pitch. "I thought you weren't coming until tomorrow."

"I guess Michael had my arrival wrong," Enzo said. His English was perfect, but his accent continued to give Sofia flashbacks. "I met your parents, though. They are very nice people."

Sofia paused for a moment to get her bearings. She wasn't going to allow this man to change her plans for the week, as she had told her mother. She needed to get over his appearance and his sexy accent right away, or things could go astray in a very bad way. She straightened up and threw her shoulders back.

"Okay," she said in as bossy a tone as she could muster. "So you're here. I want to get something straight right away."

Enzo backed away, his eyebrows raised, and Sofia continued. "I need some R and R, and I'm not here to entertain anyone but Rufus. I don't cook or clean for anyone but myself, and I expect you to respect my parents' home and give me space."

A smile started to creep across Enzo's face until he forced it to stop.

"I came here to be alone and to see some old friends," Sofia said. "I would appreciate it if you make yourself as scarce as you can."

Enzo frowned, and Sofia imagined he was accustomed to a much different reaction from women he met. Probably. With those dark eyes and slim figure, he most likely got nothing but swoons in his presence.

"Ooookay, boss woman!" He backed up another step and pushed the front door open. "You are as tough as your brother said you were."

Sofia bent down to pick up her purse. "What does that mean?"

"Oh, don't get me wrong," Enzo said, taking a little bow. "I love tough women. I promise I will stay out of your way. I promise. Don't want to get in trouble with the boss."

Sofia rolled her eyes and headed back to the car to get her bag out of the trunk. Enzo followed, and as she popped open the trunk, he reached in for her bag. "Let me get that," he said.

Sofia slapped his arm away. "No! Really! Don't you understand English? I asked you to give me space!"

Enzo backed up, his hands in the air.

"Whoa!" he exclaimed. "Bad flight?"

Sofia slammed the trunk shut and lugged her rollerbag clumsily up the uneven path, Rufus at her heels. She felt Enzo's eyes on her back and heard him mutter, "Wow, Michael didn't prepare me for this."

Four

OF THE THIRTY-PLUS TASTING ROOMS now dotting Walla Walla's Main Street and a couple blocks of side streets, Sofia had her favorites, and she was pleased to see they hadn't changed much in a year. A couple that she'd never been fond of had disappeared, replaced by new labels that Sofia hoped to try before she headed back to Seattle the next week.

The room Sofia and Janet chose to visit her first afternoon in town was quiet for a Thursday, which worried Sofia. Quiet was good after noisy Seattle, but it could mean the bloom was off this particular winery's rosé, and it too would be replaced by a shiny newcomer soon.

As they relaxed on the tasting room sofa with full glasses of a pleasantly dry viognier, Sofia looked her best friend over with a critical eye. She'd always been afraid of staying in a small town like Walla Walla, where youthful fashion sense and fitness would be replaced by grown-up complacency, but from what she saw in Janet, she had been worried for no reason. Janet's soft blonde curls were as well tended as her petite frame, and her work clothes were quite a few levels above what Sofia wore to work at the brewery in Seattle every day.

Janet appeared to be making the same assessment, and her evaluation of Sofia wasn't as benign.

"I have to say, you've looked better, Sofia," she said frowning.

Sofia laughed uncomfortably. "Gee, thanks. With friends like you ... ."

"No, I'm serious. You look tired and stressed."

"Well, that's why I'm here!" Sofia's gesture was a little too emphatic, and she sloshed a little wine onto the couch. She wiped at it, and it rolled right off. Tasting room upholstery, of course, was chosen for its impermeability.

"I know I need a little R&R," Sofia said, trying not to whine. "But I didn't come to get scolded."

She picked an olive off the plate on the low table in front of them and chewed pensively.

"It is hard, though," she explained. "The brewery is struggling. The new hard cider isn't taking off like it should. Last year, it would have flown off the shelves. Just when we got it perfected and started marketing, everyone suddenly wants hard seltzer."

"I guess it's a good thing you didn't invest in it, then, right?"

Sofia nodded. Janet was a loan officer at the biggest local bank, and she knew finance and investments. Sofia had called her when she was offered an opportunity to buy some shares in the closely held company that owned the brewery.

"Yes, absolutely. You steered me right on that. I really appreciate it. But if the brewery goes under, I'm not going to have a job. That's just about as bad. You know how hard it is to find jobs right now."

Janet took her turn at the appetizer plate and finished a couple of olives before answering.

"You can always come back to Walla Walla," she said finally. "This place is still growing. You know we got two more tasting rooms downtown last year? The town's becoming an international destination."

Sofia was proud of what her hometown had turned into, but she raised an eyebrow at her friend's assertion.

Janet waved her arms at the scene out the big picture window to the street. "Wine tours, bike tours, balloon festivals. You name it. The Whitman Hotel is booked solid all the time, not just in summer like it used to be. They're building a couple new motels on the highway and there'd be more going up if the county would allow it. I just hope we don't get too big. I don't want this place to turn into Denver or something."

Sofia chucked at Janet's enthusiasm. "I don't think you have to worry about that. Speaking of Denver, I guess you see Thomas didn't come."

"Oh, my gosh. I'm sorry. I didn't even ask. Why not? You two haven't broken up, have you?"

"No, although I think we may be the only two people in the world who think we shouldn't. My parents have still not warmed to him."

Janet nodded. "But has he given them a chance? When was the last time he was here?"

"Three years ago. I think." Sofia tried to remember. "We only stayed a day. He had some emergency that meant he had to get back to work. This time, he had to go to Denver for a meeting."

The news appeared to please Janet. "So that means, it's girl time!" she exclaimed. "What do you want to do? We have a bunch of new wines to taste, so of course we'll do that."

"Of course," Sofia smiled. It was great to be back in

a place where people enjoyed and appreciated good wine. "But I'd like to play a little golf too. It's so hard to play in Seattle. I don't like that country club that Thomas belongs to. So hoity-toity. I'd swear they'd all swing their drivers with their pinkies out if they could."

She demonstrated as well as she could without a club in her hand.

"That's not a problem at Wine Valley." Janet laughed. "And I won't make you go to our country club, although it's certainly not snooty. We can play plenty of golf without it."

"And I want to sit up there at home on the hill and look at the vineyard," Sofia continued. "I miss it so much! I love how quiet it is up there. You should come up and stay a couple of nights."

"I'd love to—"

"Oh, but I have to warn you. My brother invited some friend of his to stay up there for the next two weeks." Sofia scrunched up her nose. "Enzo. Quite the charmer," she said mocking his accent. "Or so he thinks."

"But isn't your brother still in Argentina?"

"Yes. And that is where Enzo is from. Came to learn all about wine tourism, I guess. Judging from my last experience with an Argentinian, he's probably looking for other things, too."

Janet picked a slice of cheese off the plate and waved it at Sofia. "You can't judge every Latino by what Julio did to you," she said. "He was just immature. I'm sure there are Argentinians who are out for something other than … ." She stopped.

"Yeah. You remember what Julio wanted," Sofia said. "All he wanted."

"Sofia, you were in high school. Haven't you gotten past that?" Janet finally quit waving the cheese and stuck it in her mouth.

"I would if everyone else would. Every time I come to

town, I feel like everyone is looking at me like 'Isn't that the girl who—"

Janet interrupted. "Oh, that's silly. You need to get over it."

Sofia shook her head and reached for a slice of sausage. "I hope you're right. Anyway, why don't you come up for a glass of wine and a light dinner tonight? I haven't had a chance to cook anything but frozen dinners in ages. You can stay overnight if you want."

Janet considered the offer for a moment before accepting with an upturned thumb. "Okay, I'll bring a toothbrush in case, but if I don't drink too much I'll probably come back down. I have to work tomorrow." Her face brightened. "And I'll get to meet Enzo, right?"

"I don't know. I asked him to give me space. I don't want to cook, clean or entertain for him. But Rufus will be there. I know he misses you as much as he misses me."

Five

THE SUN WAS SHINING BRIGHTLY again the next afternoon when Sofia arrived at the Wine Valley Golf Club. She walked into the pro shop and stood just inside the door to let her eyes adjust to the relatively dim light.

"Hey! It's Sofia!" John, the golf pro, shouted. "Sofia Michaelis! A sight for sore eyes. Haven't seen you in ages."

As her pupils got used to the room, Sofia noted that tall, athletic John looked exactly like she remembered, big smile and all. He was the kind of guy who made friends of everyone who came through the door. At times, Sofia had been jealous of his gregarious energy.

"Hi, John," Sofia walked up to his counter. "Good to see you too."

"How's that beautiful swing of yours?"

"I'm afraid it's not what it used to be. It's a lot harder to get out to play in Seattle. It's not just the rain. It's work. It's the courses. There's nothing there like Wine Valley."

Sofia pulled her billfold out of her purse and handed her credit card across the counter. John put up his hand to stop her.

"Nope. Your money's no good here," he said. "It's on me today."

"Gee, thanks, John." Sofia stuck the card back in its slot.

"Just this once. Don't get used to it. So, you're back in town for good?"

Sofia shook her head. "No, just in and out."

John printed out a ticket and handed it to Sofia along with the keys for a golf cart. "Why don't you move back?" he asked. "If the golf's not so good in the big city, what keeps you there?"

"A job. Ever since Mom and Dad sold the vineyards, there really isn't anything for me to do here."

"Oh, I don't know. Seems like things are booming. Just ask Janet." He gestured at the door to indicate her friend's arrival.

"Hey, sorry I'm late," Janet said.

Sophie greeted her with a quick hug. "No problem. Our tee-time isn't for a half hour. You're not late."

As Janet paid for her round—no freebies for the locals, Sofia noted—Sofia rummaged through the racks of golf clothes, looking for something on sale. It had been ages since she'd had an excuse to buy anything new for golf.

"Come on," Janet called out. "Let's go hit some balls. My guess is you're kind of rusty."

SOFIA'S SWING WAS A LITTLE sluggish, but the driving range faced northeast and a nice breeze from the southwest helped the balls fly farther. A right-handed player, Sofia faced lefty Janet as they worked through their irons and hybrid clubs and finally pulled out their drivers.

The repetitions helped Sofia work out the kinks, and by the time she set a ball on a tee and took a couple of practice swings with her driver, she felt more confident. Each time she stepped up to the ball, she reminded herself what she needed to do. Keep the head behind the ball. Keep the left arm straight, turn the shoulders, start the swing with the hips.

In a second and a half, she saw she hadn't lost all of her game in the six months since she'd last swung a club.

"Nice shot," Janet said, watching Sofia's ball soar out past the two-hundred-yard marker. "It doesn't take you long to get it back."

"I'm kind of surprised." Sofia stopped and watched Janet's drive. Her swing was smooth, but she'd never had Sofia's distance. The ball, nevertheless, caught the wind and came up just short of Sofia's.

Janet let her driver rest and watched Sofia take another shot. "That was fun last night," she said. "It was wonderful to be back up there on that hill, away from traffic and sirens."

Sofia watched her ball land before reaching down to place another one on the tee.

"Ha!" she said, while taking another practice swing. "You should live in Seattle! Walla Walla is as quiet as a funeral parlor compared with that. I'm glad Mr. Obnoxious stayed out of our hair."

"I, for one, was a little disappointed. I wanted to meet Enzo."

Sofia swung again. This time she ignored the ball flight and shook her head at her friend. "Janet! You are happily married. Why would you want to meet him?"

"Just curious. Let me tell you, Sofia, you never stop looking. Even when you don't have to. Even when you're not interested."

Sofia looked over Janet's head up the slight slope behind them and frowned. "Well, then, I guess it's your lucky day. Here he comes."

Janet spun around to watch Enzo walk toward them, a driver and a sack of practice balls in his hands. Enzo waved the club at them. He looked much happier to see them than Sofia was to see him.

"Well, hello, landlady. Fancy meeting you here!"

"Yeah, fancy that," Sofia snarled. "I can't imagine this is some coincidence, is it?"

Enzo ignored Sofia and walked up to Janet. "And who is this gorgeous companion of yours?"

Sofia threw Janet an I-told-you-so look, but Janet's eyes were focused on Enzo.

"This is Janet," Sofia answered. "A friend from high school. A *married* friend."

Enzo glanced at Sofia and smirked. "I certainly hope so," he said. "I'd hate to think all American men are blind to such beauty. *Mucho gusto*, Janet. I'm Enzo."

He leaned in and kissed Janet on both cheeks, drawing a big smile from her.

Sofia rolled her eyes, but neither Enzo nor Janet was looking. She lined up for another shot off the tee, but she gripped the club too tight and topped the ball. It skittered off the tee and bounced about 40 yards in front of them.

Disgusted, Sofia bent down and picked up her tee. "I'm done here, Janet. Let's go see if John will let get out on the course a little early."

Enzo gestured to where her shot had traveled. "Are you sure?" He laughed. "Looks like you could use a little more warm-up."

"Thanks for your evaluation, *señor*," she said, her voice squeaking with sarcasm. "But I don't think I need your advice on the golf course." She slammed her driver back in her bag. "You may know wine, but I know golf."

Sofia pulled the heavy bag onto her shoulder and started up the hill to their golf cart. She turned to watch Janet shrug and trade smiles with Enzo.

"Are you coming or are you just going to stand there making eyes at him?" Sofia hooked her bag on the back of the cart and waited for Janet to catch up. As Janet climbed the hill with her bag, Sofia watched Enzo set a ball on a tee and, without so much of a stretch or a practice swing, send it sailing out onto the range. She didn't wait to see how far it went.

"I'M SORRY," JOHN SAID, SCROLLING through the tee times booked on the computer in the golf shop. He looked up at Sofia. "You'll have to wait. Your tee-time is only 15 minutes away, and there's a group on the tee right now."

Sofia groaned.

"And," John said, "I hope you don't mind, but we're too busy for twosomes today. I had to pair you with a single. It shouldn't slow you down since there's a foursome out ahead of you anyway."

Sofia made a face and turned to Janet. "I just hope we're not paired with you-know-who."

A minute later, they stood next to the first tee, swinging their drivers to keep their muscles warm.

"You didn't tell me this Enzo was so attractive," Janet said.

"Oh, is he? I didn't notice. He looks exactly like I expected he would. Argentinian."

"Well, I thought you weren't very nice. He is a house guest."

"I didn't invite him. I wanted some peace and quiet. And I don't really care what he looks like."

Janet nodded at the cart coming down the path toward them. "That's good because here he comes. At least he won't distract *you* on the tee."

Sofia swiveled to see Enzo driving up to them in his cart. She slumped like her day had just been spoiled and turned to stare down the first fairway. She took a deep breath and muttered to herself, "I'm not going to let him ruin my first round in six months."

Enzo jumped out of his cart and bounced up toward them, driver and ball in hand. "Well, we meet again! I guess I'm paired up with you two today. Aren't we lucky?"

Sofia turned to face him. "Lucky is not exactly the word I'd use. But fine. I just hope you can keep up with us. I was the captain of the high school golf team, and Janet here was my deputy. We've played this course more times than you have shaved, is my guess."

Enzo grinned and stroked his chin, which, Sofia admitted to herself, looked like it required at least daily shaves.

"I'm intrigued by your confidence, my dear landlady," he said. "I hope I will not hold you back. What tees would you like to play today? Ladies' tees?"

"We don't call them ladies' tees," Sofia snapped. "They're forward tees. And we'll play whatever tees you choose. Are the 'men's tees' okay with you? The whites?"

"Sure. If that works for you." Enzo pointed down the fairway to indicate the group ahead was out of their way. "Go ahead and tee off first. *Ladies*."

Janet walked up to the tee box. She set her tee and ball in the ground, took a practice swing and hit her tee shot. It was nice and straight, a decent amateur's shot about 170 yards down the middle.

"Nice shot, Janet," Sofia said.

"Yes, a good start, I'd say," Enzo added.

Sofia stepped up next and set her tee and ball in the ground. Her shot rocketed about two hundred twenty yards down the middle. She stood for a moment, holding her finish, admiring it.

"Nice!" Enzo exclaimed. "I can imagine how good you were in high school."

Her attitude softened by her good tee shot, Sofia shrugged at him. "I don't get to play much anymore. I'm a little rusty. I used to drive a little farther."

"I'm sure you did. Boyfriend doesn't play?" Enzo asked as he set up for his turn.

"None of your business," Sofia answered, and stepped off the tee box to watch him swing.

Enzo focused down the fairway, apparently choosing his target and without a practice swing hit a perfect drive about 280 yards out into the middle.

Watching it, Sofia was embarrassed for herself. She knew golf better than he did?

"Wow," said Janet. Sofia jabbed her in the ribs.

"Let's go see if we can find those shots," Sofia said. "I think yours was slicing a little, Enzo." She climbed in their cart and looked at Janet with chagrin.

THREE HOURS LATER, SOFIA AND Enzo walked side by side into the clubhouse chatting about their shots on the 18th. It had taken a few holes, but Enzo's skill and course etiquette had finally broken through her resistance. He was polite, complimented her and Janet on good shots, held the flag, helped rake bunkers, stood out of the way on the putting green, and was quiet during their shots. She'd seen much less admirable behavior from most men she'd played with since competing on the golf team in high school.

"Why didn't you tell me how good you were?" Sofia asked as they took stools at the tiny bar in the back of the golf shop.

"You didn't ask. And you didn't tell me how rusty you were."

Sofia slugged him in the arm. "That's not fair. I work 60 hours a week. And I live in a place where it rains 320 days a year. We don't tan in Seattle, we rust."

"Then while you're here, we should play a few more times," Enzo said, nodding to both women.

"I thought you were here to work, not golf," Janet said.

"Well, I didn't know I'd have such delightful golfing partners, or I'd have come here on vacation instead."

Sofia grimaced. He was trying too hard.

Enzo waved at the bartender who walked in from a back room, and continued. "I plan to work afternoons and evenings. The tasting rooms are open late. That's what I'm here to see."

The bartender approached, wiping his hands on a bar towel. "What'll it be, folks?"

"Pinot grigio," Janet ordered. "Local if possible."

"Do you carry any hard cider?" Sofia asked.

"No, sorry." The bartender shook his head. "Beer, wine and hard seltzer. Sodas, of course."

"I'll just take a local brew, then," Sofia said, a bit of a whine in her voice. "Whatever you recommend."

The bartender looked at Enzo. "And you?"

"I'll have a hard seltzer. Do you have grapefruit?"

Sofia shot him a look of disgust.

"What? What did I say?" Enzo sat back from her with a chuckle.

Sofia shook her head and looked away.

Enzo shrugged and turned to Janet. "And what do you do here?" he asked.

"I'm a banker. I make loans to wineries. You know, for equipment, marketing, working capital."

"Great, perhaps you can make some introductions for me."

Sofia listened as Enzo and Janet chatted happily for a while. Then she tuned them out and stared out the window and down the fairway. It looked like it stretched all the way to the horizon and the purple hills in the distance. It reminded her again how much she missed these wide, open spaces.

Six

THE HEAT OF THE DAY dissipated quickly up on the hill. Janet and Sofia had taken Rufus for a long walk through the vineyard earlier, and now he rested contentedly at their feet on the patio. He let out a big sigh, and Sofia mimicked him with one of her own.

"I forget sometimes how beautiful this is," she said, staring off across the tops of the vines. A light breeze fluttered the big grape leaves, shifting the kaleidoscope of light shining off of them from dozens of purples to dozens of greens in a silent dance. The air was warm but fresh, so dry it couldn't hold onto an odor. "Can you believe how lucky we were to grow up here?"

"Well," Janet replied. "You grew up here. I grew up down there." She pointed southeast toward town in the valley below.

"But you know what I mean," said Sofia. "It was fun playing golf with you again today."

"It's been too long. I think we were better in high school, though."

"You should come to Seattle sometime. We can go out to the peninsula and play. Lots of great courses out there," Sofia said, her gaze into the distance stuck as if she were in a trance.

"Yeah, maybe."

Sofia shook her head to release her stare and poured a little more wine into her glass. "What do you mean, 'maybe?'"

Janet paused a moment before answering. "Tell me about Thomas," she said. "Is there still a Thomas?"

Sofia sniffed. "Of course, there's still a Thomas. I told you, he had to go to Denver for a marketing meeting."

"It's been, what, three years since you met? Is anything really happening there?"

Sofia picked at the charcuterie plate, finally selecting a slice of sausage and bending down to hold it in front Rufus's nose. He gently picked it out of her fingers.

"We're busy with our careers," Sofia said. "But, yes, I think something's happening. We're learning about each other, figuring out what makes sense for us."

Janet laughed and flicked a dismissive wave with a hand. "What do you mean? 'What makes sense?' I want to hear about feelings, emotions, not 'what makes sense.'"

"Okay, let me be honest with you. But keep this to yourself." Sofia paused, parsing her next words. "I really don't know if he's committed to us anymore."

Janet nodded. "Well, how do you feel? Are you *in love* with him?"

"Yes, I love him."

"That's not what I asked. I asked if you are *in love* with him."

Sofia stuck a piece of cheese in her mouth, delaying her answer while she considered it. "I don't know. I guess I always thought that would come later, you know. As we got to know each other better."

She reached for the wine bottle and drizzled another ounce into her glass.

"You know being here reminds me of how I felt about Julio, as bad as that turned out. I've always wondered if that was just something you felt when you were too young to know better, or if that's something you could feel when you were grown up."

"You mean good old infatuation? Or lust? Which one drove the two of you out there on the golf course in the middle of the night?" Janet asked with a laugh.

Sofia looked stern. "You know nothing serious happened, right? I told you that."

"Sure, if you think running under the sprinklers naked is nothing." Janet giggled.

"You know what I mean. Nothing sexual happened. We were just playing."

"Honestly," Janet said. "I've never known if you're telling me everything."

"Like what? What else should I tell you?"

"I mean, did you want something else to happen? Did you like him that much?"

Sofia weighed that question too before answering. "I don't know. I don't think I knew then. I was only seventeen. Sex was just fantasy. But it didn't matter, since the groundskeeper caught us and then told the entire town, and Julio pretended that something more had happened. Like some sort of conquest. Boy, that was embarrassing."

Janet took a big gulp of wine and reached over for the bottle.

"Well then, Sofia," she said, "it's good that you and I are the only ones in town who remember anything about that."

"Geez, I hope you're right." Janet wrapped a piece of cheese in a sliver of prosciutto and popped it in her mouth.

"So, explain what it is you have against Enzo?" she asked. "He's damn good looking, obviously a great golfer, and seems to want to get along. Why are you being so difficult with him?"

"It doesn't really matter, Janet. I'm already in a committed relationship. I don't want Enzo to get any ideas. I mean we're stuck in this house together for my entire vacation."

"Maybe you're overestimating your irresistibility."

Sofia reached for a piece of cheese and threw it at Janet. It landed on the patio behind her, and Rufus got up to retrieve it. "I can't believe you said that. Whose friend are you anyway?'

"I know you better than anybody in the world," Janet answered. "I'd even argue that I know you better than Thomas does. And frankly, when I met him, I wondered how someone goes through life calling himself 'Thomas'—instead of 'Tom'—and not ironically."

Sofia chuckled and fed Rufus another piece of sausage.

A moment later, Enzo walked out of the house at the far end of the patio. Rufus stood up and waddled over to him. Enzo leaned down to scratch the dog's ear and then leaned against the railing, looking over the vineyard toward the west and the setting sun. He appeared to be oblivious to the women sitting on the other side.

"Hi! We're over here!" Janet called out to him, waving her arm in the air.

Sofia slapped her arm. "Shh. Damn you, Janet. I was enjoying our peace and quiet."

Enzo turned toward them and grinned. He followed Rufus back to their table.

"Oh, I'm sorry. I didn't know you were out here," he said. "I wasn't trying to ignore you."

"Come, sit down," Janet said. "We're just talking about your golf game. Tell me, how did you get so good?"

Sofia flashed her a dirty look, and if Enzo saw it, he

pretended he didn't. He nodded at Sofia, who faked a smile. He returned it with a sincere one.

"So good?" he answered Janet. "My game is half of what it used to be."

"I'd hate to imagine what it used to be," she said. "What do you mean?"

"I was on the circuit, the professional tour in Argentina. A while ago. But I finally realized I'd never make the PGA in the U.S. I just wasn't good enough, and I decided I needed to make a living. Gave up the game."

Sofia tried to hide her interest in their conversation, but she couldn't resist turning her head to look at him. He sat down between them and waved an arm at the vineyard stretching out below them.

"This reminds me so much of Mendoza. I could feel at home here."

"Did you grow up in the vineyards there?" Janet asked.

"Yes, my father tended the vines for one of the large growers. I spent my entire childhood running down the rows, throwing sticks for my dogs. When the owner died, he deeded the property to my dad. I guess he attributed all of his success to my father's excellent care. Dad started making his own wine about ten years ago. When I returned home from the golf tour, I went right to work for him, a chance to learn viticulture from the best in Argentina."

Janet kept up her end of the conversation, while Sofia sulked. "And you know Sofia's brother?"

"Yes, we play golf together," Enzo said. He turned to Sofia. "He's very good, you know."

"Oh, of course I know," she said. "He'd never let me forget it."

She returned Enzo's look and lost her resolve to stay cool. His dark eyes smiled at her, and he looked sincere. She grinned in spite of herself.

"Well, he's been a great friend to me. Not that I've always deserved it. He helped me convince my dad that I should quit pruning vines and ratchet up our marketing."

"What's wrong with pruning vines? It takes skill and precision. Yields, sugar content, well, everything depends on it," Sofia said. She watched his expression turn serious.

"Ah, yes. But if I'm going to take over the business someday, I had to get out of the vineyard and into the office. I think my father would prefer to believe he'll live forever, and I won't have to learn what he does in there."

Sofia's cellphone buzzed, vibrating the table and startling all of them. Enzo pointed to it, and Sofia looked at the screen.

"Oh," she said. "Sorry, I have to get this. Janet, could you get our guest a glass? Perhaps we should introduce him to some quality Walla Walla wine."

Sofia picked up the phone and walked off the edge of the patio into the garden that separated it from the vineyard below.

"Hello!"

"Hello, Sofia? What took you so long to answer?" Thomas sounded impatient.

"I'm sitting out on the patio with Janet. What took you so long to call? It's been three days. Where are you? It sounds quiet there."

"I'm on my hotel room balcony, looking out at the mountains. It's very peaceful."

"I never thought of Denver as peaceful," she said. "How is it going? The meetings?"

"Oh, busy, you know. Marketing meetings. You know how they are. Boring and contentious at the same time."

"But it's going okay?"

"Oh, fine. fine. How are things there? Getting any relaxation or are you taking work calls?"

Sofia walked to the edge of the garden and turned to

watch Janet and Enzo on the patio. They were getting along very well.

"Thomas, you know it's always you who interrupts our vacation with business calls. No, I actually played a round of golf today."

"Great. How was your game? ... Uh, hold on a minute, someone just came in ... ."

Sofia could hear a woman's voice, her words muffled.

"What's going on there?" Sofia asked.

"Oh, nothing," Thomas answered. "Look, I have to go. I hope you're having a great time. I'll try to call tomorrow."

Before she could answer, the call disconnected. Sofia pulled the phone from her ear and stared at the screen. What was that all about? If he was on the balcony of his room, why was a woman talking in the background? Sofia tucked the phone in her back pocket and walked back up to the patio with Enzo and Janet watching her.

"I suppose that was Thomas," Janet said flatly.

"Good guess," Sofia answered, plopping back down in her chair.

"Thomas?" Enzo asked. "Is that your boyfriend?"

Janet answered for her. "Ostensibly. I'm not that sure, though. Sofia, what did he have to say?"

"Not much. But it sounded like things are going well. I'm glad he went. It's for our future, you know. He's up for a big promotion. This might help move things along."

Janet snorted. "Oh, I'm sure it will." She turned to Enzo. "This Thomas ... He's been dating Sofia for three years now, and, well, just let me say—"

Sofia cut her off. "Enough Janet. That's enough." She faced Enzo. "My friend has never cared for Thomas. I'd chock it up to jealousy, but ..." She reached over and lifted Janet's arm to show Enzo the big diamond ring on Janet's left hand.

"Right." Janet laughed. "What have I got to be jealous

of? I'm happily married, happy in my work, love my home-town." She paused and put a hand on Enzo's arm. "Look, all I have to say is if you were to meet Thomas, well, I think you'd wonder too." She theatrically lifted her eyebrows and her wine glass.

"Janet, I said that's enough." Sofia's voice was testy.

"So, this man is okay with you running off to Walla Walla without him?" Enzo asked Sofia. "Doesn't he worry about what handsome men you might run into?"

Sofia feigned disdain. "I don't suppose you're referring to yourself? No, he's not worried. And he doesn't know you're here."

"Oh, that's interesting. You didn't tell him?"

Sofia ignored the question. "We're very happy together. Committed."

"Engaged?" he asked. "When's the wedding?"

Sofia lowered her voice. "We haven't gotten that far."

Enzo turned to Janet. "How long did you say it has been?"

Sofia answered. "Only three years."

Enzo laughed. "Only? I have known vineyards to take that long to establish, but not love."

It was Sofia's turn to laugh. "Well, you're Latin. I guess things happen faster for you. Your hot blood and all. Perhaps it's my mother's cold Scandinavian blood that's my problem."

Enzo tilted his head down and peered at her under his eyebrows. "Perhaps he's not the right one."

Sofia blushed at his intense look. "I certainly don't think you're in a position to judge that."

Enzo sat back and smiled apologetically. "No, of course not. I apologize." He reached over and briefly laid his hand on Sofia's forearm. He sat back again. "Let's start over."

He waved his arm out at the darkening vineyard and looked up at the stars that were starting to peep out in the sky. "It is certainly a lovely evening, isn't it, ladies?"

Seven

MOST OF THE NEARLY FORTY wine tasting rooms in downtown Walla Walla didn't open before 11 a.m., but Francois met Sofia at the door of his at 10.

"Sofia!" he exclaimed, his arms wide open. She stepped into his bear hug and fought back tears.

"Oh, Frenchie, I have missed you," she mumbled into his soft, round shoulder. She sniffed and stood back to look at him. "And you don't look a day older."

"A few pounds heavier," he said, laughing and patting his protruding tummy.

"It wouldn't be you without this," she said, adding a pat of her own.

"I'm so glad you called," he said. "Are you back in town? Looking for a job? I could use a good server."

"I don't think you could afford me. I've gotten used to the big city salary, I'm afraid."

"Sit here and tell me all about it." Francois pulled a

stool away from his serving counter, and Sofia hopped into it. "And you have to try my new mourvèdre."

He slipped behind the counter and pulled a corked bottle out from a low cabinet. Sofia watched her old friend inspect a wine glass in the light of the bar and pour her a couple of ounces. Francois had purchased grapes from her parents from as far back as she remembered, right up to when they sold the vineyard. He'd always been like an uncle to her, attending her birthday parties and graduation ceremonies, and letting her help with the crush, even when she was too young to contribute much but big enough to be in the way. At sixty, he still moved with the weightlessness of a much younger man, although his thinning hair had turned silver. Sofia wondered if his famously prodigious wine consumption had anything to do with his rigor. As soon as she was old enough to understand, he had preached that wine was an age-defying potion more potent than the fountain of youth.

"I didn't know you were doing mourvèdre," she said, tipping the glass up to breathe in a big lungful of its nose. "Where are you getting the grapes?"

"Why don't you taste it and see if you can tell me," he said, leaning forward with his hands on the bar, waiting for her verdict.

"Gosh, Frenchie, I think I've been gone too long. No palate left." She tipped the glass again for a taste and swirled the tiny bit of liquid in her mouth before swallowing it.

"But what do you think?"

"Wonderful," she said. "What's the alcohol content? 13?"

"Good guess. It's 13.2," he said. "You haven't lost it entirely. Now tell me what you're up to in that big city you've grown so fond of."

Carefully choosing her words, Sofia fashioned a description of her job and her life in Seattle that sounded as upbeat as possible without bending the truth too much. No one wanted to hear her complain, not even an old family friend like Frenchie. As she struggled to put her job and her relationship into the best light possible, her mind took off on another track. If making her life sound good was so hard to do, why didn't she do something about it?

"A fiancé?" Francois lifted his bushy eyebrows. "I don't think your father told me anything about that."

"I don't think he's too crazy about Thomas."

"Thomas, huh. But you're in love, right, honey?"

Sofia opened her fingers and waggled her hand. "More or less. I'm not sure I'm any more excited about it than my parents are," she said. "Not since he cancelled his plans to come with me again. For the third time in a row."

Francois slapped the counter with his palm, making Sofia jump. "That won't do! Hey, I know just the thing for you. We're about to harvest, and I'd love to have you come and help with crush. There's a whole bunch of wineries that'll be crushing at the same time. You can look around. See if anyone catches your fancy." He wiggled his eyebrows.

"Frenchie. I know every man in this town. I grew up here, remember."

"Oh, but there are so many more wineries now, and so many new vintners. You don't know half of them."

"Well, it does sound a lot more fun than selling cider," she said, holding out her glass for another sample.

Francois reached for the mourvèdre and held it up, questioning if she wanted more of the same. Sofia nodded and he poured again.

"I know you're trying to make it sound like you're happy over there in Seattle," he said. "But I wonder if that's true. Don't you like what you're doing?"

Sofia sipped some wine and considered how to answer. "I do," she said. "As much as anyone does, I guess."

"I'm not sure about that. I love what I do. I've never wanted to do anything else."

Sofia watched as he turned away, picked up a rag, and started to shine the glass doors on the cabinets behind the bar. He looked happy.

"Well, I'll admit," she said. "I miss working with wine."

"What about it do you miss?"

"The romance of it. The subtleties of every vintage. The heritage."

She leaned forward with her elbow on the counter and her chin resting on her hand.

"And being outside," she continued. "Even in the winter. I'd rather be back here working in the vineyard, but when Dad decided to sell, I didn't have much choice. And I guess I think people still remember what happened with Julio that summer."

Francois faced her and frowned.

"Julio? Who is Julio?"

Sofia laughed. "He was our Argentinian exchange student. The fact that you don't remember him makes me very relieved. I thought … ." She waved her hand to dismiss the subject. Apparently, she could finally let it go. "Oh, never mind."

"Speaking of Argentina," Francois said, offering her more wine, which she declined, "you have a guest at the house, I hear. A man your brother knows from Mendoza?"

"Yes, trust me. It was not my idea. I was coming for a little R&R and to see Rufus, not to host some Latin would-be Romeo."

"Well, this guest of yours is coming by this morning to talk about our tasting room business." Francois glanced at his watch. "I guess he's trying to learn marketing for his family's winery."

"Oh, Jeez. Everywhere I go—" Sofia started to complain, but Francois interrupted, pointing at the front door.

"I'm guessing this is him now."

Sofia turned to see Enzo walk in. He grinned brightly.

"I didn't know you'd be here," he said. "What a surprise!"

Francois slid around the end of the counter to shake Enzo's hand. "You must be Enzo. *Bienvenido*! I guess you know Sofia here."

"Indeed, I do. We had a lovely evening under the stars on the patio last night." Enzo faced Sofia and bowed slightly. "I'm enjoying her hospitality very much."

"That's kind of you to say," Sofia said, hopping off her bar stool and reaching for her purse. "I'll leave you two to discuss business. I've got some errands I need to run for Dad."

Enzo stepped forward to kiss Sofia's cheek. She blushed and turned to catch Francois winking at Enzo.

"You don't have to leave, Sofia," Francois said. "I'm sure there are no state secrets about to be divulged."

Sofia shook her head. "Thanks for the tasting, Francois. I guess I'll see you at the house later, Enzo."

"I am looking forward to it. I am making dinner tonight, by the way. Is *coq au vin* suitable? And is Janet coming again?"

Sofia was surprised. *Coq au vin*? Would he really go to that trouble?

"Yes, uh … uh, *coq au vin* will be … uh, great," she stammered. She recovered her poise. "But, no, Janet headed to the Tri-Cities with her husband today. She won't be back in time."

Enzo's grin widened even more, and she avoided his eyes. He was getting more attractive every time she saw him. It wasn't fair.

"So, it will be just you and me," he said happily.

"And Rufus," Sofia added, walking as far around Enzo as she could without looking rude.

"Of course. I'd never forget Rufus."

Sofia fled for the door, feeling Enzo's and Francois's

eyes on her back. Just as she slipped out, she heard François's harsh whisper to Enzo: "You could do worse."

"Don't I know it," she heard him respond.

Eight

THE CAST-IRON SCONCES ON TWO sides of the patio provided a soft light, barely illuminating the walls that surrounded the dining table on two sides. The pink rays of the sunset reflected off the bottom of low clouds in the west, remnants of an afternoon thunderstorm, and painted the vineyard below in a rosy glow.

When Sofia walked out onto the patio for dinner, Enzo was lighting two tall candles on the table, which he had set with cloth napkins, crystal wine glasses, and a little bowl of flowers. Two flutes of champagne awaited them along with a decanter that aired the evening's pinot noir.

Enzo looked up as Sofia stood, amazed at the elegance he and the evening sky had conjured on the rustic patio. He smiled, and she knew immediately that he appreciated the effort she had put into dressing for dinner.

She wore the red knit dress that showed off her slim figure and her simple diamond pendant, and her hair was swept back into a soft, slightly messy French braid.

Enzo put down the lighter, as if afraid he would set something on fire accidentally while he stared at her. "Wow. You look beautiful. This is for me?"

Sofia nodded. "I thought if you were going to the trouble of *coq au vin*, the least I could do is dress for dinner."

Enzo exhaled. "Well, thank you." He pulled out a chair for her.

"Sit. Please. I'll get the soup."

"This is incredible," she said, accepting the seat. "You managed all of this and you've only been in the house for a couple of days?"

"Well, Rufus helped," Enzo said. "Turns out he knows where everything is. He even helped me pick out the wine."

He disappeared back into the kitchen with Rufus trotting after him. For a moment, Sofia considered the possibility that he had charmed Rufus as much as he was charming her, and had, indeed, gotten the dog to help make dinner.

The meal was exquisitely French, which surprised Sofia. Yes, she knew the entré would be *coq au vin,* but Enzo had stuck to a traditional Gallic presentation of soup first, followed by his entré, then a palate-cleansing salad, a small plate of cheeses, and finally, a dessert of *pot au crème* topped with a few raspberries. Each course was presented in just the right proportion to be satisfying, but not overwhelming.

"I don't know when I've ever had such a fine meal," Sofia said, spooning out the last of the *crème* from her dish. "I think if I die now, I'll know I've not been deprived of the very best in French cuisine."

Enzo smiled his thanks and offered his wine glass for a toast. "And here's to serendipity. I had no idea my visit to Estados Unidos would be so full of pleasurable moments."

"You are too kind," Sofia said. "I was such a bitch—"

"No more of that," Enzo gently cut her off. "It was perfectly understandable. I was early. I was not invited by you. And I probably come on a little too strong with most introductions. It's my country habits. Mendoza may be a famous wine region, but we're still mostly farmers."

He stood up to remove their plates, but Sofia reached out and put her hand on his forearm.

"No," she said. "I insist on cleaning up. You made an incredible meal and I will do the dishes. Put those down."

Enzo did as he was told. He laid the dishes on the cabinet by the door and returned to the table. He picked up the bottle of wine and poured a little more in Sofia's glass before sitting down.

"It is so fortunate your parents kept the house when they sold the vineyards," he said, sighing a bit as he sat. "It's so beautiful here."

"Yes. I hope I can come back here someday. It's my favorite place in the whole world."

They sat in silence for a few minutes. Sofia felt oddly comfortable next to this man whom she was so determined to avoid. He seemed to appreciate the quiet countryside and the vineyard view as much as she did. They watched the sunset colors fade on the horizon.

"Is it possible we could play some golf tomorrow morning? I think I could give you a tip or two to help your game," Enzo finally spoke up as dusk hit the patio.

Sofia laughed. "So, you think my game needs help?"

"Everyone's game needs help. Tiger Woods had a coach. But I had fun out there with you the other day. And you have a lovely swing."

"That's very flattering. But don't you have to work?"

"My next appointment with a vintner isn't until tomorrow evening."

"Okay, then. I'd love to play."

"Great. I already made a tee time. We'll be the first on the course."

Enzo paused, and he looked away, as if he had suddenly been hit by a bout of melancholy. He stared at the wine in his glass.

"What is it?" Sofia asked.

"I need to apologize for springing this visit on you. I understand you didn't plan on coming here and spending your vacation with a complete stranger. But thanks for sharing your home with me. You are a beautiful hostess, and I'm so grateful to your brother for this chance to meet you."

"Ha! I'm the one who should apologize. It was a such a surprise when Thomas told me he wasn't coming with me, and then my mother told me you were coming. You see, I have a bit of a troubled history with male house guests here, and I had flashbacks like I was going through that again."

Enzo peered at her in the waning light. "Want to give me a clue? What happened?"

Sofia thought about not answering, but the intimacy of the setting seemed to beg for a confessional.

"It was long ago. I was still in high school," she explained. "My father's friend in Argentina—the guy who helped Michael get started there—sent his son my age to stay with us one summer to learn a little about American viticulture from my dad."

Enzo guessed: "And you didn't get along."

Sofia shook her head. "No, actually, we got along a little too well. It all ended with a nighttime episode on the golf course, the police were called, and this being a small town, well …"

"… and pretty soon everyone knew," Enzo finished for her.

Sofia nodded, a sardonic smile forming. In the retelling this many years later, it seemed a lot less scandalous than it had before.

"You don't have to say any more," Enzo said.

But Sofia continued anyway. "It was really so innocent, but Julio didn't want anyone to think it was. He built it up, embellishing with lies … you can imagine what lies … and I could see people looking at my belly for the next six months. I couldn't wait to get out of here and go to Seattle for college. I even graduated from high school a semester early, just so I could leave."

"I'm sure no one else remembers it though."

Sofia looked at him appreciatively. "Turns out you're right. I guess when you're seventeen, you're sure you're invisible until suddenly, everyone's staring at you and you want to hide."

"I feel the need to apologize for my countryman. Obviously, I don't know this Julio, but—"

Sofia stopped him. "No, no. This has nothing to do with you. It was silly for me to connect the two of you. This is something I should have gotten over a long time ago."

Enzo stood up and reached out for her hand. "Have you ever walked through a vineyard at night? It's the most incredible place in the world under the stars."

Sofia smiled and rose, letting him hold her hand. "Yes, I have. And I agree."

They stepped into the garden and passed through to the vineyard, and Rufus followed them. As they walked down between the vines, Sofia looked up at Enzo's face. It was hard to see his expression in the waning light, but she sensed he was at peace. Rufus ran ahead, chasing some kind of rodent, and then came bounding back to them and nudged Sofia's hand.

She looked down at him. "You didn't really want to catch that critter, did you?" she said, patting the top of his head. She looked up at the stars as they turned to walk back toward the patio.

"This is what I miss," she said quietly. "You never see stars like this in Seattle. Maybe Venus, sometimes the Big

Dipper. But there are too many lights to see anything else."

"I wish I could show you the stars in the Southern Hemisphere." Enzo nearly whispered too, and Sofia realized they were still holding hands. It had happened so naturally, and now she decided not to resist it. "You have your Big Dipper and North Star. We have the Southern Cross. The air in Mendoza is so clear that the Milky Way sparkles like a belt of shining jewels."

Sofia sighed. "Maybe I'll come down to visit Michael sometime."

Enzo stopped and Sofia stopped with him. "And me?" he said, circling to face her and look into her eyes.

"Yes," she whispered. "And you."

"I will wish upon a star for that to happen, Sofia."

He bent his head down and Sofia closed her eyes and lifted hers, anticipating the soft touch of his lips. Just as their lips met, a raspy jingle rang out from the patio. Startled by the sound, they stepped apart.

"It's my phone," Sofia said. "That's probably Thomas." She dropped Enzo's hand and stepped back toward the patio. "I'm sorry. I have to get that. He's been so hard to get ahold of."

She could barely see his face, but Enzo's voice rang with disappointment. "Of course," he said. "Thomas. I forgot."

Sofia ran up the hill with Rufus trotting ahead of her. She picked up the phone and went inside without turning look back at Enzo. She knew that if she did, the hitch in her voice would betray her.

Nine

THEY MET A LITTLE AFTER sunrise the next morning at Wine Valley Country Club, and Sofia was glad Enzo didn't ask about the call from Thomas. She would have had to lie and tell him that it was fine. Good, even. Maybe great.

It hadn't been. Once again, Thomas had been in a hurry, and when she asked what was keeping him so busy well into the evening—it was nearly nine o'clock, after all—he scolded her for being suspicious.

"I'm not suspicious," she replied. And truth was, she hadn't been until he suggested it. Then she worried. Was there someone in Denver on the new marketing team that had caught his eye? She couldn't imagine that. He hardly seemed to have time for her, let alone another woman right then.

The call had ended unhappily, with Sofia feeling guilty about what had just about happened in the vineyard with Enzo and with Thomas angry.

She didn't want to share that with Enzo, especially since he had to know she was as attracted to him as he seemed to her. Instead, Enzo acted as if he had forgotten the walk through the vines. Perhaps she would get over this silly infatuation if he quit encouraging it. She could hope.

The morning was perfect for golf. The air was still. They teed off on the first hole as the first rays of sunlight burst over the low hills behind them. The tall, golden grass that covered the ridge to the left sparkled with morning dew. Sofia spied a coyote running at the edge of the fairway and pointed. Enzo saw it just before it disappeared into the deep thatch.

Being more familiar with the course, Sofia drove the golf cart, and Enzo didn't seem to mind. Thomas, Sofia reflected to herself, had a fit if she suggested she drive. It was as if he thought it threatened his masculinity or, at least, his masculine reputation.

The damp greens held their approach shots nicely, and they had the course nearly to themselves. With their long drives and a few good putts, they put the first nine holes behind them in little more than ninety minutes, and as they made the turn to the second nine, Sofia worried that the lovely morning was passing too quickly. Just as the thought occurred to her, Enzo echoed it.

"Let's slow down," he said. "I don't have anywhere I have to be until later today. Why don't we ditch the cart and walk the back nine?"

"My thought exactly!" she said.

She pulled the electric cart up to the cart barn, and they walked away a few minutes later with pull-carts.

"This is so much more like it!" Enzo said. "You know, we walk more in Argentina. Not many courses even have golf carts."

"So that's why you're in such good shape," Sofia said. "I hope I can walk this far. I don't think I've walked nine holes in more than five years. Since I was in college."

"We don't have to rush. There isn't anyone behind us for a few holes."

Sofia had honors on the tenth tee, having beat Enzo on the ninth hole. She swung easily off the tee and stepped aside for Enzo's turn. His tee shot was a few yards longer, but her second shot hit the green while his skidded off to the right across the cart path into a patch of scrubby ground covering. She putted in for a birdie while he looked for his ball, and then she walked over to help him search. She found it nearly buried under the foliage and laughed.

"Oh, I don't envy you," she said.

Enzo walked to the ball and shrugged. "I've seen worse."

He pulled out an iron, and without hesitating a moment, hit the ball out of the scrub in a high arc that landed on the green and rolled into the hole.

"I can't believe that!" Sofia cried. She reached over and raised her arm for a high-five. Enzo slapped her hand and walked on the green to retrieve his ball.

"I said I'd seen worse," he said, walking back to their pull carts and trying to hide his grin.

"You're a big show-off!" Sofia grabbed the handle of her pull-cart and led the way to the next tee box.

"Actually," he said, following close, "that was luck. I had no idea what I was doing."

As the morning stretched on, their progress slower now that they were walking, they laughed and talked, taking their time to line up long, winding putts and congratulating each other on good shots. Sofia tried to remember the last time she had enjoyed a round so much, and decided it probably was back when she played with Julio that summer, before he betrayed her and was sent home in infamy. Playing with Thomas was certainly no joy.

Sofia noticed that Enzo was keeping his distance, approaching her only for high-fives and a quick, platonic hug on the eighteenth green. A few times, she caught him watching her intently, but he looked away quickly, as if he knew she had noticed. It seemed that he was working hard to accept his limited place in her life.

Leaving the eighteenth hole, they walked with their carts toward their cars in the lot, reaching Enzo's rental first. Sofia waited while he loaded his clubs in the trunk.

"I'll take your cart back," she said. "I know you need to clean up for your afternoon meetings."

"Thanks," he said, accepting the favor. "I had a great time out there, Sofia. Your game isn't far off. You just need to play more."

"Don't I know it. But, yes, it was fun. Thanks."

She started to walk away, but he called out after her. "About last night …"

She turned to face him.

"I'm sorry, I should have said this earlier. I forgot about Thomas. Maybe it was the stars, maybe your dress, maybe the wine. I don't know, but I apologize. I don't want you to think I'm another Julio."

Sofia smiled at the irony. She was just thinking that in some wonderful ways, he was another Julio. But this time, she would be careful not to let those things seduce her. Perhaps if she kept thoughts of Thomas on the top of her mind, she could maintain a safe distance between them.

"No, I'm sorry," she answered. "I got carried away. There's something about a vineyard at dusk that makes me forget my real life. It was my fault."

Enzo took a step toward her. "So, Thomas was okay? Everything going well for him?"

"Yes. It was a short call. He seems really busy. We'll talk again tonight."

"Good. I'll be back late. Don't wait up."

Sofia laughed. "I wasn't going to."

She walked toward her car to load her clubs and looked

back to watch him wave and drive away.

"Oh, golf gods," she whispered, looking up into the cloudless sky. "Give me strength to resist this. Get me back to Seattle before it's too late."

She pulled out her cell phone and texted Thomas:

Thinking about you … will call tonight … hope all is going well. XO

Ten

SOFIA WAITED FOR JANET AT a table in one of the down-town coffee shops close to her friend's bank and considered filling the time with a quick call to Thomas. It would be good to hear his voice. It would bring her back to earth after the high-flying emotions of the past twenty-four hours.

"Let's see." She thought out loud. "Denver is only an hour ahead of us. So, it's only three o'clock there." She decided it would be better to wait until the end of the work-day. He barely had time to talk to her in the evenings. He certainly wouldn't stop work to chat in the middle of the afternoon.

She put the phone down just as Janet walked in.

"Whatcha drinking?" Janet asked, setting her purse down on the chair next to Sofia.

"Iced coffee."

"I guess I'll do the same." Janet walked up to the count-er, and Sofia studied her from behind. Her friend had put on a few pounds since their high-school golf team days, but she was still trim and fit. The modest business suit she wore with low, classic pumps fit perfectly, and her messy strawberry blond braid bespoke businesswoman too busy to be fussy.

"I'm glad you called," Sofia said when Janet returned. "I was trying to figure out what to do this afternoon."

Janet sat down and pulled the paper covering off the straw with her teeth. "Well, I don't have a lot of time, but I want to see you as much as I can before you leave. Usually I don't take coffee breaks in the afternoon, but we're not that busy right now."

"How was the trip to the Tri-Cities?"

"Fine. About as exciting as you'd expect. I met with some winery owners and Jason looked at a new combine."

They lived in town, now, but Janet's husband was a wheat farmer who had grown up in the business on his family's farm. He was accustomed to spending a half-million dollars or more at a time on a piece of machinery, a concept that had once blown Janet's mind. "That is until I saw what wineries spend on fermentation tanks, distillers, and bottlers," she told Sofia. "Now those numbers don't wow me anymore."

Janet glanced at the door, and Sofia turned to see what she was looking at. "Are you expecting someone?"

"Yes." Janet looked sheepish. "I'll be honest. I talked with one of my vintners the other day, and he said they're looking for a new marketing person for the wine region. I told him about you." She glanced at the door again and grinned. "Oh, here he is now."

"Hi, Will!" Janet waved and Sofia turned to see a middle-aged man dressed in winemaker's attire—jeans, khaki shirt, and sturdy boots. All he was missing was an apron.

Sofia whispered to Janet. "I'm not dressed for this. You should have asked."

Ignoring her, Janet stood to give Will a hug and introduce him to Sofia.

"I know your father well," Will said, shaking Sofia's hand. "Great man, great viticulturalist."

"Thanks. I'll give him your regards when he's back from their trip."

Janet motioned for Will to sit with them. "Can I get you a coffee?"

Will shook his head. "No, no. I've just got a couple of minutes." He turned to Sofia. "Janet tells me you may be looking for a way back into the wine business."

Sofia laughed. "Uh, this is the first I've heard of it."

Janet shook her head. "You said the other day that you miss wine—"

Will cut her off with a dismissive wave. "Tell me what you're doing now, Sofia."

"I'm working at a brewery in Seattle. We recently brought out a new hard cider, and I've been trying to build our market presence."

"And how's that going?"

Sofia frowned. "Not especially well. I think the timing was bad. Just when we thought there was room for another cider brand, consumers decided to switch to hard seltzers."

Will looked surprised. "No market research?"

"Oh, no. Plenty," Sofia said. "But between the time we got the data and got the product ready for the market, things changed."

Will nodded. Sofia imagined he understood how quickly beverage tastes and trends could change, especially for products marketed to millennials. She could have faulted the market research firm for failing to see the turn to seltzers, but blaming others for your failures was no way to impress.

"Are you interested in returning to the wine country?" he asked. "I sense some ambivalence." He glanced at Janet.

"I guess it is something I think about. But, I haven't—"

Will interrupted again. It appeared he was in a hurry, just as he said. "What appeals to you about wine?"

Sofia thought for a moment, but Will's impatient expression pushed her to answer quickly. "It's more steeped in heritage and tradition. The thing about the beer business is it's so trendy. One day it's all about ales and craft brews, then it's cider, and now, like I say, the beer drinking public is turning to seltzers. Fewer calories, I guess."

"Doesn't the wine business seem staid in comparison? Old school?"

"I don't think of viticulture or winemaking as staid. There's plenty of experimentation with technologies and new blends. It's just that it doesn't seem that it's so obsessed with changing fads."

"I agree with you totally," Will said. He placed both palms flat on the table, as if to lift himself from his chair. "I'm glad that Janet got us together. But I think we're looking for someone with a few more connections in the area—more recent ones, that is. I'd suggest you come back here, spend some time in marketing for one of our bigger producers, and in a couple of years, let's talk again. I'm sure Janet has her ear to the ground and can let you know when something's open."

Will stood. "I've got to run. I'll see you around, Janet. Good luck, Sofia."

He held out his hand to her. She stood up and took it. The shake was anything but warm, and moments later, Will was gone.

Sofia sat back down hard enough that she stung her tailbone. "Well, that was embarrassing," she said, frowning at her friend.

"What do you mean? You did great."

"I wasn't looking for an interview. Come on, Janet, let me run my own life."

"I'm not trying to run your life. I just want you to come back here." Janet glanced at her watch. "Oh, I've only got a minute."

"Janet," Sofia's voice was argumentative. "There's a big world out there. Walla Walla isn't the only great place with vineyards and wineries. I love coming home and seeing you. But even if I leave the brewery, I'm getting married. Thomas will never agree to move to Walla Walla."

"Would you move if it weren't for him?"

"That won't happen."

"How about Argentina?"

Sofia laughed. "Don't be silly."

Janet stood up and pulled her purse onto her shoulder.

"So, I'll see you tonight, right? A little wine tasting for old times' sake?"

Janet nodded and smiled. "I can't wait!"

Eleven

THE SIDEWALKS WERE CROWDED, EVEN on a weekday evening, but then, it was summer, and the tourist season was peaking. Strolling arm-in-arm with Janet, weaving among the milling oenophiles, Sofia could see that Janet's boast about the town booming was no exaggeration.

"This is the new place I wanted you to try." Janet steered Sofia around a family that nearly blocked the entrance as they argued about what tasting room to try next.

"These guys have been producing for only about five years, but they're doing some really fine Rhone blends," Janet said, introducing her new favorite winery. She made a beeline for a couple of empty stools at the tasting bar.

"And besides, they have stools up at the tasting counter. I appreciate that after a long day at work."

Sofia hoisted herself up onto the stool and watched the server behind the bar lean over and kiss Janet on both cheeks. Was cheek-kissing replacing handshakes out here in Eastern Washington the same way wine had replaced beer over the past couple of decades?

"Nice to see you, Janet," the server said. "You haven't been out much this summer, have you?"

Janet shook her head, despondently. "Too much work, Tim. But it's slowing down now." She pointed at Sofia. "This is my best friend from high school, Sofia. She lives in Seattle now."

The server reached out a hand to Sofia. Apparently only some people warranted the cheek kiss.

"You thinking of moving back?" he asked.

"Someday, maybe," Sofia said. She wondered how many more times she'd answer that question before she left. "But I've got a job and a fiancé in Seattle."

"Plenty of jobs here, Sofia." The server winked at her. "Plenty of alternative fiancés, too."

Sofia laughed. "I'm sure you're right. What are we tasting tonight?"

"Let me choose a couple for you. I already know just what Janet likes." The server walked away, and Sofia regarded his trim frame as he pulled a half-dozen glasses and started pouring tastes from different bottles.

"So, everyone knows you in this business now?" Sofia asked, still staring at the server, mesmerized by his graceful motion.

"Not everyone," Janet said. "Some of the big wineries have relationships with banks in Seattle and Denver. But most of the little guys come to us. I'm guessing we won't be paying for any tastings tonight."

"Great perk!" Sofia said, finally pulling her eyes away from the young man's frame. "I am really jealous. It seems like you've really figured things out. I didn't think any of us would end up back here when we left for college."

Janet smiled past her as the server returned with a tray of tastings.

"Here are three of our blends," he said, placing three glasses in front of Sofia. "Janet is familiar with them, but perhaps you want to test your palate and tell us what you think the varietals are?"

"I appreciate the challenge, Tim, but I'm afraid my palate is a little rusty," she said.

"Well, give these a try and wave me down when you're ready for a full glass."

Sofia handed him a credit card, but he put up his hand to refuse it. "We don't charge our friends here, Sofia. Enjoy. I'll be back to check on you."

"I guess you were right." Sofia held up the first glass to Janet for a toast. "Cheers! I'm in the mood for some great free wine."

Sofia took a sip. The dark red liquid surprised her. It was full-bodied, but it stung her tongue just a bit, as if it was peppered. "Mmmmm," she said, contended. "I'm not even going to try to guess what's in here. I'm just going to drink it!"

Settling in, Sofia pulled out her cellphone again and texted Thomas. She didn't want him to call while they were out. He'd scold her for being out late or slurring her words.

Can't call tonight. Out with Janet. I'll talk to you tomorrow.

Sofia put her phone away and looked around at the other patrons in the tasting room. As her eyes surveyed the scene near the front window, Janet elbowed her and pointed to the back of the room. "Well, look who's here!" she said. "Your nemesis."

Sofia followed Janet's eyes to where Enzo sat with an older man at a table in the back, facing her. He met her eyes and waved, but he returned immediately to his conversation. Sofia felt Janet watching her.

"Wait a minute, sister," Janet said. "I just saw that look you gave each other. What is happening here?"

Sofia feigned ignorance. "What are you talking about? What look?"

"Don't try to fool me. I know you too well. You've changed your mind about our new Argentinian friend?"

Sofia's crooked smile spread as a blush covered her cheeks. "He's definitely growing on me. We get along."

Janet leaned forward to try to catch her eye. "And?"

"And nothing." Sofia tried to relax the smile off her face. "Except we almost kissed the other night."

"I knew it! I'm not easily fooled, Sofia. So, what now?"

"Nothing, Janet. I'm engaged. I said we *almost* kissed. But I pulled myself together and took Thomas's phone call instead."

Janet laughed. "You mean a phone call interrupted you? What would have happened if Thomas hadn't called right then?"

Sofia took another sip and felt her body relaxing. She leaned forward with her elbows on the bar and rested her forehead on her free hand. "I don't know. I really don't know," she said.

Janet waited for her to continue.

"But don't read too much into it," Sofia said. "It was the wine, the sunset, the accent, you know. The romance of it all. I know what was happening, and it wasn't real."

"But—"

"No buts, Janet." Sofia dropped her hand and turned to her friend. "I want to change the subject. Really. I'm marrying Thomas. I'm going back to Seattle, going back to my job, and getting married. So, let's drop it, okay?"

"Okay!" Janet was grinning. "I'll drop it. But I can't really think of anything better to talk about."

Sofia laughed with her, and they simultaneously drained their glasses and reached for their next one.

Twelve

THE LATE AFTERNOON SUN THREW a thin ray of bright light across the kitchen floor through the north-facing window. If it hadn't, Sofia wouldn't have walked over to pull the blinds closed, and she wouldn't have noticed Enzo standing in the doorway to the dining room, his arms crossed, leaning against the jamb. She realized he must have seen her minutes before, as she was dancing, apron on and chef's knife in hand, to the ancient tunes of Abba. The music blared from the cheap boom-box her mother kept in the kitchen, convinced that no one needed high-quality sound if all they were going to listen to was sixties and seventies pop music.

"What are you doing?" Sofia stopped, still holding the big knife as if it would shield her from embarrassment.

"Watching you dance. You look so happy." He grinned, but he didn't budge from the door frame.

"Well, I had a great day today. Saw some old friends.

Went to the driving range to work on my game a little."
Sofia wondered why she was delivering this stream of excuses for being content. "Thanks for your tips yesterday. I
think it helped."

"Very welcome," Enzo said, still leaning and grinning.

Sofia started to blush. She moved around the kitch-
en island and resumed her work. She tipped up a freshly
husked corn cob on end and sliced down, cutting the ker-
nels off in perfectly matched blocks of three rows at a time.

"And I love to cook." She blabbed on. "I'm cooking you
some realio, trulio American food. A Cajun vegetable dish.
Lots of butter. I hope that's okay. And we're having barbecued chicken. I don't want you going back to Argentina
thinking we have nothing to offer here."

She glanced up to take in Enzo's slouch and sly grin.
Was he trying to be sexy or was that just one of his easy
talents?

"The last thing I would say," he said, his eyes frozen on
her, "is that America. Has. Nothing. To. Offer."

Sofia felt a hot flash rush through her body, but at the
same time, she was perturbed that his flattery hit so effec-
tively. "When it comes to cuisine, I mean, my Latin friend,"
she said sternly.

She finished the corn cobs and started chopping a red
bell pepper she'd cored in the sink earlier. She looked up to
see if he was still there. He was.

"You could make a girl self-conscious," she said.

Enzo smiled, perhaps in an apology of sorts, and stood
up straight. "Do you need some help in here?"

"As long as it'll get you to quit staring, sure," she said.
She pointed the knife at the refrigerator. "Do you mind taking the chicken out of the refrigerator and cutting it apart?"

"Love to. Is there another apron?"

Sofia nodded at a tall cabinet in the corner. Enzo
pulled out a long white apron, hooked it over his neck and

tied the strings in the back. For the next few minutes, they worked side-by-side, humming along with "Thank You for the Music."

Out of the corner of her eye, Sofia saw Enzo glance at her a few times, but she pretended not to notice. She cut up an onion, wiping her nose on the back of her hand, diced up a couple of stalks of celery, and tipped the chopped vegetables into the bowl.

"*Waterloo!*" Enzo yelled. *"The history book on the shelf is always repeating itself,"* he sang, loudly and not particularly well. He put down his knife, wiped his hands on his apron, and reached for Sofia's elbow. He turned her toward him and coaxed her into dropping her knife and joining him in a jitterbug. Rufus got up and left the room, perhaps worried about being stepped on.

Sofia's feet picked up the rhythm, and she sang along with him. *"Waterloo! I was defeated, you won the war. Waterloo! I promise to love you forever more."* They danced around the island, singing and laughing at themselves.

The song ended, and Enzo raised both arms for a celebratory high-five. Sofia bent over to catch her breath.

"Don't tell me I wore you out!" He laughed. "We are going to have to get you out from behind that desk in Seattle before you can't dance anymore."

THE EARLY EVENING SUN HAD retired early to make way for a weak thunderstorm, but thanks to the broad eaves over the patio, Enzo could still barbecue the chicken outside, collecting only a few drops of rain on his shoulders as he went back and forth from the grill to the kitchen. The light breeze that accompanied the mild storm wafted into the kitchen through the screen door, cooling off the room and scenting it with water-splattered dust of summer.

They sat at the kitchen table, Rufus at their feet, listening to the distant thunder and the patter of rain on the patio stones. Sofia finished her second piece of chicken and licked her fingers for what she figured must have been the 100th time.

"You barbecued this just perfectly," she said, pointing at Enzo with the thigh bone. "Not burned but cooked all the way through."

"It was a great meal. Hats off to you."

"It wasn't nearly as good as your *coq au vin*. And you did half the work."

Enzo grinned and wiped his hands on his napkin before picking up his wine glass.

"We do make a good team, don't we?" he said.

"Yeah, we do." Sofia lifted her glass, and they clinked them together.

"Speaking of teams," Enzo said, "you know there's a tournament next weekend at Wine Valley. Mixed couples. Do you think we could win it?"

Sofia shook her head. "I know you could, but I shot an 85 yesterday. I don't think that's a winning score."

"But you're improving. And I shot a 68. Together, who knows...?"

"And I'm supposed to go back to Seattle on Saturday."

"What's there to go back for? Do you have a date?" Enzo scooped up the last of his vegetables.

"Yes, a date with my job." She pushed her empty plate away and sat back. What would it hurt to stay a little longer?

"Well, on the other hand," she mused, "I do have more vacation coming, and I've done all I can with that marketing campaign for our cider until we can see the latest results."

Enzo watched her, a smile growing on his face as she continued to consider the idea. "And Thomas isn't due back until Wednesday. Maybe … ."

"Then let's do it!" Enzo exclaimed.

"Can I sleep on it and see how I feel in the morning?"

"No. I think you should decide right now. There aren't many slots left in the roster."

Sofia stood up shaking her head. She gathered their plates and scraped the bones into the trash while she thought it over. "Let me see if I can change my flight."

"Yay!" Enzo clapped excitedly, like they'd already won the tournament, and Rufus barked in agreement.

"Hey, don't get too excited," Sofia said. "It's still possible I'll have to fly home on Saturday. And besides," she picked up and shook a handful of dirty silverware at him, "we still have all these dishes to do."

Two hours later, they were still sitting under the eaves on the patio with Rufus, finishing another bottle of wine and watching the light rain, their conversation having dwindled to a companionable silence.

"I really need to hit the hay," Sofia said.

"What does that mean?" Enzo asked, and Sofia laughed.

"I guess I'm getting so used to your accent that I forget American English isn't your first language. It's an idiom. I guess from when people used to sleep in barns, or on straw mattresses. Something like that. I'm not really sure."

She stood, and Enzo looked up at her with sad eyes. She was tempted to lean down for a good night kiss, but she didn't trust herself. She knew where it could lead.

"Goodnight, Enzo," she said. "I'll call the airline tomorrow morning." Sofia walked to her side of the house, turning off lights as she went. Rufus padded after her and curled up in his usual corner on the foot of the bed. Sofia sat next to him and stroked his head.

"He's an all-right guy, isn't he, buddy?" she asked. Rufus's eyes looked up, but his head was down for the night. "Okay, I'll let you sleep. And I'll keep my opinions to myself."

She changed into her night shirt, brushed her teeth, and crawled in to bed next to him. As she reached up to turn off the bedtable lamp, she noted the time on her phone. It was almost midnight.

"Oh, shoot! she said. Rufus moaned. "I forgot to call Thomas again."

She sat up and texted.

Sorry. Too late to talk. Got busy. Love you. Talk tomorrow?

As she lay back down, it occurred to her that she'd texted him three times in the last two days, and he'd never responded. Things must be going very well or very badly in Denver, she decided. She'd hear about it soon enough. She pulled the covers up to her neck, closed her eyes, and immediately fell asleep.

Thirteen

HER CELLPHONE'S RASPY TUNE WOKE Sofia before the sun did.

Thomas, she surmised. She leaned over, tipped the phone up to her face, and sat up, surprised. Her mother? Why was she calling so early? She knew Sofia wasn't a particularly early riser.

"Mom," Sofia answered. "Is everything all right?"

"Sofie," her mother replied. "I thought you told me Thomas was going to Denver."

Sofia tossed the covers off and swung her legs over the edge of the bed. Rufus stood up and stretched before jumping down.

"Yes," Sofia said. "He has a marketing meeting there. Until next Wednesday."

"Then why is he sitting here in Sun Valley? Across the restaurant from us? And who is that woman he's sitting next to? She's practically sitting on his lap!"

"I have no idea, Mom. I'll call you back."

Sofia hung up. What would Thomas be doing in Sun Valley? Had they moved the meeting, and he hadn't told her? But how could they afford to fly an entire marketing team up there? The room rates this time of year were astronomical.

She threw a bathrobe over her shoulders, dropped the phone into its pocket, and opened the bedroom door. Rufus padded down the hall and straight to the back door of the kitchen, ready to go out and do his morning business of peeing, sniffing for critters, and securing the perimeter of the yard. Sofia left the door open to let in the fresh air cooled by last night's rain. She glanced out the window to see Enzo's rental car was already gone.

She pulled her phone out of the pocket, planning to call Thomas, but she laid it on the counter instead and drew a carafe of water to make coffee. She wanted to be wide awake before she made that call. Already she sensed the conversation would be difficult. There was no way he brought the marketing team up to Sun Valley. Whatever he was doing up there didn't have anything to do with work.

Her stomach churned with anxiety. She waited for the pot to finish brewing and filled a cup. She sat down at the kitchen table and chose Thomas's phone number from the top of her speed dial list.

It took five rings before he answered. "Sofie?"

"What is going on? You told me you were going to Denver."

"What do you mean?"

"I mean, you're supposed to be in Denver. My mother just called to tell me you were sitting across the restaurant from her in Sun Valley with another woman. Would I be crazy in guessing that might be your new marketing director?"

"Uh … ," Thomas stuttered. "Uh, uh, hold on, I need to get outside. Reception is horrible in here."

Sofia waited, listening for any clues that might tell her where he was and with whom.

She heard the swoosh of a what sounded like a revolving door and then bird chirps that indicated he had made it outside. "What's this about?" he said.

"Are you serious? I just told you I know you're in Sun Valley, and you ask me what this is about?"

A long pause filled the distance between them before Thomas answered. "Sofia, I can explain."

"I think that's a very good idea." Sofia's jaw was so tight she could hardly form words. Her hand was shaking violently, and she punched the speaker and laid the phone on the table.

"I don't know what to say. I ... I ... ," Thomas started.

"Not much of an explanation, Thomas," she retorted. "Just tell me the truth, Thomas. I want the whole truth."

Sofia waited for an answer. Rufus walked back in the kitchen and nuzzled her leg. Time for his breakfast. She reached down and put her hand on his back.

Still Thomas said nothing. Was it silly to ask for the truth when it would be unlikely she'd get it?

"You know, I'm not sure I want to know," she added.

"I'm sorry. The trip to Denver was—"

Sofia interrupted. "There never was a trip to Denver, was there? Thomas. This whole Denver trip was a lie, wasn't it?"

Again, he didn't answer.

"Was it?" she repeated.

"No. Uh. " Thomas hesitated. "You're right. There was no trip to Denver."

Sofia waited for more. Finally, he continued. "I'm sorry, Sofia. We'll have to talk when we get back. We can't do this on the phone."

Sofia let out a whine. "But Sun Valley? Sun Valley is where we met, Thomas. You knew my parents were going to be there. Just how cocky can you get? And who is she?"

Suddenly, Thomas's tongue seemed to find the energy to move. "Sofia," he said, "I'm sorry. I thought maybe I could figure this out if Anna and I got away from Seattle for a few days. I could figure out how I feel about us. And now I know." He paused. "I can't keep leading you on like this. I'm in love with her."

"With Anna and not with me."

"I love you, Sofia. I really do. But you're right. I'm not in love with you." Sofia closed her eyes, hearing the echo of Janet's question: Are you *in love* with him?

"Ever? Were you ever in love with me?" she asked.

"Just not anymore."

Sofia looked up at the ceiling and let the stinging in her eyes deliver a stream of tears. She took a deep breath. Oddly, despite the tears, she felt more relieved than sad.

"You know, maybe this is for the best," she said, trying to hide a sniffle, "getting this over with now. I've known for some time that we weren't ready to get married. And lately, I've started to think maybe we never would be. I love you, Thomas, but I'm not *in love* with you either." She hoped she sounded more certain than she felt.

They let the silence linger for a long time.

"We can talk more when we get back to Seattle," Thomas finally added.

"Right. We can do that." She punched the hang-up button on her phone without saying goodbye. She looked down at Rufus. "And what kind of a guy calls himself Thomas, anyway?"

Her phone's ringtone started again, vibrating the wood table. She looked down and saw it was Enzo. She swiped down to decline the call. "The last thing I need is to talk to you right now." Immediately, it rang again. "Why am I suddenly so damn popular?" Exasperated, she looked at the display again, and this time she answered.

"Hey, have time today to go shopping?" Janet asked cheerfully.

"I … I … Thomas … ." Sofia choked and sobbed.

"I'll be right there," Janet said.

FIFTEEN MINUTES LATER, WHEN JANET arrived at the door, Sofia had changed into sweatpants and had fed Rufus. They returned to the kitchen, and Sofia sat, hugging her knees to her chest. By then, her tears had run their course, leaving her cheeks crusty and leaving Sofia feeling hollowed out.

Janet declined a cup of coffee. She reached into a cabinet and pulled out the vodka. She poured a glass and set it in front of Sofia.

"What's this?" Sofia frowned.

"It's vodka."

"I only drink wine, and it's still morning."

Janet nodded emphatically. "Right. But wine is for happy times. And lots of people drink vodka for breakfast. Screwdrivers. Bloody Marys." She turned, pulled out another glass, and poured some for herself.

Sofia lifted the glass and inspected it. "I don't see any juice here."

"Think of it as a screwdriver with a little less orange juice and a little more vodka."

"I can't believe you're making jokes when I just broke up with my fiancé"

Janet snorted. "Look, I feel bad for you. But first, he's not technically your fiancé, is he? I see no ring. And I don't know if it's really a break-up if you were never getting married in the first place. And third, I never liked the guy."

"Come on Janet. A little sympathy here. I loved him. Once upon a time, like yesterday, I thought we'd have a future together."

Janet sat down next to her and sipped her vodka, looking thoughtful. "I can't figure out how he hid this Anna person from you. They must have been seeing each other a lot."

Sofia lifted the glass to her lips and wet them. She put it back down. "I didn't see anything. Maybe I was working too hard. Maybe I didn't want to see anything."

She put the glass to her lips again and took a long sip. The vodka burned her throat and she coughed.

"Hey, shouldn't you be at work?" she asked when she could talk again.

"This is more important," Janet said. "It's not like this is the busy season. All the farmers are getting ready for harvest, not thinking about loans right now. None of the vintners worries about finances until after the crush. Besides, I called you to see about shopping, remember?"

Sofia sniffed sarcastically. "Somehow, that slipped my mind." She took another sip of vodka. It still burned, but less so. "Thanks for coming over. I know there's nothing you can do, but it helps to talk with someone."

"I wish I could do something more. Like murder Thomas. Has he ever cheated on you before?"

"Not that I know of."

"How about lying? Has he lied to you?"

Sofia considered the question. "Yes. A few times. But it was silly stuff. How many martinis he had on the way home from work ... that sort of thing."

"Wow, this kind of betrayal has to be hard."

Sofia nodded. She raked her fingers through her hair, pushing her bangs straight back. Then she shook her head. "Maybe it's not as hard as it should be. I think I was already starting to pull away. I could feel he was. But I still didn't see this coming. You should have seen our anniversary dinner. He ordered Dom Perignon!"

Janet snorted again. "He struck me as that kind of guy. Big on the show. And big on himself."

"Maybe," Sofia muttered. She wasn't sure she agreed.

"Maybe what you saw was just how serious he was about his career. He's going to go somewhere. It takes that kind of commitment if you're going to succeed."

"Relationships take commitment too, you know."

"Don't lecture me, Janet. I'm not the one who's in Sun Valley with my new marketing assistant," Sofia said, tipping up the glass and draining the vodka. "Heck, I don't even have an assistant."

Janet finished her vodka and the two sat in silence for a couple of minutes.

"It may take a while before I put myself out there again," Sofia said. "I need to focus on my career. Find a way back into the wine business. You know," she paused, "I haven't dated anyone but Thomas since I finished college and started my job. I haven't even looked at another guy in three years."

Janet smirked. "Until Enzo."

Sofia slapped Janet's arm. "What are you saying? I am not 'looking' at Enzo. He's staying here because Michael invited him."

"Oh, come on. You told me the other night he was growing on you. Didn't you almost kiss?"

Sofia pouted. "I can't believe you are bringing that up now. Your timing sucks, my friend." She stood up and pulled the carafe from the coffee pot and poured herself another cup. The last thing she needed to add to this impending depression was more alcohol.

Janet nodded and twisted her lips. "I'm sorry. I don't know what I'm saying. I guess I'd really like to see you with someone who makes you happy."

Fourteen

WITH EVERY SWING OF THE club, Sofia felt better.

Out on the driving range, nearly finished hitting two hundred practice balls, Sofia considered how the almost violent act of smashing the clubhead against defenseless little white balls over and over again enlisted muscle, sinew, and bone in the service of clearing the mind. With something like seventy things to remember in every one-second swing—among them: keep the head behind the ball, keep the left arm straight, maintain the triangle formation of arms and chest, start the swing with the hips not the arms, keep the head level, maintain the spine angle, finish with 90 percent of your weight on your front foot, turn the hands over beginning at impact—there wasn't a lot of brain power left to noodle one's angst. It was a bit like a deep, dreamless sleep. With her conscious mind focusing on the swing, her subconscious could work out her problems. Or not.

With six balls left, Sofia decided to forget all seventy

things and just focus on generating as much brutal power as possible. She tried to imagine the ball as Anna's face, but realized she had no idea what the woman looked like. "I guess Thomas's face will have to suffice," she muttered.

Apparently, the work she'd put in on her technique with the first 194 balls had done its trick. Every one of the last six shots went straight down the middle and farther than she'd ever hit a ball with a driver in her life. "Huh!" she huffed, breathless from the effort, watching the last ball sail far past the two-hundred-yard marker. "Maybe I just need to swing harder."

She looked back at the pile of clubs she'd left lying on the ground next to her bag and saw Enzo standing behind her, smiling.

"How long have you been standing there?" she asked. "You should have warned me."

"Looked like you're working on more than your golf swing," he said. "I didn't want to disturb the process."

"How—?"

"Janet told me. She called me and told me what happened."

"That wasn't for her—"

"She was only worried about you. She thought maybe I should come and check on you. It's great to have good friends like that."

Sofia pursed her lips. It was hard to argue with any of what he said. It probably would help not to be alone for the next day or so. A little sympathy and camaraderie could mend a lot of hurt.

"Look, I'm sorry. I don't know this guy Thomas, but I can't imagine he found anyone as great as you."

Sofia looked off into the distance and tried not to tear up. It wasn't as if she didn't know breaking up with Thomas was the right thing to happen. It was something else: the experience of failing, the end of a shared history, the loss of a friend. It all made her sad.

"Maybe I'm really not so great."

"I think you are." Enzo stepped toward her and offered her his arms. She accepted. His hug was solid and comforting without a hint of erotic intent. She rested her head on his shoulder for a good minute. She couldn't remember ever receiving an embrace as consoling and calming as this.

Enzo gently pushed her away. "Hey, come on. Let's get out of here and go for a walk."

Sofia wiped the tears from her cheeks with the back of her golf glove and bent down to pick up a club. Enzo helped her put them away, and then he picked the heavy bag and led the way back up to the parking lot. She flipped open the trunk of her car, and he tossed the bag in.

"I'll meet you at your house," he said. "We should stop there first so we can take Rufus with us."

Mention of Rufus made her smile for the first time that day.

RUFUS HAD GONE CRAZY AS soon as he realized he was going to get to ride in a car, and he ran circles around it until Sofia got the door open so he could jump in. Enzo drove to Lion's Park on the east side of town with Rufus hanging his head out the backseat window.

Enzo parked and hooked Rufus on a retractable leash, and the three of them headed downstream along the canal.

They watched Rufus sniff and mark and sniff and mark with happy abandon, saying nothing to each other, for a quarter mile. Sofia breathed deeply, imagining she was expelling any negative vapors that had built up since the call from her mother that morning.

Finally, Enzo spoke quietly. "I tried to call you to tell you we got the last spot in the tournament on Saturday. Actually, someone cancelled, or we wouldn't—"

Sofia interrupted. "I don't think I can do it."

Enzo nodded. He didn't argue. He looked up at the tops of the trees and at the wetlands beside the trail. "It is really beautiful here. I can see why people never leave," he said.

Sofia let out a little laugh. "Oh, lots of people leave. And you wouldn't say that in January in the middle of a blizzard that blows in all the way from the Cascades. It's not so beautiful then."

"I suppose," he said. "But if it weren't for winter, the vines would get no rest."

Sofia looked over at him, humored. "Are you always thinking about vines? About grapes and wine? What is it about wine that produces that kind of devotion?"

"I don't know." He paused and rubbed his chin. "Maybe it's the way the vines have to suffer in order to produce the sweetest fruit. The way grow in rocky, dry soil, and survive freezing winters."

They walked a few more feet before he continued. "Maybe it teaches us something about life ... that it's not the easy path that makes us strong."

That made Sofia chuckle. She flashed him a sardonic look. "If I were a suspicious kind of woman, I'd think you've used that line before."

Enzo looked back at her, grinning. "What makes you think I haven't?"

"And how has it worked in the past?" she asked.

Enzo looked down the path ahead and shook his head. "A little better than it did just now."

They walked a little farther in silence. A light breeze made the sunlight flicker through the trees onto the trail. Little critters scampered deep in the leaves and the grass beside them, and Rufus stopped them now and then to stick his nose into the ground cover. A squirrel raced across the road in front of them, and Rufus pulled hard on the leash. Enzo stopped him with the leash brake and gently pulled him back.

"You're good with him," Sofia remarked.

"Yeah, well, I've had dogs forever."

A few steps later he added, "Mine is a simple life, Sofia. Wine, golf, and dogs. Now you know everything there is to know about me."

"Hmm. No girlfriends? No wives? No concubines?"

Enzo looked puzzled. "Concubines? I don't think I know that word."

"Mistresses," Sofia said.

He laughed. "Ah! No. No mistresses. But, to tell you the truth, I was dating a woman for a year or so." He paused, and his face looked like he was trying to figure out how to explain.

"It's part of the reason I'm here," he said finally. "To get away."

Sofia frowned and then worked to rid it from her face. "You never said anything about her."

"Not much to say." But then he elaborated anyway. "Christina. Christina Montoya. I'm afraid she is more interested in my ... no, let me rephrase that. She is more interested in our winery than in me."

"Why do you say that?"

"Her family and mine have been competing for years over whose vineyards make the best wines. She has been estranged from her father, and I think she's trying to get even with him."

"By dating you?"

Enzo nodded. "Yes. She makes all the right moves, says all the right things in public. But in private, she closes off. It's like she's only with me to get her father's attention." He looked at Sofia with a crooked smile that deepened his dimples. "Perhaps I'm not handsome enough?"

Sofia blushed. "Ummm. Something tells me that's not it."

Enzo mugged a funny face.

"Why? Do you think I'm handsome?"

Now Sofia laughed fully for the first time that day. "You are begging for a compliment?"

"Yes, I am," Enzo said and echoed her laugh.

They walked a little farther and Sofia spoke again.

"But you felt more for her than she did for you. Is that the problem?"

"It was. But this time away ... it's been good for me. It's helped me put those feelings aside finally. I don't miss her like I once thought I would. What I thought was love was only fear at losing her. When I go back, it will be over."

Out of the corner of her eye, Sofia saw him look over at her meaningfully, as if he were waiting for her to approve. She looked down at Rufus and avoided his eyes.

"So, you haven't talked to her since you got here?" she asked.

"I've been busy."

"Not that busy." Sofia bumped into him playfully, but Enzo's expression didn't change. They kept walking.

"You know, I don't miss Thomas either," Sofia said. "I realized that the second day I was here. Actually, it's been good to be away from him. Like freeing. But I thought I'd feel different after a week apart. Now, I do, but not in the way I thought."

Enzo said nothing.

"And," she added, "by the way, Rufus doesn't like him."

"Well, that should have been a deal breaker." They laughed together. "Why don't you tell me about your life in Seattle," he continued. "I've always wanted to visit there."

ENZO WAS SITTING OUT ON the patio, absent-mindedly scratching Rufus's head. Sofia watched him for a minute through the glass door before sliding it open with her foot, a bottle of wine in one hand and a bowl of olives in the other. Enzo glanced up, looking like he was having trouble leaving his daydream, and smiled.

"Another beautiful sunset," he said. "Do you ever get tired of them?"

Sofia's eyes followed his eyes out over the vineyard. "No," she answered. "Never." She paused, frozen by the view. "We get beautiful sunsets over the water in Seattle, too. But only about two months of the year. Rest of the time, it's too cloudy to see them."

She shook herself away from her gaze and put the olives and wine on the table.

"Thanks. Two of my favorite things—wine and olives," he said. "You know what my third favorite is?"

Sofia's heart jumped. "No, what?" she whispered.

"Rufus." Enzo bent down to let the big dog smother his face with his big tongue.

Sofia laughed. "Why was I thinking ... ?"

"Thinking what?"

"Never mind." Embarrassed, Sofia turned to grab two wine glasses from the cabinet under the eaves. "By the way," she said over her shoulder. "I changed my flight so we can play on Saturday. I'm staying another week."

Enzo wound himself out of his seat and stood with his arms open and the biggest grin Sofia had seen yet. "The best news ever!" he exclaimed. "I thought you would, so I didn't cancel our slot in the tournament." Sofia stepped into his big hug, but immediately, a jealous Rufus stood up and squeezed between them.

Sofia laughed and stepped away from man and beast and reached for a corkscrew in the cabinet drawer. She handed it to Enzo. "You open the bottle. We have to plan our tournament strategy."

Fifteen

THE TOURNAMENT'S SEVENTY-TWO GOLFERS MINGLED in the pink light of dawn, spreading over the putting green and out to the driving range. They milled around the golf carts lined up for the shotgun start, studying the tournament rules and the tournament scorecards clipped to the steering wheels.

Sofia looked anxiously for Enzo's rental car as she chatted with old friends from her high school golf team and older golfers who played with her parents. Enzo wasn't late yet, but there wasn't much time left for him to warm up or practice putting.

Finally, she saw him pull up to the club drop, leave his bag on the stand, and then maneuver into one of the last parking spots left. She trotted out to meet him as he walked back toward her and toward the clubhouse.

"You don't have much time. Going to warm up a bit?" she asked a few yards before reaching him.

"I overslept," he said as he approached with a sheepish grin. "I think all those late nights on the patio are starting to take a toll."

"What? Do you go to bed at sundown in Argentina?"

"You probably think that's funny, but yes," he said, matching her stride back to the sign-in tent and pulling her in for a sideways hug. "If you've hit balls already, I'll just putt a few. Get the feel for the greens."

They reached the tent, and Enzo ducked inside to check in. When he re-emerged, Sofia grabbed his arm.

"I have some people you should meet," she said. She led him to a knot of men and women, all about their age, chatting, laughing and exchanging bets over the coming contest.

"Hey, guys," she shouted. They opened their circle for her and Enzo, and she introduced him.

"Another Argentinian, huh?" said Donna, a woman Sofia had known forever but never much liked, setting several others to laughing. Sofia punched her in the arm.

"I can see what you see in them, though," Donna responded, winking and rubbing her arm as if Sofia's jab had really hurt.

"Enzo's here for a couple of weeks, studying wine marketing," Sofia explained. "He used to play professionally back home."

A few impressed murmurs replaced the giggles, and a couple of the men stepped up to shake Enzo's hand. "Played here before?" asked one, and Sofia left Enzo to tell his own stories while she made a final trip to the clubhouse restroom.

SOFIA AND ENZO PULLED UP to their first tee of the tournament and jumped out to greet the other two of their four-some. Betsy and Carl Werther were of an age somewhere between Sofia and her parents, and although she had known them for years, she had never played with them.

"I heard you were back in town," Betsy said to Sofia, giving her a quick, platonic hug. "Are you staying or going back to Seattle?"

"Going back," Sofia said, and stepped back to let Enzo introduce himself to the couple. Why, she wondered, did everyone think she might come back to town? Was that a thing these days? Sofia had seen that the wine business—both production and tourism—was booming, but it was it really bringing people back? Or maybe people who stayed just liked to think they knew a good thing before she did, and that she might just now be catching on.

Sofia was reluctant to go back to Seattle. But was it the vineyards and the wine business? Or was it simply her job? She liked Walla Walla and was proud of her family history there, but she still didn't feel the draw that everyone seemed to be alluding to. Maybe it had been Thomas that kept her in Seattle, and now there was no more Thomas, she could decide what she wanted her future to look like.

Carl stepped up to the tee box and took a couple of easy practice swings like a man who played golf regularly. No hitches, no shyness on the first tee like Sofia remembered feeling when she first started playing golf.

Whack! The ball few down the middle of the fairway about two hundred yards—nothing an amateur golfer would be ashamed of.

"Nice shot, man. Keep them in the middle like that and you'll never get in trouble," Enzo commented as he walked up to place his tee in the ground. He stepped back, picked his target, and as usual, stepped up and teed off without a practice swing. The ball sailed well past the one-fifty-yard mark, landing at about 255 yards, only eighty yards shy of the green.

Sofia watched Carl's face. At first, he smiled, and then as he followed the ball, his eyes widened, and his jaw dropped.

"Well, I guess we know who the real competition is going to be today!" he said. He clapped Enzo on the back as they headed back to the carts.

At the forward tees, Sofia hit a great drive as well, nearly reaching Enzo's thanks to the sixty-yard advantage the tee box gave her, and Betsy kept hers in the fairway. Their round was started.

The tournament was set up as a shamble, which allowed each couple to play their second shots from where their best tee-shot landed. With Enzo's long drives and Sofia's short-game skills kicking in, she and Enzo penciled in a few birdies the first nine holes. Betsy and Carl took the stiff competition well.

"I always play better when I play with good golfers," Betsy commented after she putted in for a birdie on the ninth hole.

Sofia thought they couldn't have picked another couple that would have been as pleasant to play with.

At the turn, Enzo and Sofia grabbed a couple of beers and relieved themselves in the clubhouse restrooms. As they waited in the shade of their golf cart for Betsy and Carl to catch up to them on the tenth tee box, Sofia gazed out at the purple hills far to the west and sighed deeply.

"What was that for?" Enzo asked.

"Just thinking I can't remember a better day in my entire life," she said, still staring at the view.

Enzo tapped her on the shoulder, and she turned to face him. He smiled and leaned forward, and she met his lips half-way. The kiss was brief, cut short by the arrival of their playing partners. But it set Sofia's head swimming, and she hesitated before stepping out of the cart.

"I didn't realize you two were—" Betsy started to tease as the men stepped up to their tee box.

Sofia cut her off. "We're not. I mean we're not what that probably looked like."

She felt her face heat up. She wished she didn't blush so easily.

"Well, I don't know why you're not," Betsy said. "Seems like a pretty nice match to me."

As the men waited for the group ahead to clear the fairway, Sofia remembered that she and Julio had first kissed on this golf course too—and how their relationship had ended here, with the policemen leading two naked teenagers back to where they'd left their clothes, and then escorting them back to Sofia's parents. It was time, she decided, to quit thinking of it as a nightmare. It wasn't. It was fun and funny and, yes, in the end embarrassing, but the love and the reckless abandon were special. Had she ever captured that since?

On the tough tenth hole, Enzo chipped in for an eagle, and Sofia walked over and pulled his face down to hers and gave him a noisy smack on the lips.

"Bravo, partner," she whispered. He flashed his big grin and pulled her to him. This time, their kiss was long and passionate, and Sofia backed away from it out of breath, her heart pounding. They walked back to the cart with Enzo's arm over her shoulder and hers around his waist.

"Liar," Betsy said.

Although she was tempted to embrace Enzo every time one of their putts dropped, Sofia kept her distance for the next few holes, and rewarded his great shots with only a smile. Displays of affection on the golf course were disrespectful to both the playing partners and the game, and Enzo apparently believed that as well.

As the last ball fell into the final hole, though, they were ready to celebrate. They hopped toward each other for an energetic high-five, but their hands missed. Doubled over laughing, Sofia felt Enzo's arm reach over her back, and she rose for another passionate kiss. She didn't want it to end, and for a long time, it didn't. Betsy and Carl drove back to the clubhouse, leaving them alone on the green.

Sixteen

Sofia breathed deeply to tamp down her emotions as the crowd of golfers gathered on the patio for a late lunch and the announcement of the day's winners. She had a pretty good feeling that their gross score, two under par, might hold up as the best of the day. But that wasn't what was making her smile.

They sat at a table with their day's partners, Carl and Betsy, as players usually do at couple's tournaments, and talked over their good shots and bad shots before they forgot them. They toasted birdies and laughed about the shanks that led to bogies. The hamburger and steak fries were fine, but Sofia had a hard time focusing on her food. She kept glancing at Enzo and seeing a completely different man than she had met less than a week ago. And he looked back at her in a way she had never anticipated days before. As he talked to Carl or Betsy, she studied his expressions, and when she spoke, he watched as if seeking hidden meanings in her face. She could hardly wait for the party to break up so they could start their evening on the patio over the vineyard.

"Hello, hello. Can you hear me?" John, the golf pro, stepped up to the edge of the patio just above the drop-off to the fairway below, microphone in hand. The speaker beside him squawked, and he adjusted the dial.

"Before we hand out the trophies to today's winners, I want to thank you all for coming out and enduring this horrible weather." He pointed out at the sunny fairway, and the golfers laughed politely.

"And thanks to our staff for putting on an absolutely perfect tournament. Let's give them a hand."

Sofia joined the others, cheering and clapping for the staff who stood across the patio from John, their backs leaning up against the clubhouse.

"And, now, without further blabbing from me, I'd like to present our winners." The patio fell silent. "In third place, with a net score of 146, Betsy and Carl Werther."

Sofia and Enzo stood and clapped wildly as their playing partners got up and walked up to John. He handed them each a small trophy of a golfer in a finishing pose engraved with the tournament name and date. A photographer stepped up and took their picture standing next to John. They returned to the table, smiling proudly.

"And in second place, with a net score of 144, a perfect par, Teresa and Blake Thompson."

A couple seated across the patio got up and went through the same routine. Once they returned toward their seats, John continued.

"And in first place, with an amazing, yet official and attested, combined gross score of 134, a 128 net, are our own Sofia Michaelis and her new partner, Enzo Benedetti!"

New partner? Sofia tried that on for size in her mind. Could Enzo be her new partner?

She blushed as the golfers stood, clapped, and whooped for her and Enzo. Enzo took her hand, and they walked up to John.

"And they might be the best-looking couple out here today too," John added, making Sofia's face grow even hotter. Enzo accepted the big trophy and turned to let Sofia help him hold it up high. The photographer stepped forward and snapped a picture.

It didn't surprise Sofia when Enzo turned and put his free hand on the back of her head. She leaned forward, eyes closed for a celebratory kiss.

Just as their lips met, a clubhouse door banged open, and everyone turned to see a diminutive, attractive blonde stumble out in stilettos, a short, tight skirt, and the biggest hairdo Sofia had ever seen in her life.

"Enzo!" the woman shouted. "I look all over for you! I should know you be on the golf course."

The woman strutted across the patio to Enzo as Sofia stepped back. Just before she reached them, the woman seemed to suddenly spy Sofia. Briefly, she paused, but then she approached Enzo, pulled his face down to hers, and kissed him passionately.

The photographer, apparently afraid to miss Walla Walla's photographic opportunity of the century, squeezed off a few quick shots of their lips smashed together.

Sofia studied Enzo's face as it was bent to the woman's. Rather than closing his eyes, he strained to look over at Sofia. All the effort in the kiss was the woman's, but he didn't pull away. Sofia stood back, now holding the trophy alone.

"*Felicitaciones, mi cariño. Ganaste otra vez?*" the woman chirped as she finally stopped her smooch. She grabbed Enzo's hand, pointed at the trophy, and looked at Sofia with a patronizing smile. The woman poked her hand toward Sofia to shake.

"Hello. I'm Christina, Enzo's girlfriend from Mendoza.

It looks like you are to be congratulated also?"

Sofia accepted Christina's limp clasp and quickly let go. The other golfers, who at first seemed intrigued by the scene, had already turned away and resumed their conversations. John, however, watched the strange trio, frowning.

Christina stood between Enzo and Sofia, looking back and forth. "You play together today? You must be very good, Sofia. He never play with me. I don't do golfing, really, you know."

"No, I didn't know. I'd never guess." Sofia didn't try to withhold the sarcasm from her voice.

Christina smiled, apparently not recognizing the tone, and turned to grab Enzo's hands. "Can we go now? I'm starving. And I want you show me around. This is so quaint little place. But is Walla Walla a real name?"

Sofia started to walk back to their table, but Enzo reached out for her arm.

"Sofia, wait! I will give you a ride home," he pleaded.

Sofia pulled her arm free. "No, I drove myself, remember? You slept in. And, in retrospect," she nodded at Christina, "it appears to have been well-timed."

She took a step away. "And everyone here knows me, so I'm sure they'll want to thank me for giving them another embarrassing story about Sofia Michealis and her Argentinian to remember."

She turned back to Christina. "It was wonderful to meet you, Christina. I hope you enjoy your stay at my family's home." She looked to Enzo. "I'll be out of there before you get back from your dinner and tour of the city."

"But your flight isn't until next week," he said.

"I think I'll stay with Janet for a couple of days," Sofia answered, forcing a benevolent smile. "We haven't had much of a chance to see each other." She held out her hand to Enzo. "Goodbye, Enzo. Safe travels home."

Sofia's hands were sweating, and her heart pounded

as she snuck back to the table with Carl and Betsy. She tried to ignore Betsy's expression—a mix of sympathy and mortification—and put on a big, happy smile. She held up the trophy victoriously, and let Betsy take a picture of her standing with it.

Sofia sat down, and they stumbled into a jumbled conversation that went nowhere. Sofia watched Enzo and Christina walk around the patio toward the parking lot. Enzo glanced back at her, and she looked away.

Seventeen

Sofia placed the trophy she and Enzo won on the mantle over the big stone fireplace in the living room of her parents' home. She stepped back and looked. It wasn't quite centered. She adjusted it and stepped back again. A tear dropped onto the wood floor at her feet. She wiped angrily at her eyes with the back of her hand and swore.

She stood and stared at the tall golfer atop the award. His arms were extended high above his back and his weight was solidly balanced on his front foot. How many times in a round, she wondered, did she execute a perfect finish like that? How many times did Enzo? She grimaced. He completed every swing as if it were going to be memorialized in just such a statue as the one atop the trophy.

Yes, he was perfect. Perfect in most ways, anyway. Perhaps not when it came to taking control of his love life. If he really didn't love Christina, as he said, he should have convinced her of that long before she flew all the way to this backwater town in southeastern Washington to ruin Sofia's otherwise perfect day.

She turned and walked out to the patio through the open door and stared at the late afternoon light reflecting off the fluttering grape leaves below. Rufus lifted his head off his paws, yawned, and put it back down. He was lucky. He got to stay there for the rest of his life. She was going back to Seattle the next morning. Who knew when she'd get back to these glorious afternoons?

She stood with her hands on her hips and flashed back to the evenings she'd spent out there with Enzo. How much time she'd spent resisting her attraction to him! For what? For Thomas? Thomas who never kissed her the way Enzo had that afternoon. Twice. And what a brutal tease those kisses had been. He'd be back in Argentina with Christina in no time, and Sofia would be back in Seattle, loveless and alone, working at a job she didn't like in an industry she didn't respect.

"Just how sorry can I feel for myself?" she asked aloud. "Get your life together, Sofia. It's no one's fault but your own that you have nothing to go back for." Seattle had one of the country's hottest job markets. Her marketing experience was valuable across industries; she just had to decide what she wanted. And only four other cities in the country had a higher percentage of young adults living solo. There were plenty of bachelors there. She just had to put some effort into finding one. If she wanted to. Now she wasn't sure. Maybe the best antidote to the Thomas and Enzo fiascos was a very long time alone.

After a minute, Sofia shook off her self-pity and her memories, and tossed her car keys in her hand. She walked back through the house, followed by Rufus, grabbed her rollerbag, and pulled it out to the car. Rufus lay down on the sidewalk with his head on his paws again and whined a little. Sofia threw her bag in the trunk on top of her golf clubs and turned to take a last look at the house.

"Goodbye, Rufus," she said. "Your buddy Enzo will be back shortly. Bite his girlfriend for me."

She lowered herself into the driver's seat. As she turned the corner onto the highway, she saw Enzo's car approaching, signaling its turn onto the driveway. She stared straight ahead. If he recognized her, if he waved, she didn't see it.

Sofia's head drooped over her coffee cup. Despite Janet's attempt to make her comfortable, Sofia hadn't slept much. And although her friend had made pancakes and bacon—their favorite breakfast way back when they played on the golf team together—Sofia couldn't eat.

"I didn't know how I felt about him until it was too late," she muttered, just barely loud enough for Janet to hear. "Honestly, just 10 minutes before she showed up, we were celebrating and talking about me coming to visit him in Argentina. Then, she struts in. And I just stood there like a jilted lover at the altar with the whole town staring at me. Me making a fool of myself with another Argentinian. Geez, I'm pathetic."

"But what did he say?" Janet asked, tearing pieces of bacon off a slice by hand and chewing them one-by-one. "Was he happy to see her?"

"I don't know. He let her kiss him. Right there in front of everyone. Right after everyone saw him kiss me."

Janet shook her head. "Ugh, how embarrassing! So, she stayed with him? Up at your house? That just stinks!"

"That's why I had to get out of there. And why I have to get out of here today." She snorted derisively. "I'll bet she doesn't even like dogs."

Sofia looked up at Janet. "Do you know she doesn't play golf?"

Janet's mouth formed a fine line. There wasn't much she could say that would help, and it looked like she was trying not to say anything that would make matters worse.

Slowly, Sofia sipped her coffee, until it was finally too cold to drink. She pushed it away.

"I guess I'd better go. My flight leaves in an hour." The two women stood up, and Janet gave her a hug.

"You'll be okay alone in Seattle? Want me to come and stay for a few days?" Janet asked.

"No. I think I need some time alone to figure things out. Maybe I'll quit my job and come back here eventually. Turns out Rufus is apparently the love of my life."

"I'd love to have you come back. But don't rush into anything. You've been through a lot the past couple of days. No rash decisions. Okay?"

Sofia nodded. "I won't. I promise."

She grabbed her rollerbag's handle and started to the door. Janet passed her and held it open. She kissed Sofia on the cheek as she stepped out.

Sofia rolled her bag down the front steps, and as she reached the sidewalk, she looked up and stopped.

Enzo was leaning against his car at the curb, arms crossed over his chest. He straightened up, dropped his arms, and walked toward her. He placed his hands on her shoulders.

"You can't leave," he said. His eyes were pleading. "I can't let you leave. Not without me."

"What do you mean?" Sofia demanded. She looked around him for Christina. "Where is she?"

"She's gone. Back to Argentina. I just took her to the airport."

"But you two looked so … ."

"Miserable?" Enzo finished for her. "Or did I just look like I didn't know my head from my tail?"

Sofia looked away from his face and shook his hands off her shoulders. "Why did she come?"

"I was ignoring her texts. She says she was worried

about me. Turns out, she had reason to be. I had fallen in love with someone else."

Sofia shook her head and turned her back to him.

"I'm sorry, Sofia," Enzo said, talking over her shoulder. "Even before I left Mendoza, I knew that it was over with her. But when she showed up like that yesterday, I didn't want to embarrass you by making a scene in front of all of those people."

Sofia stood with her arms crossed over her chest. He walked around to face her.

"I remembered what you said about Julio humiliating you in front of the entire town. I wanted to get out of there as quickly as possible. I needed to go somewhere else to tell Christina that we were over. I couldn't do it there in front of everyone."

Sofia was looking away from him.

"Sofia?" He bent to look at her.

Sofia closed her eyes for a moment, and then looked up at the trees, sunlight winking through as a light breeze rustled the leaves.

"You are telling me it's over between you?" she asked.

"Yes. I knew it a week ago. Sofia, I knew it the minute I met you."

She looked into his face. "But you have to go back to Argentina. Sooner or later, you'll get back with her. She'll make sure you do."

"Not if you come with me."

Sofia frowned. "Come with you? What are you talking about? My home is in Seattle. I work there. My life is there."

Enzo nodded and reached for a hand. Reluctantly, she allowed him to hold it.

"Look," he said, "you're not crazy about your job. You want to get back to working with wine. Lots of wineries in Argentina—not just mine—need help with marketing. I think you should come down to visit your brother. Maybe you'll decide to stay. Maybe you'll let me love you."

The word "love" surprised and muted her. She caught her breath and thought for a minute. She was crazy to believe him. She would be crazy to quit her job and fly to another hemisphere on the chance that she'd found the love of her life in Enzo. That he could make room in his life for her.

She tried to stay calm, but she couldn't stop the smile working its way across her lips. Her heart was pounding, telling her what she wanted. Enzo. And it sounded like he wanted her. Finally, she looked up at him. "Are you serious?"

"I want you. I won't leave without you."

Sofia held his eyes as he stepped close.

"Sofie. I love you." He put a finger under her chin and lifted her face toward his. He kissed her lightly.

Sofia closed her eyes and let out a sob. Could she trust this? Could she believe he loved her?

Could she not?

"I love you too," she said. She put her arms over his shoulders and pulled him in.

Eighteen

SOFIA BURST THROUGH THE DOOR onto Enzo's patio, where he sat with his parents, having a late afternoon cocktail.

"Sorry I'm late," she said, nodding at the elders.

Enzo stood up and grabbed Sofia's hand. "*Lo siento*," he said to his parents. "We need to talk in private."

He led her at a trot down between the vineyard rows as the sun set in the west behind huge, snow-capped mountain peaks. The big dog, Vino, jogged ahead of them, stopping every few yards to sniff the wake of some critter that had passed through before.

Once they were out of earshot of the patio, Enzo slowed down. "Now, I can't wait any longer. Tell me what happened!"

"I didn't think I had a chance." Sofia paused to catch her breath. "Back in Walla Walla they said I didn't know enough people to do marketing for a wine region. But here, they said with your help and my brother's, I can make all the connections I need. I figured, why not? So, I said yes. I took the job. I start next week."

"So, you will stay here in Mendoza?"

"Si, Señor." She grinned. "I am going to stay here as long as you want me."

"That will be forever!" He stopped and picked Sofia up with his arms around her waist and twirled around. Vino loped back to them and barked. Enzo let Sofia down and kissed her softly. He took her hand, and they continued walking between the vines.

"I don't think I ever realized how beautiful dusk is until I spent those evenings on your patio with Rufus," he said, looking out over the vines toward the setting sun.

"And with me?" she asked.

Enzo smiled mischievously. "Oh, were you there too?"

Sofia laughed, and reached down to scratch an ear of the big dog walking beside her. "Well, I never knew I could love another dog as much as I love Rufus." She joined Enzo's gaze at the horizon. "And I never knew I would find a place I loved as much I loved that patio back home," she whispered. "But this is just as beautiful."

Enzo stopped again and turned her to face him. "Welcome to your new home, my love."

Their kiss lasted long after the sun finally dipped behind the mountains and the vineyard grew dark.

Love on the Links

One

WHAT BETH LOVED MOST ABOUT her fifth-floor condo in Seattle was the view of Puget Sound she had from its west-facing balcony. Yes, there were a few warm days when she wished the evening sun didn't shine directly through the big sliders into the living room, but no one in Seattle ever complained about getting too much sun.

She appreciated the balcony for another reason: Chi-Chi. The big dog loved the sun, and every chance she could get, she lay out there, soaking up the heat of the rays. If Chi-Chi could have spent all her daylight hours on the balcony, she surely would have. Luckily, the malamute mix wasn't a barker, and Beth let her out whenever she was home, although the dog preferred Beth's big queen bed once the sun set.

None of this made Dan happy, however. He would have preferred ChiChi live somewhere else entirely, and it was partly because of their canine disconnect that Beth kept brushing off Dan's insistence on setting a date for their wedding.

On the balcony one summer evening, Beth pulled her feet out from under ChiChi's shaggy body and drained the last of the wine from her glass. She picked up the bottle she and Dan had just finished and stood.

"I'm going to start making dinner." She pulled the sliding glass door open. ChiChi looked up for a moment before deciding to stay right where she was, even if it meant sharing the balcony with Dan. Her big head plopped back down, and she sighed audibly.

"But we're not done with this conversation," Dan argued. "I really want to make a decision now."

"I'm not ready to set a date," Beth answered. She fell back down on her chair and slumped forward.

"You love me. You want to get married. Right?"

"Sure." Beth moved her head up and down, but it wasn't a convincing nod. "I think. I just don't understand why we have to decide this now."

Dan looked at her with a long face, his eyelids drooping as if he were exhausted. "You know what the problem is?" he asked. He didn't wait for her answer. "We love each other, but we don't have enough in common. I love golf and you love dogs. Your friends are bohemians and canines, and mine are married grown-ups with kids. I think what we need is to develop a mutual passion."

Beth couldn't disagree, but as she stared at the reflection of the setting sun rippling across the sound, she couldn't imagine what mutual passion—or even mutual like—they could develop at this point in their three-year relationship.

"That makes sense, I suppose," she said. "But that isn't going to help me get dinner ready tonight." She pushed herself back up out of her chair, but Dan reached over and put a hand on her arm to stop her.

"I think you should learn to play golf," he said. He

reached into a rear pocket and pulled out what looked like a brochure—folded in half to fit alongside his billfold. He unfolded it and studied it like he'd never seen it before.

"Right. And I think you should learn to love dogs," Beth answered.

"That's not going to happen," he said, continuing to peruse the brochure in his hand. "Once ChiChi is adopted, I don't want you to get another one."

"I'm not promising that. I've never lived without a dog. I would own one instead of just fostering if I weren't trying to make you happy."

"Okay, we'll cross that bridge … ." Dan stopped. His voice had started to rise as it always did when the topic of Beth's canine obsessions was raised. He lowered it. "But how about golf?"

"I'm no good at it," Beth said flatly, remembering their disastrous outings to the driving range and the course the summer before. "And when you try to teach me, we always end up fighting."

"That's why I think we should do this." Dan tossed the brochure in front of her.

Beth looked at the front of the colorful trifold. Three gorgeous women stood in a line, each holding a golf club as if ready to swing, smiling big, toothy grins. In front of them, clearly endangering his life by standing there, a man held up his arms as if demonstrating some immutable physical law that controlled the universe—or perhaps just the perfect golf swing.

A smart trick, Beth thought: showing women, not men learning to play golf. This brochure was designed with men like Dan in mind—men who liked pictures of gorgeous women. And, more specifically, men who wanted to convince their own gorgeous significant other that golf could be fun for women. Or at least that golf instructors were really good looking.

"How long have you been plotting this?" Beth said, tossing the brochure back without looking inside. "When did you get that brochure?"

Dan ignored her questions. "You're between jobs right now, so I thought it would be a good time," he said instead. "And I have too much vacation time built up. I need to take some time off or I'll lose it. I think we should go to Palm Springs this fall and take couple's lessons."

"Or we could go to the Westminster Dog Show. Maybe you'll see a dog breed you like," Beth countered.

"It's not about breeds. It's about the species." He pointed at ChiChi. "They're messy. Golf? You put the clubs in the garage, change your shoes, and you get on with your day. Dogs—it's not so easy. Whenever you go somewhere, you have to put the dog in a kennel. We can't even go out to dinner without having to hurry home to let ChiChi out. Not to mention the ridiculous dog hair everywhere."

ChiChi lifted her head briefly at the mention of her name, but quickly let it drop again with a thud against the deck boards.

"That's why I shouldn't take up golf," Beth argued. "It's a day-long commitment. ChiChi would be cooped up inside all day. And I already have no time to see my friends. Not to mention that golf is expensive."

At that, Dan smirked. "Do you recall how much you spent on ChiChi's last vet visit? And she's not even your dog!"

"Touché." Beth hated it when Dan used that tone of voice—the one that sounded like he was all reason and logic and smarts, and she needed a scolding like a child. She picked up the brochure again. "But how much is this golf school?"

"Less than ChiChi's root canal."

"Not funny," Beth muttered. She opened the brochure and started to read. What Dan said made some sense. They did need to find new ways to engage with each other now that the initial spark of their romance had cooled—as unimpressive as it was in the first place. Maybe she could learn to play golf. Maybe she could get good at it. She used to play tennis, and she used to think she was fairly athletic.

But even if she did take up the game, she had no plans to give up on dogs. If she could play golf, he could put up with ChiChi.

Two

THE STARBUCKS EMPLOYEE CAFETERIA WAS in a big industrial space with huge ducts painted in bright primary colors overhead and concrete floors underfoot. Beth tried to smile at everyone who looked her way. She had no idea who might be interviewing her that afternoon, and which of these people she'd be working with soon, if she were lucky enough to get the job.

Ever since she'd stepped inside the building an hour before, she'd been envious—not so much of the subsidized lunch or the open floorplan, but of the company badges everyone else wore. The paper visitor tag stuck to the lapel of her jacket made her stick out as an outsider.

It had been a few months since she'd worn a corporate badge at her former company. Once she'd been furloughed in the pandemic, the company decided she wasn't needed—permanently. With all corporate meetings cancelled, no one needed an events coordinator, and once companies learned that their business could continue fine by Zoom, she got the bad news in writing.

"This is no reflection on your performance, and it does not affect the amount of severance you will be paid per your employment contract," the bad-news letter concluded. Her former boss called and assured her that she would receive an enthusiastic review if anyone called for a reference. Now, the severance money was quickly running out, and it had taken longer than she had hoped for employers to get back to scheduling employee marketing or customer events. A chance at this dream job—at a successful company with a worldwide brand in what was reportedly a fun working environment—was almost too good to be true.

"Are you nervous?" her friend Debra asked, as they finished the French fries they were sharing for lunch along with their healthy but uninspiring salads.

"Oddly not," Beth said. "Should I be? I mean, I really want this job, but I've been doing this sort of thing for five years. Surely I'm qualified."

"You wouldn't have gotten the interview if you weren't. Just remember, a lot of the interview will be about whether you're a 'good fit'—not about your experience of qualifications."

"Well, how do I prove I'm a good fit? How will I know what it looks like?"

"You won't. But the interviewer has a list of things to look for."

"Do you know what they are?"

Debra laughed. "Heck no! Every department is different, and every manager has his own quirks. You're about to learn the meaning of serendipity, my friend. Either you fit or you don't."

"Seems more like luck of the draw than serendipity," Beth mused.

"Well, just be yourself. If you're not a good fit, you don't want the job anyway. It wouldn't be any fun. Most important is to convince them you're a team player. Team is everything around here."

Beth sank into her own thoughts. She wasn't necessarily a social butterfly and, in fact, was at times socially awkward, which made her choice of a career in event planning a bit ironic. But she'd always gotten along with her co-workers at big events by grinning and bearing—and going home afterwards to a cold bottle of sauvignon blanc.

"I'm glad I got this interview today," Beth said, shifting topics. "We're leaving tomorrow."

"The golf trip?" Deb flashed a sympathetic smile. "You're really going through with this?"

"If nothing else, it will be nice to be in the sun for a week. If I flunk out of the golf lessons, I'll sit by the pool and drink cocktails with little umbrellas."

Deb sighed, jealous. "Maybe I should come with you. I could use some warm-weather R&R. But I'm not crazy about this golf thing. I'm afraid you'll really like it and we'll never have time together anymore. You'll be on the golf course with Dan all the time."

"If I get this job, then we'll see each other at lunch every day. And I doubt I'll be good enough after a week that Dan will want to play with me."

"I don't know," Debra said. "You've always struck me as pretty athletic. I'll bet you're a natural. Is Ellen taking ChiChi for you?"

"Yes, Mom loves her."

Beth glanced at her watch. "Whoops, you'd better run. I'll get your tray. Run upstairs now or you'll be late for your interview."

THE NEXT MORNING WAS RAINY again, and Beth had to run in the dark from Dan's car to her mom's front door, hoping ChiChi's thick coat wouldn't soak up too much water. She had the dog's rain coat in the bag she'd prepared for Chi-Chi's visit, but she didn't have time to put it on her before Dan rushed them out of her apartment.

The door was unlocked, and Beth let herself in. ChiChi ran past her mom and headed for the spot in the kitchen where her food bowl was kept.

"So that's my hello?" Ellen said, looking at the dog's wet trail.

"Hi, Mom." Beth leaned in and kissed her mother on the cheek. "Here's the leash, some pills for anxiety, and some treats."

"Anxiety?" They followed ChiChi to the kitchen.

"Yeah, I actually think it only happens around Dan, but you never know."

"I'll have to admit, I'm surprised Dan is letting you travel with him," her mom said, putting the big bag of dog stuff on the kitchen counter.

"Well, we're getting separate rooms," Beth said, "so he didn't have to explain something embarrassing to his mom."

"That doesn't surprise me," Ellen said, shaking her head. "How did my little bohemian end up with Dan?"

Beth just shrugged.

"You're coming back when?"

"Saturday. A week from tomorrow. Dan wants to get back in time to have a day in the office by himself before the week starts."

"You mean on Sunday?"

"Yup. Oh, and by the way, he still doesn't know that I've adopted ChiChi. He thinks I'm still just fostering her. So don't say anything to him."

"Doesn't he wonder why no one has taken her yet? She's so gorgeous!" Ellen bent down, her face close to Chi-Chi's. "You know you're gorgeous, don't you?" She rubbed noses with the dog.

"Dan's so blind to dogs, he can't see how wonderful she

is," Beth said. "Especially for a malamute. They can be so difficult."

"I never thought I'd see you with someone who doesn't like dogs," Ellen said, straightening up.

"Okay, Mom. Enough Dan-criticism already. I've got to run. We're catching that seven a.m. flight to Palm Springs." She bent down and hugged ChiChi.

"You be a good girl for Grandma, okay Sweetie," she said. ChiChi followed her to the door. "Bye, Mom."

Beth leaned in to kiss her mother on the cheek again and ran outside through the downpour to the car. She jumped in and brushed water off her coat.

"You're getting the seat all wet," Dan said, putting the car in gear.

Beth looked at him, puzzled. "Sorry. What do you want me to do? Levitate?"

Dan grimaced with disgust and shook his head. He pulled away from the curb. The rain pelted the windshield, and Beth watched it wash in sheets off the streets and sidewalks into the gutters.

"I don't know if I'll ever take to golf, but I'll sure be glad to get out of this rain for a week," she said, glumly.

"I predict you're going to like golf. A few lessons can make all the difference," Dan said. "I might have trouble getting you to come back here."

"If it were all about the weather, I think you're right. I've lived here all my life, and sometimes even I get sick of the rain."

Dan leaned forward to look up through the splattered windshield at the dark sky. "Sorry I had to work so late last night," he said. "I needed to get the team all set before we left."

"That's okay. I went to bed early. I was really tired."

"How'd the interview go yesterday?"

"I don't really know. I think I had answers for all their

222

questions. But Debra said something about how it all comes down to 'the right fit.'"

Dan nodded. "Yes, it does." He probably knew, Beth thought. He'd been part of that kind of corporate world for more than a decade at Amazon's headquarters.

"How do you figure out if someone's the 'right fit?'" she asked.

"If it's a guy, I like to play golf with him. You can learn a lot about a person on the golf course that you can't learn in an interview." He stopped briefly at a red light and turned right onto the highway toward the airport.

"And if it's a woman? You don't take her on the golf course?"

"Most of the women I interview don't play golf."

"Then you do you determine 'fit' if she doesn't?"

As usual, Dan ignored the question he didn't want to answer. "See that's another reason why you should learn to play golf. It will give you a leg up on the competition when you're looking for a job."

"Well, only if the guy who's hiring is a man who plays golf," she said, trying to keep the sarcasm out of her voice. It was early. They had eight days together in front of them. Striving for a more neutral tone, she added, "I doubt that one week of lessons is going to make much of a difference."

"If you go in with that attitude, it probably won't," he said, reaching across the console to grab her hand. "Come on. Promise me you'll try."

Three

BETH AND DAN DUCKED THROUGH the downpour into the departure terminal in Seattle and shook themselves off in a way that reminded her of ChiChi. Three hours later, their coats tucked into garbage bags and stuffed into outside pockets of their suitcases, they walked out of the Palm Springs Airport terminal into bright sunshine.

"Now, this is more like it!" Beth exclaimed. She pulled her phone out of her purse and turned it on. "It's 85 degrees here! I haven't seen 85 since that one day in August."

She stuck her phone into the back pocket of her jeans and looked up at the bright blue sky, the steep grey-brown slope of mountains just west of the town, and the palm trees swaying in the breeze.

"I could get used to this," she said.

Dan was paying no attention to her, focused as he was on reading emails on his phone. He looked up just as a town car pulled up to the curb with his name taped to the window, and a driver in uniform hopped out.

"You ordered a town car?" Beth asked. "What are we? Celebrities?"

"It's a perk of being a big wig at Amazon," Dan said, rather smugly. "Don't complain. It's much more comfortable than a cab."

"What's wrong with Uber?"

Dan stepped off the curb and shook the driver's hand. As Beth slid into the back seat, Dan stood watching the man load their golf clubs and suitcases into the trunk. He got in beside her when the trunk slammed closed.

"So, is this how it goes when you travel for work?" she asked.

"Pretty much. Why? Does it bother you?"

Beth shrugged and looked away, out the window as the driver pulled out and turned the air conditioning up to gale force.

"You'll get used to it," Dan said before turning back to his cell phone.

Beth watched as they rolled past vast, empty desertscapes next to huge residential developments, some that looked sad and aging and some brand new—so new that the tops of the replanted palm trees were still tied into tight, upright ponytails.

Twenty minutes later, they pulled up to the Westin Hotel, its shady, arched portico leading back past the check-in lobby and the time-share sales office toward the restaurants and swimming pools.

"We're staying here?" Beth asked. Suddenly she felt like a rube. How could anyone spend their entire life in a sophisticated city like Seattle and never stay a single night in a fancy resort hotel? she wondered. She'd organized plenty of events at them, but she'd never once been a guest at one. Perhaps getting married to Dan would come with benefits she'd never imagined.

The driver opened her door first, and she stepped out to look down a cascading fountain at a wide, lush lawn between rows of majestic palms. The whole watery display seemed to serve no purpose other than decoration.

"I thought this was a desert," she mused, only realizing she'd said it out loud when Dan grabbed her arm.

"Yup, it is," he said brusquely. "Let's hurry. I'm starving. We have just enough time for lunch before we meet the instructor on the driving range this afternoon."

"Don't we have to check in?"

"All taken care of," Dan said.

As they walked down the arched portico to the restaurant, Beth wondered why Dan always seemed so tired when he got home from his business trips. This kind of travel seemed awfully easy to her.

BETH WATCHED WITH EMBARRASSMENT AS Dan shoveled his lunch soup and sandwich down as if a wildfire was approaching and it would be his last meal for the foreseeable future. For all his advanced degrees and all of his sophistication when it came to business, he easily slipped into a kind of bachelor, barbarian comportment when no one but she was looking.

"You have soup on your shirt." She pointed to the orange tomato stain just below the buttons of his golf polo.

Dan dabbed at it ineffectively with his napkin and pointed at her salad.

"Better hurry," he said. "I don't want to be late. Jake is very popular and we're lucky to get him."

"Jake?"

"Our golf instructor. Didn't you read the confirmation letter?"

"Yes, but I guess I didn't memorize it."

Dan slurped the last of his soup and tossed down his spoon. "I sure hope you get your heart into this, or it will turn out to be a big waste of money," he said, wiping his chin.

"It wasn't my idea to spend this kind of money on golf lessons," she reminded him.

Dan grabbed the leather portfolio the waiter had left with their lunch check, threw in some tens, and snapped it closed. "Come on now. Eat up. We should get going."

"I'm finished," Beth said, folding up her napkin and laying it across her plate. "Not impressed with this salad anyway."

Four

FOLLOWING DAN DOWN THE SLOPE from the restaurant to the roped-off lesson area, Beth glanced over at the pool complex. It looked heavenly.

It was noon, and most of the lounge chairs were still unoccupied. Only a handful of people sat at the bar tables under colorful umbrellas. She heard a whir of a margarita machine and the clink of ice cubes being scooped into glass. Perhaps she would be over there soon. If she could just get through this first afternoon and show Dan that he'd be happier taking lessons without her.

The man Beth assumed was Jake stood before a large pile of golf balls, swinging an iron back and forth with an ease that made it look like he'd been born with a club in his hand. He turned as they approached, and Dan strutted forward, his hand extended. He grabbed Jake's and pumped.

"Hi, I'm Dan Norris," he nearly shouted. "And this is my fiancé." Either his adrenaline was spiking at the thought of showing off his golf swing or that tomato soup was full of amphetamines.

Beth walked up behind him and shook Jake's hand, considerably less excitedly. "I'm Beth. I think Dan forgets I have a name sometimes."

Jake winked at her. "You might be surprised how common that is," he said. He stood back, his club still in his hand and looked them over.

"Welcome, Dan and Beth," he said. "I see you're from Seattle. I'll bet this sunshine feels pretty good."

Beth smiled and nodded. She liked the look of the instructor, even if she wasn't terribly excited about why they'd been brought together. Just a few wisps of dark hair curled out from under his golf cap, framing a nicely tanned, lean face. His strong cheekbones framed a wide smile and left just enough room for his Ray-bans to rest on his nose like an eyeglass model. He was tall with a muscular chest and long, sinewy arms. He continued to flick the club a few inches back and forth. Was it nervous energy, or had he swung a club so many times in his professional career that he didn't even realize when he was doing it?

"As you probably read in the brochure, I am Jake Engels, and I am going to help you take whatever golf game you came with to a new level this week," he said. "We'll work hard, but we'll have some fun too."

Beth hadn't come in feeling very positive about that, but Jake's gorgeous smile was changing things. On the other hand, Dan's feet were shifting impatiently. He kept looking at his clubs as if he couldn't wait to start pounding balls out onto the driving range.

"I think you should know," she answered. "I really don't have a golf game. I'm pretty much starting from zero. Or less than zero."

Jake's grin seemed to get even bigger. How was that possible?

"Not a problem!" he said. "I've helped people who didn't even know what end of the club to hold. Most get to the point that they enjoy the game. The good thing is that golf is one of those things you don't have to be really good at to enjoy."

"Can we cut the chit-chat and get started?" Dan interrupted. "I'm paying for instruction, not for cheerleading."

Jake took the jab well. "Sure, Dan. I understand," he said, his voice unchanged. "Why don't the two of you grab your favorite club from your bag and warm up a bit. I'd like to watch your swings so I have a bit of an idea of where we're starting from."

Beth watched Dan pull his driver out of his bag and step a few feet away to take some warm-up swings. She didn't have a "favorite club," so she followed his lead and grabbed her driver too.

Jake came up beside her and reached into her bag, pulling out an iron.

"Why don't you take the seven iron," he said, handing it to her. "It's a nice, comfortable club to hit. A mid-iron. Probably an easier place to start."

Beth nodded and stepped up to a pyramid of balls on the tee. She watched Dan put a tee in the ground on the next tee over, knock some balls off his pyramid, and put one on a tee. He took another practice swing, lined up for a shot and swung. Beth had been intimidated by his golf prowess before, and now she didn't feel any better. She doubted she'd ever be able to swing that fast or hit the ball that hard. The ball flew out to the right side of the driving range and landed somewhere beyond where Beth could see.

She looked over at Jake and shrugged. He smiled and nodded at her pyramid of balls. "Go ahead. Just swing easy," he said. Could he read her mind already?

Beth reached down and took the top ball off the pyramid and put it on the grass. She was happy she knew enough about golf to not use a tee with an iron. She stood back for a practice swing and tried to swing the club fast and hard like Dan did. She felt silly, but she stepped up to the ball and swung again. The club hit the ball and skidded forward about 25 yards, never leaving the ground.

She turned to Jake and raised her arms. "See! I'm no good. I shouldn't even be out here."

Dan lined up to take another shot with his driver, and Beth turned to watch.

"Beth, isn't it?" Jake said.

"Yes."

"Beth, don't watch Dan. You aren't going to learn anything that way. Just go ahead and hit a few more balls. Slow and easy. And don't be so nervous. No one is watching but me, and I've seen people whiff the ball a dozen times in a row. You made contact, and that's a good sign."

Beth did as she was told and was relieved to see Jake move over behind Dan to watch him instead. She took a deep breath and lined up another shot.

"Nice swing, Dan," Jake said. "I think if you slowed it down just a tad and stayed in the shot just a split second longer, you'll get a little more accuracy and less of a slice."

Dan twirled around and lifted his chin. "It's not a slice. It's a fade," he said. "I do that on purpose."

"Great," Jake said, rewarding Dan's confidence with a big smile. "If you're going for the power fade, perhaps aim a little more to the left then, and you'll end up closer to the middle."

"Are you serious?" Dan sounded angry. "Let me ask you something, Jake. What's your handicap?"

Beth listened closely. She knew Dan bragged about his "single-digit" handicap, which was a nine—just barely single-digit. He'd told her it meant he generally could expect to score nine strokes over par in an 18-hole round.

"I'm a plus two," Jake said, nonchalantly. Beth knew

what that meant, too: Jake would generally expect to finish a round a couple of strokes under par. That, she knew, was the kind of handicap professional golfers had, but one that was rare for amateurs like Dan. "What's yours?"

"Uh …" Dan muttered something that Beth couldn't hear and lined up his next shot a little to the left, and his slice—or was it a fade?—sent the ball right down the middle.

"Well, look at that," Jake teased. "Just like you planned it."

Dan pretended not to hear him and knocked another ball off the pyramid. Jake moved back over behind Beth.

"How's it going here, Beth?" he asked.

"I don't think I'm learning anything," she said, shrugging again.

"Yeah, I just wanted you to warm up a bit. Now, let me show you the first thing I want you to learn." Jake moved in behind her, his long arms along her sides. He shook her club loose from her hand, and stood it upright, holding it with just an index finger in front of her.

"Put your left hand on the grip like this," he said. He demonstrated and then moved his hand away.

Beth felt his warm torso against her back and wondered how she was supposed to concentrate on the club, but she tried to follow. "Like this?" she asked.

"Yes, but looser. Don't squeeze," he said. "Now put your right hand over the left thumb like this." As she tried to imitate his placement, he gently lifted her right thumb and moved it counterclockwise.

Jake backed away, and Beth felt the air cool against her back. Was she sweating?

"There," he said. "Now waggle the club a little and see how that feels."

Beth lifted the club off the ground and swayed it back and forth. "Weird," she said. "It feels weird."

"That's because you've gotten used to a bad grip," Jake explained. "The grip is what sets up the entire golf swing. Without a good grip, we put ourselves at a disadvantage from the start."

Beth looked up as she waggled the club and saw Dan watching her, frowning.

"Don't stand with your feet so far apart." He pointed at his own feet. "More like this."

"Dan," she said. She dismissed him with a wave. "I'm listening to Jake here."

"I know," Dan insisted. "But your stance isn't any good."

"Dan is right," Jake said, stepping in between them to block Dan's view. "But let's take one step at a time here. Now, with your new grip, take a full swing, just to get a feel for it."

Beth started to swing, and Jake walked back behind Dan. "Dan, I see you're driving the ball well. How's your short game? Chipping? Putting?"

"Not as good," Dan admitted.

"Why don't you grab a short iron and show me your approach shot," he said, pointing at Dan's bag. "Maybe hit a few hundred-yard shots. Take a few practice shots, and I'll be right back with you."

"Now, Beth," he said, moving back to face her. "Let me see how that grip is holding up."

A couple of hours later, Beth had started to get more comfortable with the new grip, and Jake had given her a few more tips about turning her shoulders and keeping her left arm straight. She was starting to get tired, though, and she paused longer and longer between shots. Finally, she let her club fall down and shook her arms.

"My hands are getting sore," she said. "Do you think maybe we've done enough?"

"You're gripping the club too tight," Dan shouted over his shoulder. "Loosen up a little."

Beth watched as Jake shook his head, took a deep breath, and winked at her.

"I think that's all for this afternoon, anyway," he said. "Let's call it a day." He bent down and picked up the clubs Beth had left lying by her golf bag. He stuck them back where they belonged and handed her a towel.

"So. I'll see you folks bright and early tomorrow," he said. "Eight-thirty. Is that okay?"

"I'm not sure this is a good idea, guys," she said, looking at Dan. "Why don't you just take the lessons. I'll come and watch some, but I don't think I'm going to like this."

"Absolutely not," Jake interjected before Dan could answer. "You've already made a ton of progress, Beth. I won't take no for an answer. I'll see you both tomorrow morning. Have a great evening, you two."

He turned and started to walk back toward the clubhouse but, after a few steps, he stopped and looked back at them. "Just leave your bags here," he said. "I'll have the bag guys come and get them for you. We'll store them overnight."

"Thanks," Beth called after him.

Dan put his arm over Beth's shoulders and steered her up the slope. "He's right, Beth. Don't get discouraged. It takes a lot of practice, but you can get there. Come on. Let's go get a cocktail at the hotel."

Maybe, Beth thought. Maybe she could "get there" if Dan would get off her ass. She'd give it one more day—or at least one morning. And then, if it still seemed hopeless, she'd head for the pools and that drink she'd been dreaming of. The one with the umbrella.

Five

MIDWAY THROUGH THE LESSON THE next morning, even Beth could tell she was improving. Dan was slamming ball after ball down the practice range, signaling clearly that he didn't think Jake could teach him anything. But as Jake stood next to Beth to show her how to move her hips as she swung, Dan stepped toward them.

"You need to pause a little bit at the top, Beth," Dan said.

He took his own club back and held it at the top of his backswing to show her. It was the third time he had butted in that morning, and it wasn't helping Beth concentrate on Jake's advice.

But it was Jake who protested.

"Dan, we're going to make no progress here if you keep throwing in your two cents." He waved Dan back.

"Well, when I see she's doing something wrong—" Dan started to explain.

"And how has that worked in the past?" Jake asked. "Has she had trouble learning from you before?"

Beth was surprised when Dan stepped back, chagrined. "I just want to help," he said weakly.

"I know you do. But this isn't helping. I'm happy to work with both of you, but I have to ask you to back off when I'm working with Beth."

Dan looked away and sighed. It didn't seem like he was having any fun.

"How about if I just go up and see if I can get a tee-time?" he said. "I'm kind of tired of practicing."

"Sounds like a good idea, Dan," Jake said. "I think the main purpose here is for Beth to learn. Am I right?"

Dan and Beth both nodded.

"So, why don't you go play, and we'll continue here? I'm happy to give you a refund for half the price of these lessons."

"No, that's okay," Dan said, dropping his clubs back into his bag. "A one-on-one lesson costs about the same as for two. I'm glad to pay. You just help Beth."

"Great," Jake said as Dan pulled the bag over his shoulder and headed up the hill. "Thanks, Dan."

Beth and Jake watched him retreat toward the clubhouse, and Beth let out a sign of relief.

"Have fun, honey," she called after him. "I'll see you at cocktail hour."

Once Dan was safely out of earshot, she turned to Jake.

"Thanks. You don't know how hard—"

"No problem." Jake cut her off. "You'll never know how common that is. You can't learn from your spouse—male or female. It's not possible. Now, let's get back to work. You're making incredible progress already."

Jake took the club she was holding out of her hand and handed her a different one from her bag. "You're really quite athletic," he said. "What other sports do you play?"

"None," she answered. "I ride a bike, hike. But I used to play a little tennis. Back when I was in college."

"Ah. That makes sense. That hand-eye coordination is important in golf, too. Why don't we work another hour, have lunch, and then go out on the course this afternoon?"

"Do you think I'm ready? I still can't hit the ball very far."

"No, you can't," Jake said. "But I want you to enjoy the game, not just hit balls. We can just do a few holes, if you'd like. And we can play a scramble."

"What's that?"

"You hit, I hit, and then we take our next shot from the spot of the best one." He pointed to the club in her hand. "Now, let's work a little more on your follow-through."

Beth was happy the morning's lesson was over. Once again, her arms and hands were tired, and hitting the ball out into the big grass range was starting to feel monotonous. As she sat with Jake on the patio and sipped a grapefruit juice and vodka, she relaxed, knowing they weren't going to return to the range that afternoon.

"What made you decide to take golf lessons?" Jake asked after the waiter had taken their order for sandwiches.

"Well, we're supposed to be getting married ..." She let her voice trail. Suddenly she wasn't sure this was something she wanted Jake to know. Why not? she wondered. Was she—could she be—so quickly attracted to him? He was a golf instructor. He was supposed to be congenial and a bit of a flirt. Caught in thought, she didn't finish her sentence.

"Congratulations," Jake said. "Supposed to?"

"'Supposed to,' yes," she said. "I'm not as sure as Dan, but that's neither here nor there." She tried to adopt a breezy, devil-may-care tone. "Dan thought we needed to have more things in common. So, golf it is."

"It is a great sport for couples," Jake agreed.

"I suppose. So, do you play with your wife? Partner? A girlfriend? Anyone play golf with you?"

He grinned. Had she been too transparent?

"No, I just came off the tour. Haven't had any time to meet anyone. And trust me, you don't want to date any of those women who follow the tour around. They're looking for one thing."

"What?"

"Money."

Beth chuckled at herself. She had expected him to say "sex." Why was that? How silly could she be?

"Of course," Jake continued, "they would have figured out pretty quickly that I wasn't making much."

Beth laughed. He was certainly modest. It only added to his appeal. Too bad that hadn't rubbed off on Dan a little.

"So, you played on the PGA Tour?"

Jake shook his head. "Not the regular tour. I never got past the Korn Ferry Tour." He looked up at her blank expression. "It's like the minors in baseball."

"Wow, you hit the ball as well as you do, and you got stuck in the minors?"

"Well, it takes a lot more than hitting the ball to succeed."

Beth nodded. She'd heard this before. "You mean 90 percent mental, like Dan always says?"

"Yup, that's exactly what I mean," Jake said as the waiter put their sandwiches down. "Now, let's eat and then we'll go see what we can do out there on the course."

Six

THE THREE HOURS BETH SPENT playing with Jake that afternoon were like none she'd ever spent on a golf course before.

They were fun.

As she stood up to the first tee box, her hands shook so violently that she was afraid she would drop the club. Jake stood in front of her and put his hand on hers, stopping her before she swung at the ball.

"Let's go for less than driver," he said.

She looked up, puzzled. "What do you mean?"

He took the driver out of her hands and replaced it with a five-wood out of her bag. "Drivers are hard to hit. I know men who never use them, and many women prefer the smaller head of a fairway wood."

Beth had to admit: it felt intimidating to swing the huge head of her driver at the ball. Not only did it seem too big for the task, the shaft was the longest of any of her clubs. With that much distance between her arms and the ball, it seemed unlikely she'd hit anything.

"Take a practice swing with that one and let your arms relax," Jake said.

Beth shook her arms to release the tension, but her heart was still racing. "I feel naked," she muttered.

"Everyone does," Jake answered. "It's called Naked on the First Tee. There's a book by that title. Let your shoulders drop. That will help."

Standing over the ball, she looked up at him and grimaced. "There are too many things to think about!"

"Don't think," he said. "Just relax and watch the clubhead hit the ball."

"What if I miss?"

"Then you can try again."

Beth took a deep breath, let her shoulders drop from her ears where they'd been stuck, and swung. Miraculously, the ball sailed forward and straight. She stood watching it fly and then roll down the fairway. She'd never hit a shot like that when she'd played with Dan. Ever.

"Wow," Jake said, his hands on his hips, watching with her. "See what you can do? Let's go play that ball!"

"But aren't you going to drive?" she asked. "You can hit it much farther."

"Sure, I can, but I think we should take advantage of that great drive. Come on, jump in." He hopped behind the steering wheel, and she barely got in before he gunned the cart.

Most of her shots that afternoon were much less glorious than that first one off the tee. But instead of turning grouchy, as Dan always did when she whiffed the ball or hit it sideways, Jake just laughed, and she laughed with him.

At first, when she lined up for her shots, his eyes on her made her nervous. But after he praised her few good ones, she looked forward to performing for him. If she hit a horrid shot, he threw down another ball for her to hit and told her to relax. Indeed, relaxing was the key to playing well, she discovered as they went along. "It's a stupid game" was Jake's mantra, which took the seriousness out of the silly venture. The more she laughed, smiled, and relaxed, the better she played.

Halfway down the last fairway, Beth was tired. It was only a par-three, and after her tee shot, her ball still sat sixty yards from the green. A good shot with her wedge should have put the ball near the pin, but instead, she shanked it into the bushes on the right.

"I'm spent!" she said, letting her club fall to the ground.

"Yes, I can see that," Jake said. He walked up to her and picked up the club. "Here, let me show you something." He handed her the club and stood behind her, putting his hands over hers on the club. He started a backswing as if they were going to hit together and stopped when Beth thought the club was only halfway back.

"See this?" he said, holding the club still. "This is as far as you need to take the club back. In fact, when you're tired, you try too hard and you swing too big. Remember, less is sometimes more."

Slightly dizzy, Beth turned her head to face him. His arms stayed along her sides, their faces only inches apart. For a long moment, they held their position, searching the other's eyes.

Beth fought the urge to lean forward just a little and brush her lips against his. And yet, at the same time, she feared he was going to kiss her. But she couldn't move.

Jake smiled, relieving the tension, let go of her club, and backed away.

"I'm sorry," Jake said, looking away. "I didn't mean to do that." His shyness was part of his charm. Unlike Dan, he didn't show any evidence of what her fiancé had displayed as a sense of entitlement to any space he wanted to occupy.

"That's too bad," she half-teased. "I was hoping you did."

"Let's go putt," he said, waving at the green and avoiding her eyes. "The only way to end a round is with the sound of that ball going in the hole."

As they drove the long nine-hole distance back to the clubhouse, she put a hand on his forearm. "Thanks, Jake. I had so much more fun than I expected."

"I'm glad you enjoyed it," he said. It seemed he had regained his composure. "See, the secret is taking the pressure off yourself. Just enjoy the swing. How many times in your day do you get to do something so free and physical as swinging a golf club?"

"I am starting to get that feeling. Is that what Dan feels? Is that why he likes it so much?"

"I don't know Dan very well, but at his level, he probably really enjoys competing. Remember how he asked me what my handicap was?"

"Yeah, why?"

"Well, a guy does that if he's trying to prove something to himself. It's a way of competing without even swinging a club. You just compare numbers. He probably does that on the course, too. And that's okay. It's a game. You can play it to compete, or you can just play it to enjoy swinging the club or to take in the beauty of the golf course."

Beth looked out at the green fairways as they zipped down the cart path, past holes 10 through 18.

"It is a lot more peaceful out here than I ever knew," she said quietly. "It helps if you don't have someone yelling at you every time you take a swing."

"I'm sorry that's what has happened," Jake said. "But you and Dan seem happy together otherwise. Maybe this will bring you closer together."

"That's what Dan thinks. That's why we're here. To get closer together. We're supposed to get married."

"'Supposed to' again?"

Watching Jake squint as he took that in, she wondered if she should talk about her ambivalence over her marriage. Jake was not only kind and patient, but got better looking and nicer the closer she got to him.

"It's good to share hobbies," he said, ignoring her stare. "What else do you two share?"

"Not much. We're both pretty serious about our careers. I love books, but Dan doesn't read. I love dogs, and Dan really doesn't like them. He loves golf, but up until today, I didn't have much to say for it."

"Well, there! We've made progress already!"

Jake laughed and Beth had a close up look at the smile that intrigued her the afternoon before. How long had they known each other? It had been just over twenty-four hours, she realized, and yet here she was, more comfortable sitting in the cart next to him than she ever was sitting in one next to Dan.

"It is a great sport whatever your skill," he said.

"I suppose," she said. "But is teaching beginners like me any fun?"

Jake looked at her and smiled as he pulled up to the cart barn. "With beginners like you who learn so fast, yes, it's fun."

"I can see why you teach, Jake. You are really good at this."

They had just enough time to exchange affectionate grins before Dan ran up to their cart and opened his arms to Beth, begging a hug.

"You won't believe how great I played today!" he exclaimed.

She wondered how long it would be before he thought to ask how her game had gone.

Seven

DAN WAS IN HIGH SPIRITS after his afternoon golf game, surprising Beth. She was used to him complaining about how he played, which never seemed to be as well as he thought he should.

As they settled at a table in the middle of a white-tablecloth restaurant in a high-end hotel in Palm Desert, he reached over the table with one hand and wove his fingers into hers.

"You look gorgeous tonight," he said, his eyes soft.

Beth grimaced. That schmaltzy look was usually a precursor to another insistence that they talk about a wedding date. She decided to preempt it by encouraging a recap of how he had scored on all eighteen holes that afternoon. His play-by-play usually bored her to tears.

"Did you have fun today?" she asked.

"Yeah. I got paired up with a couple of guys. Great golfers. I think we're going to go out again tomorrow morning."

"Who won?"

"Won? You've never asked me that before," he smiled brightly, looking both surprised and pleased.

'Well, I think I'm starting to understand what attracts you to the game. You like the competition.'

At that, he chuckled condescendingly. Beth decided to let it pass. She was in a good mood, and her afternoon on the course was the reason, too.

"Of course. It's a game. That's what games are. Competitions."

The waiter delivered a glass of wine for Beth and a beer for Dan, and they studied their menus. Beth settled quickly on the sand dabs, an expensive entré that Dan was unlikely to oppose, given the good mood he was in.

Why am I attracted to him? she wondered as she watched him look over the menu items and sip his beer. She tried to remember back to three years before, when she first saw him at a company picnic she was catering at Amazon. He worked there with Jason, Deb's boyfriend, and Deb was anxious to introduce them.

"He's going places in that company," Deb had assured her. "I guess he's really good at what he does, and you know he's got to have a fortune in stock options."

Beth had argued that, in her experience, rich men weren't easy to like and were usually too full of themselves to leave room for anyone else's personality.

"That's not fair." Deb repeated the old mantra: "It's as easy to fall in love with a rich man as a poor one."

Despite her expectation that she would be disappointed, she found Dan surprisingly accommodating that afternoon. He wasn't dismissive of her work in catering, which she expected him to be, and he hung around the food table. On a date a week later, he asked about her family and her past, something that men often didn't do until they had finally finished delivering a full narrative of their own lives.

245

When they took a kayak out on the lake a sunny Labor Day another week later, Dan took his shirt off to soak up the sun. Sitting behind him, she was surprised by the muscles in his back and arms and chastised herself for her assumption that guys like him—corporate executives—couldn't be fit. Where did that come from? Even though Dan had risen in the company to where he was heading up operations of one of the company's retail divisions, it was clear that he not only saw the inside of a gym, but that he spent a considerable amount of time there.

After that, they started seeing each other every week, usually for dinner, and gradually, their relationship progressed to nearly daily meetings, only interrupted by Dan's frequent business trips, and evenings when Beth had to supervise company events. She welcomed their growing commitment at first, but once Dan started badgering her about getting married, she felt herself pulling back. Was this commitment phobia? Or was she just growing bored with him? He was smart, rich, and ambitious; but he was also uninterested in the wine, books, and dogs—her three passions. He had no travel bug and had actually told her once he had no desire to go anywhere he'd hadn't been before.

But perhaps predictably, the more she pulled away, the closer he clung. And slowly she figured out something: he wanted to be sure his future at Amazon wasn't jeopardized by an impression that he didn't have a stable family life. Ironic, Beth thought. As if Jeff Bezos was some kind of role model.

She figured that someday she would get married. And eventually she might even decide to have children—or a child. But first, she wanted to travel and get her own career on track.

But the biggest obstacle to their union was Dan's dislike—or at least indifference to—ChiChi. How could she ever commit to living the rest of her life without a canine best friend? She hadn't lived without one in the house her entire life. Dan was the only reason she had decided to foster ChiChi at first, instead of adopting her after her last dog died.

Dan put down his menu and leaned forward, his smile still reflecting his great day on the golf course.

"I think you'd really like George," he said.

"Who's George?"

"One of the guys I played with today. He's smart and funny. He used to work in L.A. for a software company."

"So, you had a lot in common, I guess?"

"Yeah, project management headaches. And golf." Dan tipped up his glass and drained his beer. "We're at about the same level. Same handicap."

"Oh." That handicap comparison thing again. If men weren't measuring themselves against each other in some such way, how would they know who was on top?

Dan signaled for the waiter, and they ordered dinner. Dan asked for another beer.

"And you, miss?" the waiter asked.

"Nah, I'm driving," she said. It wasn't true—they were taking cabs. But Dan didn't correct her. She twirled what was left of the wine in her glass and took a sip.

The waiter left. "Oh, hey," Dan said. "I forgot to ask. How'd the rest of our lesson go this afternoon?"

Beth used her napkin to wipe the smile off her face. She didn't want to raise any suspicions about how much she had enjoyed Jake's undivided attention. She lowered her voice.

"Great. We went out on the course this afternoon. Just nine holes."

"Wow. Were you ready for that?"

"What do you mean?"

"Well, you weren't hitting the ball that well yesterday."

Beth pushed his insult aside. "Didn't matter," she said. "Do you know what a scramble is?"

"Of course. I've been playing golf since I was five."

"Well, anyway, that took all the pressure off. And I hit some pretty good shots."

"Of course, Jake must have made it easy," Dan said. "You probably played from all his shots."

"Nope," she said. "If I hit a good one, we used it. Sometimes he didn't even hit."

"That's wonderful."

"We're going to do the same thing tomorrow. Driving range in the morning and another nine holes in the afternoon."

"Okay. So, you don't want me to come back to the lesson?" If Dan was jealous of how much she was enjoying playing with Jake, it didn't show.

"Do you want to?" she asked.

"Not really. I don't think Jake had much to teach me," he said to Beth's relief. "I'd rather join George and Ryan again. If that's okay with you. You don't think I'm abandoning you, do you?"

"No, it's fine," she said, trying again to hide a smile. "You and I are at two totally different levels, anyway, and—"

"Oh, I almost forgot," he interrupted. "We're going to join the guys for dinner Monday night. They know this great hamburger spot in La Quinta, and they want to meet you."

Eight

BETH SAT ON THE BED, her cellphone on speaker, looking out the window at the view of the Coachella Valley lights between her hotel room and the mountains in the distance. The full moon had just risen and painted the steep slopes a pinkish gray, and the setting sun far on the other side faintly backlit the stubble of pine trees way up at the top.

"How is ChiChi?" Beth asked, realizing at once that she should have asked her mother how she was first.

"Well, I'm fine and she's great," Ellen answered, a bit of snark in her voice. "She told me if you don't come back, she'll be happy to stay with me."

"You're spoiling her, aren't you?"

"Not a bit. She just knows she's loved here."

"You're not letting her on the furniture, are you? You know how much Dan hates it when she's on the furniture. I'm trying to teach her to stay on the floor."

"Oh, no," Ellen asserted. "I wouldn't do that."

"You're lying, Mother," Beth said, smiling at the mental image of her mother and ChiChi cuddling on the couch, her mother reading a thick historical novel, and the dog snoozing with her head on Ellen's lap. "I can hear it in your voice."

Ellen sighed loudly, a sound intended to get Beth off her back.

"Get off the couch, ChiChi!" Beth yelled into the phone. "Oh, that worked. Good girl, ChiChi," her mother intoned.

"She's still up there, isn't she?" Beth shook her head. It was a losing battle, but one she secretly liked losing. Just don't tell Dan, she thought.

"Yeah, she is. I don't know why Dan gets to decide who gets on your furniture or mine. It's not his house."

"No, but if we get married, it would be nice if ChiChi were trained right. It would cut down on the arguments," Beth said, wondering why she used the words "if we get married" instead of "when we get married." When had she started doing that?

"Honey, I don't think people should go into a marriage with thoughts of how to avoid arguments. It should be a joyous decision, not a strategic one."

"I don't want to talk about this now, Mother. We haven't set a date. I still have time to think about it."

"Well, how are the lessons going?"

Relieved at the change of topic, Beth's voice brightened. "Oh, great, Mom! Jake says I'm a natural!"

"Jake?"

"The instructor. He called me athletic. Imagine that! Me, an athlete?"

Her mother laughed loudly, and ChiChi barked. Clearly, the dog's ear was within inches of the phone.

"I'm not surprised. I always thought you were," her mother said. "And how is Dan doing?

"Oh, Jake kicked him out of the class." Beth knew it was an exaggeration, but it was the better story. "He wouldn't quit giving me tips. It was funny. You should have seen Dan's face. I don't think anyone has told Dan to get lost in a very long time."

"I kinda wish I'd been there," Ellen said.

"Yeah, you would've enjoyed it as much as I did."

THE NEXT MORNING THEY STOOD side by side, looking over the driving range shrouded with a low-hanging cloud, Beth wondered if Jake had dreamed as much about her as she had about him. He said nothing of the sort, of course, instead he pointed at the mountain tops poking up above the fog in the distance.

"You should be here when the snow covers those peaks," he said. "The bright white against that intense blue sky is magnificent."

"What, you're a poet too?" she teased.

"Clearly not. But I do think there is some magic to this valley. Not that I want to stay here forever, but I do try to appreciate what it offers as long as I'm here."

"Where would … " Beth started to ask, but as she turned to face him, she saw that he'd already picked up her bag and was headed over to the practice sand bunkers.

She shrugged. "Later, then." She followed him to the edge of a deep, sandy hole that lay right next to a smooth, lush green. Jake jumped down into the sand with one of her clubs in his hands. A couple dozen balls lay scattered at the bottom, and Jake raked one over to his feet.

"If there's one thing that's going to save your score in this game," he said, "it's getting out of the sand in one shot. You'd be surprised how many extra shots recreational golfers rack up because they never learn what to do in here."

Beth was amazed at how quickly he had shifted gears from mountain-gazing to serious instruction. She jumped into the sand, struggling to keep from falling against him.

"The keys to a great sand shot are simple," he said, "and few. But you can't resist them. You really can't do it any other way."

It sounded almost fascist, Beth thought. My way or the highway. But what did she know?

"Three things," Jake said, demonstrating. "You want to slap the sand two inches behind the ball. You want to turn the club face to the right and point your hips slightly to the left of the target—the hole." He pointed at the flagstick on the green. "And you want a very sharp up and down motion. Got it?"

"Slap sand, two inches behind the ball, open club, point the hips left, sharp up and sharp down," she repeated, as he hit another ball onto the green. "Sounds like six things, not three," she said, counting on her fingers.

Jake stopped chopping balls out of the sand and looked at her. "You are something," he said. "You are really something."

Beth put her hands on her hips and faked a frown. "What does that mean?" Was she flirting with him again? She needed to take this lesson seriously—it was expensive and time was short, after all—but the vibe between her and Jake kept interrupting her concentration.

Jake's eyes narrowed as if he were wondering the same thing—was she flirting and should he make her stop it? Finally, he shrugged and looked back down at the ball closest to his feet.

He demonstrated one more perfect shot, the ball obediently popping up and onto the green, and handed her the club. "Okay, now you try."

Beth pulled a ball up to her feet with the club and swatted at it, trying to imitate Jake. The ball skidded forward in the sand a couple of feet and stopped.

"Huh, not so easy," she muttered. She raked another

ball toward her, but Jake reached out and caught the shaft of her club.

"Wait," he said. "Which of those three things did you do?"

Beth stood up straight and thought for a moment. "None of them," she answered.

"Right. Most people think if they just jump into the sand and blast away, the ball will be so afraid of them it will hop right out of here. Not so."

"I wasn't thinking—"

"No, you weren't thinking," he scolded.

"You know, sometimes you tell me not to think, and sometimes you tell me I'm not thinking. I don't know what to do."

Jake just laughed.

"Now let's try again. And, yes, think this time."

A half-hour later, Beth was making some progress. About a quarter of the balls she hit ended up flying way over the green onto the driving range beyond. Another quarter never left the sand, but about half of them ended up on the putting surface, even if they stopped far from the hole.

Jake climbed out of the sand and reached a hand down to help her. She grabbed ahold and pulled herself up as he quickly backed away. He shouldered her bag and walked around the trap to the putting green, now dotted with the balls they hit out of the sand.

"Time for a putting lesson," he announced. He pulled out her putter and moved some balls around. He described and demonstrated his three keys to putting, and this time Beth didn't correct his count. She watched closely, and when he handed her the club, she focused on following his tips.

"Wait," he said, reaching in for the putter to stop her. "Let's look at your hands."

He stood behind her, much like he had twice before,

with his arms at her side. Viscerally aware of his body again, she caught her breath.

"You want to hold it lightly, like you're holding a baby bird," he said. "Relax. Here. Put your left hand here." He guided her hand onto the club. "And your right one here. And swing back and forth, keeping the club head square to the hole."

Beth could hardly hear him for the sound of her heart pounding in her ears. What was it about him that was doing this to her? She hadn't felt this way about Dan's presence for a long time. If ever? Jake stepped back a little, and she took a deep, shaky breath, closed and opened her eyes. She tried to move the club back and forth like he had. It wobbled.

Jake stepped close again and put his hands on top of hers. Together they swung the club back and forth, and then stopped. She turned her head to look at him and this time, Jake didn't move. His eyes moved to her lips, holding there for a moment, and then he let go.

"I am so sorry," Beth blurted. "I don't really mean to do that. You must think I'm really awful. Jesus, what if Dan …"

"No, no. It's my fault," Jake protested. He shook his head, turned, and walked away.

"I hardly think so." Beth shook her arms out and looked out across the driving range at the mountains. Should she say something about what was happening between them, or was it better left unsaid? Make an excuse? Try to defuse the tension?

"Look, I'm sure this happens to you all the time," she whispered at his back. "Let's just forget it," she said.

Jake stopped a few yards away and turned back toward her. He nodded, his grin a bit sheepish. "Yes. Let's do. Why don't you show me if you got the idea?"

He walked around in front of her to watch.

Beth took a deep breath, focused on the head of the

putter and swung it back and forth until the motion finally felt loose and easy. She stepped up to a ball, swung smoothly, and watched it drop in the hole.

"Bingo! See, you are a natural, just like I thought!" Jake said. "Why don't you hit a few more and then we'll stop early for lunch. Maybe we can sneak out about 11, between the early risers and the people who book the cheap greens fees after noon."

Nine

INSTEAD OF SITTING IN THE outdoor café for lunch again, Jake suggested they grab a sandwich at the cantina and head directly out to the course. He had an appointment late in the afternoon, and Beth had promised she'd meet Dan about four o'clock for drinks at the pool bar.

As they drove out to the first tee box, Beth opened her hoagie and squirted some mustard out of the little foil packet onto the pastrami. She was surprised how all the sun and the exercise of swinging clubs had boosted her appetite. She usually had salads for lunch, but since she'd started taking lessons, a salad was not enough. She wanted bread and meat and cheese. And a slice of tomato, if it came along. A leaf of lettuce was okay but not necessary.

"There's something I wanted to ask you about," she said, after swallowing the first bite. "But maybe this isn't the right time."

Jake steered the cart with one hand and balanced the

wrapper for his hotdog on his lap. He had just taken a big bite. "Whaa??" he said, his mouth full of bun and dog.

Beth laughed. "Sorry," she said. "Go ahead and eat."

Jake nodded, chewed his mouthful, and pulled their cart up to the tee box. He took a swig from the huge diet soda that came with his dog and chips. "Now I'm good. What did you want to ask?"

"Maybe this is not the right time. I mean you may want to keep your distance from me. Outside of the lessons, I mean."

She paused, thinking about their near-embrace that morning and the one the afternoon before. Is that what she should call those close encounters? She wasn't sure. But now Jake was looking at her like she was nuts.

"I'm really sorry if I made it strange between us."

Jake scowled—not an angry grimace but a confused one. "Look, I don't want you to overthink this," he said.

"But weren't we just talking about how golf is really a mental game. Why wouldn't I overthink it?"

"Yes, I said that," Jake said, laughing. "But there's more to it than that. Golf isn't just brawn and brains and no feelings, but actually, it's a lot emotion. Why do you think a tour player wins a tournament one week and can't make the cut the next? It's not because he forgot how to swing a club or lost muscle tone. No. It's because his heart wasn't in it."

Beth smiled. It seemed they were at a point where they couldn't avoid talking about what they were experiencing. "Are you trying to say your heart is in this?" She pointed at him and then at herself with her sandwich.

Jake took another bite of his hotdog. Beth figured he was buying time as he tried to decide how to answer.

"Yeah, I guess that's what I'm saying." He looked ahead, down the cart path, as if afraid to meet her eyes. "Look. I really like you. But I understand you and Dan are—"

"Yes," she said, her voice dropping. "We are."

Jake shook his head. "Then I'm confused. What is it you wanted to ask me?"

"Well, it's really not that big a deal." How had they gotten off track so? She wasn't sure they were even talking about the same thing anymore. Or in the same language.

"Then out with it!"

"Okay," she said. "This is what I wanted to ask." She put her sandwich down on her seat, stepped out of the cart, pulled her five-wood out of her bag, and took a couple of practice swings while talking. "I know I'm not very good yet, but I think I'd like to get some real clubs. I mean clubs made for me. I just bought these off the shelf at a sporting goods store. They're not very good, are they?"

Jake let out a breath. He looked relieved. He pulled his driver from his bag and joined her on the tee box. "They're okay," he said. "But I agree. So, let me guess. You want me to help you pick something out?"

"Yeah."

"Oh, heavens. Is that all? I thought … ." He shook his head and took a couple of practice swings.

"Let's do it!" he exclaimed. "Instead of golf tomorrow afternoon, let's grab lunch over by the golf store in Palm Desert and go shopping."

"Thanks. I didn't want to impose on you. I mean, I didn't know if I should ask you to go with me off this course."

Jake ignored that. "So, this afternoon, we'll play a few holes, and then I think we should quit early and do a rules lesson."

"Rules? What does that have to do with learning how to play golf?"

"Everything."

"But that doesn't sound like any fun."

"No, but rules keep the game fair. Buck it up, Beth. Everyone needs to learn them."

Dan pointed his club down the fairway. "It's time for

me to tee off," he said. "I can't hit far enough to reach that group on the green."

Beth looked where he was pointing. She couldn't see far enough to make out the group on the green, let alone hit far enough to reach them.

"Okay, let's go!"

She watched as Jake's ball flew high, straight and far, and felt a rush that she had to admit was pure animal attraction. How was she ever going to get over this thing between them if he kept swinging like that? She took a deep breath before she stepped up to the forward tee.

THE RULES LESSON TOOK ABOUT an hour, and by the time Jake had given her what he called "the basics," she was yawning. It wasn't so much that she was bored. It was more the heat of the day, combined with a big sandwich at lunch, and sitting still right after hours of physical activity.

"So, you think you have it now, sleepyhead?" he asked, his smile teasing.

"It all seems like too much to remember," she said, stifling another yawn.

"Well, it is. That's why you have a rules book." He pointed at the compact book he'd given her. "You can always look it up. But you can remember the basics. Don't ground your club in the bunkers. Play the ball as it lies. For the tougher stuff, like 'out of bounds' and 'line of sight,' look them up in the book."

"Does anyone know them all?"

"Only the rules officials. The men and women who officiate at tournaments. But let's drop this now. I have a few minutes before I have to leave, and I want to hear more about you. Tell me about yourself."

"Are you pretending that this is part of the lesson?" She leaned back and stretched her arms high over her head.

Jake looked at his watch. "No, lesson time is up. But I

have most of a beer and you have a full glass of wine. Don't want them to go to waste."

"So, what do you want to know?"

"Honestly," he whispered, leaning forward. "I'm very curious about you and Dan. You don't seem, well, can I say it? You don't seem perfect for each other."

"Well, I guess that's obvious to everyone but Dan." She wasn't sure she wanted to share more. There had already been too many awkward moments between her and Jake on the course. She could imagine how sharing her ambivalence about Dan could make things worse.

Or better.

"How did you meet?" Jake was clearly not going to give up until he got some answers.

"Okay. I'll give you the abridged version," she said. "At my last job, I was assigned to a company event at Amazon where he works. I always thought of Amazon as full of young guys, you know. Bachelors. Techies. Making lots of money and not very interested in meeting women. But it was a company picnic, and for some reason, it seemed like all families. Dan was obviously alone, and he works with a guy who dates a friend of mine. He came by the table where I was managing the food service, and we started talking. I had no idea then that his passion was golf and that he hated dogs, or it would never have gone anywhere."

"But it did."

Beth smiled sadly. "Yes. I guess it's one of those bad habits that gets so engrained you can't shake it."

"Bad habit? I never heard anybody talk about their relationship like that."

"Obviously, an overstatement. Really, I like him a lot. When he's not on the golf course, he can be a lot nicer."

"So you're a caterer or something?"

"I'm an event planner, actually. At least that was my job. I'm between jobs now, as they say in polite company. In the pandemic, the catering business I was working for went under. So, I'm looking. I had an interview at Starbucks before we left, and I'm hoping I'll land there when we get back."

"Did you ever think of moving to the desert? Get out of the rain?"

Beth grinned. "Why? Would that matter to you in some way?" she teased.

"Well, maybe someday I'll need a caterer," Jake said. He shrugged as if to say "you never know."

Beth chuckled. "You know, I really like you, too."

"You think that's what I was saying?"

"Was it?"

Jake held her eyes for a few moments, his smile fading. "Yes. I guess it was."

"But you must meet a thousand women out here on the driving range." She gestured toward the lesson area down the slope.

Jake nodded. "I do. Yes, I do."

"Do you ask all of them if they want to move to the desert?"

That made him laugh. "Boy, you are tough, Beth. Good questions. You should be a TV reporter."

She stuck her fist out toward his face as if she held a microphone. "And your answer?"

"I'm afraid this isn't going to help," he said, serious all of the sudden. "Never. Honestly, I have never asked anyone that before."

Beth couldn't miss his expression. It was a cross between bewildered and sad. She took a deep breath. "Well, then, I suppose I owe you a serious answer. I couldn't live here. It's too hot. And the sun shines all of the time."

Jake laughed. "Only someone from Seattle would complain about too much sun! You love your rain."

"Actually," she countered, "we're a bit ambivalent about the rain. We like it; we're used to it; we brag about it. But even for us, a sun break now and then is awfully nice."

Jake looked up over her head toward the entrance to the patio. Beth turned to follow his eyes. Dan walked toward them, and he didn't look pleased.

"So, what's going on here? I thought we were meeting at the tiki bar at four?"

"Oh! I didn't realize how late it was," she said. "Jake was just giving me a rules lesson." She held up the rules book Jake had given her.

"Look, man, I'm sorry," Jake interjected. "I lost track of time."

Dan answered him with a scowl. "Sure. I'm sure you did," he said, and turned back to Beth. "Come on. Let's go. I'm thirsty and hungry."

Jake stood up and threw a twenty-dollar bill on the table. "See you tomorrow morning, Beth."

He bowed slightly to Dan. "Enjoy your date."

Ten

Beth arrived at the roped-off lesson area of the driving range the next morning before Jake for the first time. She was diligently following the stretching routine he had taught her when he scampered down the hill toward her.

"Sorry." He was breathing heavily, having apparently run some distance to get there. "My car is in the shop, and I had to walk over."

"Walk?" Beth laughed. "It looks like you ran the whole way." She continued to warm up, now swinging a couple of clubs like baseball bats, a drill to build upper body strength.

Jake watched her as he caught his breath. Two days earlier, his gaze would have been intimidating, but now, she was getting used to his scrutiny. She hoped it would eventually help her get over the jitters she always felt when strangers watched her on the tee box.

"Are we going to go shopping today?" he asked. "Is it okay with Dan?"

Beth stopped swinging. "But if you don't have a car ...."

"Oh, don't worry. The shop is delivering it to the parking lot here mid-morning," he said. "I'm really looking forward to helping you find new clubs."

"Great." She put her clubs back in the bag. "What are we working on this morning?"

"Uhhh ...," Jake pinched his lips together and scratched the back of his head. He looked like he wanted to say something but didn't know how.

"What? Is there something wrong?"

"I just need to say I'm sorry about yesterday afternoon."

"Sorry for what?"

"For keeping you late. I'm not sure I did your relationship with Dan any favors."

Beth waved his words away. "Oh, don't be sorry. And don't mind Dan. For a guy who is certain that I should marry him, he sure seems insecure, doesn't he?"

"You think he thought ... ?"

"Oh, yeah. He always thinks ..." She shrugged.

"It must get tiring."

She shrugged again. "Well, I guess the good thing is he really cares."

"About you or about getting married?"

Beth squinted at him. He had just summed up her dilemma, hadn't he? Was Dan just committed to getting married and fitting in with his Amazon colleagues? Or was he committed to marrying her? She decided it was a question better left unanswered for the moment.

"We're here for a lesson, right, Jake? What are we going to work on today?"

"Right," Jake smirked, making fun of his distraction. "You're right. I think we should work on pitching and chipping. The short game is more important than most people realize."

He picked up her bag and pointed toward the sand trap

and green of the short-game practice area. "Let's go over there and get started."

By LUNCH HOUR, JAKE APPEARED to have shed whatever concerns he'd brought to the morning session, and Beth relaxed. She didn't want the good rapport they had built—or maybe it was even more than that—stifled by Dan's poor attitude. After grabbing a sandwich for the road, Jake drove them down to the PGA Superstore on Highway 111, the main artery through town.

Beth was at a loss as she followed him down the aisles of Ping, Callaway, Tour Edge, Titleist, Cleveland, Taylor-Made, and Cobra club sets. It seemed like he was just wandering through the displays, looking randomly at different brands. Did he have some parameters in mind as he considered them?

Finally, he stopped and waved for her to catch up with him. "Here. Come here, Beth. I think this would be a good choice for you. It has a fairly forgiving club head design, but it will work for you for a long time. And we can order them totally custom for your height and swing speed."

Beth pulled one of the woods out of its slot in the display and waggled it close to the ground. She didn't have any idea what she was looking for, but she was fairly sure that what the club looked like didn't rank high among the selection criteria.

"Can I try them?" she asked.

"Absolutely. In fact, you must." Jake pulled a couple of irons and a hybrid out of the slots. "Follow me."

With the iron still in her hands, she followed him toward the big, tented area where people were hitting balls off of artificial turf mats into stiff tarps about twenty yards away. Jake took the club she carried and handed all of them to an attendant standing at the front of an empty bay. The guy looked like a pro linebacker—big, wide-shouldered, and square-jawed. A bit intimidating, but with a quick smile.

"Jake, you old snake!" The big man laughed. "Found a new victim, have you?"

Jake and the man shared a quick one-armed man-hug.

"Brian, this is Beth. One of the quickest studies I've ever had the pleasure of coaching," Jake said. "She's looking to buy her first custom clubs."

Jake turned to her. "Brian and I go way back, back to our college days at ASU. He helped me get the job at the resort."

Brian leaned the clubs against a bag stand. "What do you have here?" He picked up one of the irons and swung it. "A bit advanced for a beginner, don't you think?"

"I told you, she's got potential. I want her to have clubs she can grow into."

"Hmm." Brian nodded. "Well, then seems like a good choice. We can customize them, fit them with a lighter shaft."

"That's what I told her. She wants to take a few swings."

Brian put some tape over the club faces and handed the shortest iron to Beth.

"Step up to the plate, lady, and let's see what you've got." Brian pointed at the square green mat.

"Boy, you really know how to put a girl on the spot, don't you?" Beth frowned at Brian.

"Just ignore him," Jake said. "You have a better swing than he does."

Beth grimaced. She stepped onto the mat and took a quick practice swing. Realizing it was a poor, rushed effort, she took a deep breath and took a long, easy swing, just like Jake had taught her. Then she raked a ball into place, looked at her target—the middle of the tarp—took another deep breath, relaxed her shoulders, and tried to execute a swing she could be proud of. The ball arced nicely and struck the tarp right where she intended.

She turned and looked at Jake for his reaction.

"Nice swing, Beth," Brian said. He sounded sincere.

Jake elbowed him. "I told you. She has learned all of this in just a few days."

"A natural," Brian said.

"Yup." Jake's grin was bigger than her own.

Brian looked at her with a serious face. "Be careful, my dear," he whispered harshly. "I think your instructor is a bit infatuated."

Beth tried to wipe the smile off her face, but it wouldn't move. More confident now, she raked another ball into place and took another easy shot. She watched it hit the target and turned to Brian and winked.

"Can you blame him?"

Eleven

As the host led Beth and Dan to a table far back in a dark corner of the fancy steakhouse Dan had chosen for dinner that evening, she made herself a promise. She was going to say nothing that increased Dan's insecurities and say as many things as she could to wipe away any suspicions he might harbor about Jake. The afternoon shopping trip made her face up to what she hadn't accepted yet: that Jake was as smitten as she was, and it was up to her to stop it. A relationship with a golf instructor wasn't a real thing. It was the plot of a silly romance novel.

"Well, this is nice and cozy," Dan said, as they sat. He nodded his appreciation to the host. "Isn't this just perfect?" he asked Beth.

"Yes, lovely. But it seems like such a waste to not be outside as much as we can while we're here. We'll be back in the rain soon enough. At least we should be sitting at a window."

Dan rolled his eyes and his face sunk into a pout. "Here I thought I'd done something right for a change," he said.

Already! Already she had said the wrong thing. Beth stomped the heel of one of her shoes on the toe of the other to punish herself.

"No, no!" she said, reaching across the table for his hand. "Of course, this is perfect. I guess I'm realizing we have only five more days here, and I'm wishing it were more like five more weeks."

"Yes, me too. But right now, I'm starved. Golf can really work up an appetite."

"Yes, it does."

"So, you're enjoying your lessons? Are you learning anything?"

"Funny you should ask. Jake says—" She caught herself. No more mention of Jake! "I'm hitting the ball much better. I'm more relaxed. Maybe I'm an athlete after all."

Dan opened the wine list. "Really?" he said, studying the offerings. "I've never thought of you as athletic. Brainy, yes. Beautiful, without a doubt. But not athletic."

Beth was ready to chastise him for thinking so narrowly of her, but she caught herself. "I used to play tennis. Remember?" she said instead.

"Oh, yeah," he answered, not looking up from the menu. "I never really liked tennis."

"Right." Beth watched him peruse the list for a minute. She focused on his face, how handsome it was. She thought about how much he wanted to marry her, how successful he was. These were good things. These were worth hanging on to. Whatever her reservations were, she needed to keep her head on her shoulders and not let her foolish infatuation with a golf instructor sway her judgment.

"But I'm starting to see what you like about golf," she said as he put down the menu and looked up.

"That's great! Because there's something I would like to

propose tonight. I've been thinking about it all day."

"What's that?" Beth's heart skipped. Was he going to push for a wedding date again?

"Let's wait until we get some champagne in front of us," Dan said, flagging down the waiter.

"Sure." She forced the word out.

Dan pointed to a line on the menu, the waiter nodded, and walked away.

"How did you play today?" she asked.

"Great. Ryan and George are a hoot."

"They played with you again today?"

"Yup. And tomorrow." Dan looked the happiest he had all week.

"How is it they can play every day?"

"They have some sort of membership cards. They get a discount."

Beth shook her head. "No, I meant, don't they work anymore? You said George worked in L.A."

"Used to. I get the feeling they come from money. You know. Trust funders, maybe?"

"Ah." She nodded. They opened their dinner menus and bent their heads to study them. The waiter arrived with an uncorked champagne bottle in a bucket of ice on a stand and set it by the table. He lifted the bottle.

"Sir, would you like to taste?"

"Nah," said Dan. "Just pour."

Once the waiter completed pouring and left, Dan lifted his flute toward her, and Beth obliged, touching her glass to his. She sipped. Another thing to appreciate, she thought. Dan was a guy who could afford a great vintage like this.

"Before we get to what you wanted to say over champagne," she said. "I'd like to ask you something."

Dan nodded, and she continued. "Do you think it's a good idea if I get some clubs made?"

"You mean custom clubs?"

"Yeah. Jake took me to the Superstore today, and this guy, Brian, he helped me figure out what I should get." She figured if Dan thought some stranger named Brian was involved, and not just Jake, he might put up less resistance to the idea.

To her surprise, he looked pleased.

"I think it's a great idea," he said with enthusiasm. "You should order them. I'll get them for you as an early wedding present."

Beth hadn't thought much about how she would pay for them. In a way, they would be a good wedding gift, cementing their new, shared pastime. On the other hand, would that be another way he could force a quick wedding?

"Or, if you can pay for them," she suggested, "I can pay you back as soon as I get a job."

"Whatever," he said. "But this is a perfect segue to what I wanted to ask."

He took another sip of champagne. Fortification? she wondered. How bad was this request going to be?

"Okay, I'll just out with it," he said. "I was thinking since you've taken to golf so well, maybe you'd be willing to make our honeymoon a golf trip. Maybe Hawaii? Or even New Zealand?"

Beth realized she wasn't going to be able to avoid the wedding discussion. She tried to smile.

"Dan, we haven't even set a wedding date yet. How can you be talking about the honeymoon?"

"Well, that's just it. I'm thinking if we want to plan the perfect golf honeymoon, we need to plan ahead. It's not easy to get reservations at some of the best resorts. If we choose where we want to go for our honeymoon, then we'll know what time of year we should go, and it will help us set a wedding date." He looked immensely pleased with his logic.

"That seems sort of upside down or backwards, doesn't

271

it?" She had intended to avoid arguing with him over dinner, but here it was. The same old dispute, just a different approach.

The waiter arrived, giving them a respite for a moment. After they ordered and the waiter left, Dan looked just as disappointed as she expected he would.

"Okay, you tell me how we decide this thing," he said. "I've been waiting a year for you to agree to a date. Nothing seems to move you forward."

Beth nodded. "I'm sorry, but I just don't understand the hurry. What's the rush?"

"Look. Everyone I know is married. I feel like the loser at work. They all talk about their kids and their family vacations. We've been dating three years now, and no one believes me when I say we're engaged."

So that was it! "Is that a reason to get married? Everyone else is doing it? To prove something to your co-workers?" Beth asked.

Dan closed his eyes and squeezed them together with a thumb and finger. "No, of course not. But we should get married because we're in love. That's what people in love do." When he looked at her again, his eyes were pleading.

"Right" was all she could think to say.

"I'm beginning to wonder if you want to get married."

"Someday, yes," she answered. But that didn't change Dan's worried face. "No, of course I do," she assured him hurriedly. She sighed. "How about we say a year from now. Next November?"

Dan's face immediately brightened. "Okay! Great!" He lifted he glass again. "Now we have something to celebrate!"

He put his glass down and squinted as he thought. "If it's November, how about New Zealand?" he asked. "Or Australia? It's summer down there."

"Sure, honey," Beth said, trying to hide the resignation in her voice. "Either one."

272

Twelve

By the end of her lesson Monday morning, Beth was starting to feel like a golfer. Like someone who could play the game with anyone. Sure, she'd never outscore Dan, but she could hit the ball reliably down the fairway, she knew what club to use given where her ball lay, and she had figured out how to hit a ball out of the sand on the first shot at least half the time.

"Maybe I really can do this," she said. "Maybe I can really play golf someday."

"You already can," Jake said. She looked up. She hadn't realized she'd said her thought out loud. She grimaced but Jake was smiling.

"Just think," he said. "Four days in and you're hitting balls like you've been playing for years."

"Well, months, maybe."

Jake nodded. "Yeah, months. But just wait 'til you get those new clubs. Did you talk with Dan about them?"

"Yes. He said he'd get them for me as an early wedding present."

Jake looked away. When he returned his gaze to her, he'd forced what was obviously a fake smile.

"Well, that's wonderful. I'll call Brian and have him order them. Let's go catch some lunch and get out on the course. They're predicting some rain this afternoon, and I'd like us to get at least nine holes in."

"Okay." Beth was happy. Although it made little sense, it was a relief to have finally settled on a wedding month. The pressure was off. She'd agreed with Dan, and now she believed all her ambiguity and uncertainly would disappear. Instead of making her feel more trapped, the decision freed her from worrying about it.

Jake chose a table for them at the edge of the patio. From there, they could watch golfers on the eighteenth green shake hands and climb into their carts at the end of their rounds. The temperature had dropped a few degrees, and the pleasant weather added to Beth's good mood. It seemed to rub off on Jake, and before their food was placed before them, he had loosened up. Perhaps having the question of Beth's marriage settled was helping him too.

Wanting to retain their good spirits, she asked him tell stories of his professional career. Other than his reason for leaving the tour, he'd told her nothing about it. It turned out he had a great sense for storytelling, and even though his time on the tour hadn't been particularly successful, it hadn't killed his sense of humor.

He told her about a time when he slipped on the mud into an alligator-infested swampy slough in Florida and surfacing to face a mouth full of giant teeth.

"All I could think about was 'where is my pitching wedge?'" he finished, guffawing at the memory. "This monster was about to bite me in half, and I was worried about a hundred-dollar golf club!"

Beth laughed so hard she had tears in her eyes. Bending toward him and putting her head against his shoulder, she tried to catch her breath. "I can just see you in there, covered in green slime!" As she lifted her head and took a deep breath, she looked out toward the course.

"Oh, no!" she said, suddenly serious. Jake turned his head to follow her eyes.

Dan stood with two other golfers just beyond the ledge that divided the patio from the grass around it. He was looking right at her, his angry eyes telling her that he had just watched her place her head against Jake's arm. Did he see their joy? Their companionship? Did he feel excluded?

"Oh, no is right." Jake turned back to face her and whispered. "That's George with him, isn't it?"

"Yeah, I guess," she said. "But I don't know what difference that makes. I'm already in trouble."

"It might be worse than you think," Jake said. He looked apologetic. "I'm sorry. I think this could be difficult."

The only way to make things look better, Beth decided quickly, was to act like nothing had happened. She smiled and waved cheerfully at Dan. "Hi, honey," she called out.

Dan scowled and shook his head before walking away. The two men with him stared at Beth and Jake a little longer, and then turned and followed him.

EARLY THAT EVENING, BETH SAT with Dan and his friends at a high-top in a hamburger joint that Ryan and George said was the best in the whole Coachella Valley. What made it so great, Beth surmised, was the number of huge TVs that hung from the ceiling behind the bar and all the way around the dining area. The roar of the Monday Night Football broadcast blasted out of at least a dozen big, black speakers.

When they had driven from the hotel to the restaurant, Dan didn't mention that he'd seen her on the patio at the golf course with Jake. Either what he saw didn't bother him as much as she expected, or he was saving his reaction for a later time. Beth had no way to know and she was too afraid of the argument it could engender to bring it up.

Likewise, Ryan and George greeted her and acted as if they hadn't seen her and Jake either. As she shook their hands and then hopped up onto the barstool, they looked her over as if they'd never seen her before. Or maybe, she thought, that was just the shameless way they looked at all women.

"So, what do you do up there in Seattle?" George asked as she helped herself to a glass of beer from one of the two half-full pitchers in the middle of the table.

"I'm between jobs, but I set up events for corporations," she said. "You know, things like investor meetings, new product launches, employee meetings, picnics."

It all either went over George's head or he hadn't really been interested in an answer. He turned immediately back to the football game on the TV right above them and took a big gulp of beer. Without turning away from the game, he asked a question she figured was really closer to what he wanted to know. "So, how are your golf lessons going?"

"Okay," she said. She glanced up to see what football action had all the men so rapt. The referees in their black and white-striped shirts were huddled, and the announcer was speculating about what penalty was being discussed. It seemed a bit silly to spend so much energy trying to guess when the answer would be divulged in less than a minute. But then, she never really understood the devotion football fans had for the announcers—male or female. She knew women who were just as riveted by the play-by-play and penalties as Dan and his friends were.

"I think I might take to this game after all," she said, completing her thought.

"Football?" Ryan asked. "Well, why not. Greatest game on earth, other than golf, of course."

George slugged his friend in the shoulder. "She's talking about golf, dodo," he said. The penalty finally revealed on the TV, he turned back to her. "And what do you think of Jake?"

She expected the question, but out of the corner of her eye, she saw Dan shaking his head and pumping the palm of his hand downward. It was his "tone it down" signal.

She turned to catch Dan's eyes, but he quickly focused on the TV again.

"Well," she answered George. "I don't know much. He's the first instructor I've ever had. How will I know if he's any good?"

"But he's charming right?"

This time, Dan didn't even try to hide his frustration with George. He rolled his eyes and buried his forehead in his hands.

"Did you put him up to this?" Beth asked her fiancé. "Is this some kind of test?"

"Should it be?" George asked.

"George!" Dan bellowed. "Lay off. Really."

"Of course, you did," she said, speaking to Dan. "Why don't you ask me what you really want to know? Too afraid of the answer?"

Dan looked frightened and tongue-tied. If he had planned this inquisition, it wasn't going well. But then he was saved by Beth's ringing phone. She picked it up and looked at the caller ID.

"Sorry, guys," she said, sarcastically. "I'd love to continue this line of questioning, but I have to take this."

She jumped down from her stool and walked outside.

"Hey, Debra," she answered. "What's up?"

"I've been trying to reach you all day," her friend at Starbucks said. "Aren't you looking at messages?"

"Oh," Beth realized she hadn't thought about checking her phone all day. "No, I guess not."

"Well, then you must be having fun."

"A blast," Beth said. "I'm really catching onto this golf thing."

"I'll bet Dan is pleased."

"Well, yes and no. I'll explain it all later. Bottom line is that I haven't been playing with him."

The line went silent for a few moments. Beth guessed that Deb was trying to figure out what that meant. "Then, who are you playing with?" Deb finally asked.

"My instructor."

"Good looking?"

Beth shook her head. Was that all women thought about? How men looked? But maybe turn-around was fair play.

"I haven't noticed," she lied.

"Liar." Beth laughed heartily. "But I'll wait till you get back for details."

"I promise I'll tell you everything. But why'd you call? What's up? Are you still in the office?"

"Yes, but everyone else is gone, so I figured I could call you and give you the good news. The hiring manager for that position you interviewed for? She called me today to talk about you. It's sounding good, Beth. I thought you'd like to know."

"Yay!" Beth had nearly forgotten about the interview, but now she was excited again. "That's great news. What'd she ask you?"

"The usual. 'The right fit' kind of stuff. I told her you'd be great. So, anyway, I thought you should probably keep an ear open for your phone. She might be calling soon to offer you the job."

Behind her, Beth heard Dan open the restaurant door. She turned to see him peeking out.

"Who are you talking to?" he asked. He sounded irritated. "We're going to order food."

"Hold on a second," Beth said into the phone and pulled it away from her face. "It's Debra," she told Dan. "She has good news about the Starbucks job." She waved him away. "I'll be right there."

Dan went back inside, and Beth put the phone back to her ear. "I've got to go Deb. We're having hamburgers with Dan's new golf buddies. I guess they're missing me."

"You're so popular! Okay. Call me if you hear anything."

Thirteen

A COUPLE OF HOURS LATER, the football game over and un-impressive hamburgers ordered and consumed, Beth sat at the hotel bar with Dan, expecting them to finally talk about what he saw at lunch. He'd ordered a martini, but instead of drinking it, he was staring off in the distance and scowling. He appeared reluctant to start the conversation.

She wanted to get it over with.

"I thought you were happy that I was getting into golf," she said.

"I am. I just think maybe you're spending a lot of time with Jake," he said. For a guy who just spent a couple of hours drinking beer with his new best buddies, he sure was in a foul mood.

"Yes, I am," she said. "Yes, I am. You paid for lessons and backed out of them. I'm taking them. You are playing golf, and I don't complain that you're spending a lot of time with George and Ryan."

Dan said nothing, so Beth continued. "Anyway, does this concern of yours have anything to do with George?"

"What?"

"Come on. That third degree he was trying to give me at dinner. He was grilling me about Jake."

"No. Okay. Kinda." Dan tipped his martini up and swallowed it in one gulp. That was unlike him. He'd never been a drinker. "Jake stole George's girlfriend."

Beth laughed and then caught herself when she saw Dan's horrified expression.

"Are you serious?" she asked. "No one 'steals' someone else's girlfriend. What do you think women are? Objects on a shelf that someone can shoplift? If George's girlfriend left him for Jake, I can't say I'm surprised."

Dan shook his glass at the bartender who nodded and started to mix another one.

"I just don't think you should be having lunch with him anymore," Dan said. He was dead serious.

"You've got to be kidding," Beth said. Now she was getting angry. This was so silly. "What? Are you jealous? This is ridiculous."

"If he's making moves on you, you aren't the first. He does this all the time. Don't think you're special. He's just doing what he does. All the time."

"This is insane." Beth lowered her voice to a harsh whisper. "You don't trust me. Is that it?"

Dan accepted his fresh martini with a nod. "No, I don't trust him."

"So, who am I supposed to have lunch with? Or do you think I should just have lunch by myself?"

"I'll meet you for lunch tomorrow," Dan said, as if he had been wanting to do that all along. He'd never mentioned it before. "We're playing a second eighteen in the afternoon, but we'll take a break after the first round and I'll meet you on the patio."

"How big of you." Beth smirked. "Are you sure George and Ryan won't be jealous?" She stood up, slammed a ten-dollar bill on the bar and left her own martini untouched. "I'm going to bed."

Dan didn't lift his chin from the bar as she walked away.

SITTING ON THE PATIO THE next day, Beth looked at her watch again. It was almost one o'clock, and she'd been waiting for Dan for forty-five minutes. In another ten, she had to meet Jake for their afternoon round on the course. Her phone buzzed.

"Well, it's about time." She scowled.

She picked it up. A text from Dan:

I'm sorry I'm late. Be there in a minute.

She waited another five minutes and gave up. She hadn't ordered lunch, as she expected to eat with him. She laid down a five-dollar bill to pay for her iced tea and to somewhat compensate for taking up a table for nearly an hour, and started to walk to the entrance. Putting her billfold back in her backpack, she nearly ran into Dan.

"Honey, I'm so sorry," he said. He held her shoulders and huffed breathlessly. "We had a frost delay, and we got a late start. I tried to hurry, but the course was really backed up."

"Terrific, Dan," she said, nearly spitting her words. "You don't trust me to have lunch with my golf instructor, and this is your solution."

He shrugged, and it occurred to Beth that she'd seen a lot of that on this vacation. For a man with such high self-esteem and such authority at work, he had turned into quite a wimp out here in the desert.

"Is this going to be what happens on our golf honeymoon?" she asked. "You take off with the boys, and I get to have lunch by myself? Sounds wonderful. I can't wait."

She tried to walk around him. He caught her arm.

"No, stay," he begged. "I want to have lunch with you."

She shook off his grasp. "Too late, Dan. My lesson starts up again in five minutes. With Jake. Maybe you can get George and Ryan to join you."

FOUR HOLES INTO THEIR AFTERNOON practice round, Beth was ready to give up. She'd not driven well from any of the tee boxes, and her fairway shot on the fourth hole barely left the ground, spitting straight off to the right at about a 90-degree angle from where she was aiming.

All afternoon, Jake had let Beth fume and swear without remark. That he could read her so well floated in the back of her mind. If he had commented on every shot—good and bad—her temper would have boiled over. This was one of those times when it was best for everyone to leave her alone, and Jake must have sensed that.

But after the horrid shank she had just produced, he stepped up beside her and picked up the club she had thrown on the ground.

"What do you think happened there?" he said, looking over at the ball resting in the brown rough.

"I don't know." Beth moaned. "I lifted up?"

"Yes, think about keeping your head steady—"

Beth turned away and walked to the cart without listening. She sat down hard and crossed her arms over her chest. "You know what, Jake. I don't care. I never wanted to learn how to play this stupid game in the first place."

Jake slipped her club into her bag and steered the cart over to collect her errant ball.

"What's wrong this afternoon?" he asked, his voice low.

"What isn't wrong?" Beth was angry enough to cry, but she wasn't going to embarrass herself with tears over Dan's behavior. "I hate this game."

Jake pulled the cart up to her ball and stepped out to retrieve it, while she sat, stubborn, her arms still crossed.

Instead of steering back to his ball in the middle of the fairway, he turned the cart and headed back toward the clubhouse.

"You know what I think?" he said. "I think we've had too much golf. I have an idea. Mind if we get out of here for a couple of hours?"

"Pfftt." Beth stewed. "I really don't care."

With the cart accelerator floored, Jake whipped up to the door of the cart barn. "I know just what we need," he said.

He grabbed Beth by the hand, pulled her out of the cart, and headed toward the parking lot with her in tow.

"But my clubs ... ," she protested.

"Don't worry. The guys will take care of them for us," he said. "Come on. We're going to have some fun."

Ten miles away and forty minutes later, Beth and Jake were winding up a ferociously contested game of putt-putt. The silly windmill, clown's mouth, and troll's tunnel wiped away Beth's rage and took her mind off anything serious— like marrying Dan. Especially marrying Dan.

Lining up to take a putt on the final hole, Beth stopped and looked up at Jake.

"Thanks," she said, her smile sheepish. "I needed this. You knew just what to do."

"Yeah, well," he said motioning at her putter. "Hurry up and putt. I'm thirsty and I have just the spot picked out for our next stop."

Beth laughed and stood looking at him for a few more seconds before whacking at the ball and watching it spin a 360 around the hole before it dropped in.

LATER, AS SHE SANK INTO a comfortable barstool at an outside bar not far from the miniature golf course, she raised her skinny can of hard seltzer to his beer for a toast.

"Wow, that was fun," she exclaimed. "What a great thing to do."

"My pleasure." Jake was all smiles.

"You're a lot of fun," she said.

"You are too."

"No, I mean that was just what I needed. And you knew it."

"And Dan wouldn't?"

Beth shook her head. "I don't want to talk about Dan anymore. Not today, okay?"

That seemed to cheer Jake up even more. "Absolutely," he said. "Why don't you tell me more about what you do—that catering thing. I think it might be something I could use."

"Okay," Beth said, surprised at his choice of topic. "Well, I manage events. I arrange everything from the sound system to the flowers to the food to the wait staff to the venue. I'm really good at it. I'm really organized."

"I'll bet you are. Maybe you can help me find someone like that."

"Why would you need someone like that?"

Jake took a big swig of beer. He looked a bit hesitant, and she encouraged him to answer with a circular wave of her hand.

"Here it is," he said. "I'd like to start my own golf school. I could easily find three or four other instructors to join me. There are plenty of unemployed PGA instructors around—just about everywhere. But I know nothing about setting up venues and figuring out the logistics. You know, lodging, meals and stuff."

"Doesn't it take a lot of money to do that? I mean for marketing and renting driving ranges and the stuff?"

Jake nodded. "I did make some money on the tour. Not a lot, but I live pretty cheaply, and I have some savings."

Beth considered what it would require to organize a golf school that wasn't sponsored by a golf resort like the one she was attending. It wouldn't take long to figure it out. A few phone calls, a spreadsheet, a review of golf school marketing materials. But he was asking her to help him find someone, not to do it herself.

"I'll check around with people I know and see who I can recommend," she said. "Most event planners do weddings, but there's a few like me who stay away from bridezillas."

Jake laughed. "You seem to have a fairly broad disdain for weddings," he said. "But thanks. Anything you can tell me would be great."

They fell into a companionable silence. Beth lifted her head to the slight, dry breeze that blew across the patio and stared out at the mountains.

"You want to talk about it?" Jake said. Beth frowned, trying to understand his question.

"About what?"

"Well, things seemed fine this morning on the driving range. But you came back from lunch upset."

Beth turned away from his eyes. "Dan stood me up for lunch," she muttered.

"Frost delay?"

"Yeah. How'd you know?"

"It was posted in the clubhouse this morning."

"Why didn't you tell me?"

Jake smiled crookedly. "I didn't know what your plans were. You just told me you were busy at noon and couldn't eat with me. You didn't tell me why."

Beth acknowledged the fact with a nod. "So, Dan shows up an hour late."

"I'd never do that."

Beth ignored that. It was easy for him to say, but it was unlikely that he would need to prove it in her lifetime. She searched his eyes for sincerity. If she was reading him right, he was offering himself up as an alternative to Dan. But was this real, or was this just a golf instructor thing, like George had suggested?

She breathed deep for courage and plunged in. "Do you know George?" she asked.

"You mean George as in George and Ryan, the Bobbsey Twins?" He sneered. "Sure, I know George. Is that who Dan played with this morning."

"Every day. And George has apparently convinced Dan that you are one dangerous dude, out to steal every man's woman."

"I'm not surprised," Jake said, nearly under his breath.

"Want to tell me what happened?"

Jake shook his head. "You know, I really don't. All I can say is it wasn't whatever George thought it was."

"That doesn't surprise me." She finished her seltzer and motioned to the bartender for another. "But you know ... " she paused. She wasn't sure she wanted to continue. "You know what happened the other day? Between us? On that putting green? And the day before on the fairway?"

"So I suppose George told you I do that all the time," he said, sardonically. He was hurt. "Any chance I get, I trap women on the putting green between my arms."

Beth put her hand on Jake's forearm and squeezed it lightly. "I don't care what George told me. But I do wonder. Does this happen to you all the time? Or is there something special here?"

"You mean between us?

Exasperation seeped from Jake's lips. He looked away. "It doesn't matter, Beth. You're getting married. You're planning your honeymoon. What difference does it make how I feel about you? I've only known you for a few days, and you're leaving in a couple more. Our last lesson together is tomorrow morning. It's not even a full day."

She was as sad as he was, she realized. She had felt warm and happy with his arms along hers. She loved the way being outdoors and laughing with her seemed like enough for him. He didn't need to prove—any more than she did—that he was marriageable, could settle down and make a family, could make a million dollars a year in stock options. Those were Dan's measures. Not hers. And apparently not Jake's.

And now she'd accused Jake of something she shouldn't even have listened to.

"I'm sorry," she said. She held up her left hand. "But see? No ring. Things could change, Jake. If I knew for sure how you felt about me, maybe things could change. Maybe the desert wouldn't be so bad for me. But I'd have to know if we'd have a chance ..."

She was stopped by Jake's face. He didn't just like her. She knew it was more than that. And while she had vowed to stop encouraging him, her feelings overrode her resolve. She held her breath, and they held each other's gaze. As he leaned toward her, she closed her eyes. His lips were warm and full, and she let herself sink into them.

Then her phone rang, startling them both. They quickly jerked apart, and Beth looked at the screen.

"Oh! This is the call I was waiting for." She looked at Jake apologetically. "Can you hold on a just a second?" She stood up and walked a few feet away. She listened and nodded.

"Yes! Yes, of course. I can start next Monday. That will be great,"

She looked over to see Jake's smile fall away. "I'll see you then," she said and hung up.

"That was the call! I got the job!" she said, sliding back onto her bar stool.

Jake stared at his beer and said nothing. Beth nudged him with her elbow. "Isn't that good news?"

He shrugged. Then he looked up and forced a smile. "Congratulations, Beth. I'm sure you'll be great at it."

He stood up and pulled a few bills out of his wallet. "We should go. You have a lot to get ready for. I won't hold you to your last lesson. Maybe you should get back to Seattle as soon as you can."

Beth reached out to stop him. "But I don't want us to end it like this." At least she didn't think she did. But would it be better to stop this flirtation before it got deeper, harder to pull away from?

Jake answered for her. "You have to go back to Seattle. It's probably better now than …" He started to walk away. She jumped down and followed him.

"Our timing sucks. We could have …"

She couldn't figure out what more she could say. They walked to his car.

Fourteen

J<small>AKE PULLED UP TO THE</small> hotel portico and waited for Beth to get out, but she didn't move, unable to figure out what to say.

"Look," Jake said without looking over at her. "Let's not belabor this. You need to get back to Seattle. I've got another client starting tomorrow afternoon. We should just say goodbye now."

Hurt by his sudden frostiness but understanding his disappointment, Beth nodded. "Okay. I guess you're right. Goodbye, Jake." She leaned over the console, brushed her lips against his cheek, and got out of the car.

He drove away without looking back. Finally, as he disappeared around a corner, she turned and walked into the lobby.

She was digging in her backpack for her room key when Dan suddenly stood in front of her, holding a dozen huge roses. He was wearing neatly pressed summer-weight wool pants, a button-down shirt and his loafers. What happened to his golf attire? He looked like he had just taken a shower; his hair was slightly damp and combed back from his forehead.

"What's this?" she asked, pointing to the flowers. "Meeting George for dinner?"

Dan grimaced. "I'm sorry, Beth," he said. "I'm so sorry about lunch. I should have left the guys and met you at noon like I promised." He pushed the flowers toward her. She took them silently. Dan stepped closer and kissed her on the lips. She didn't kiss him back.

"And I'm sorry about George, about him harassing you last night. And me grilling you. I should have trusted you."

Maybe not, she thought, turning away. It was Jake's kiss, not Dan's that burned on her lips.

"I got the job," she said quietly.

"Great!" Beth jumped as Dan's voice went from a near whisper to a shout. "Congratulations! We have to celebrate!"

When she didn't look back at him, he walked around to face her.

"Aren't you happy?' He kissed her again and backed up. He looked confused at her cold response. "Well, you should get cleaned up, and we'll go to dinner. You must be famished. I'll call in a reservation."

Beth shook herself out of her funk. Yes, dinner would be good, given that she had no lunch. "Nothing fancy," she said straight-faced. "Let's just stay here, eat at the restaurant. I don't feel like going out."

"Okay. That's fine," Dan said, walking her to the elevator. "You're doing your last lesson tomorrow, right? You should rest up tonight. And maybe we should leave early. Get back to Seattle? Maybe Friday instead of Saturday? You'll want time to get ready. And I'm going to be swamped at work when we get back."

"Right," she said flatly. "I'm skipping the last lesson.

Maybe we should play tomorrow, just the two of us. Let's see if this trip was worthwhile. But without George. And then let's leave on Friday."

"Sure!" It sounded like he was missing her clues entirely. She wasn't excited about dinner or golf or leaving. Nothing seemed to matter right then.

As the elevator door opened, he let her walk in alone. "You clean up, and I'll go to the clubhouse to get us a tee time for the morning. What time you want to meet for dinner? 6:30?"

"Sure, whatever." The elevator doors closed, and Beth rode up, her face buried in the roses.

By THE TIME BETH'S SALAD arrived at their table in the dining room of the hotel that night, she had already consumed two full flutes of champagne and was starting to regain her sense of humor. What had she been thinking? That she and Jake would live together in Palm Springs—a place where a big, shaggy dog like ChiChi could never be comfortable—working on her golf game? How would she keep him away from the next good-looking beginner who graced his practice tees?

Yes, his kiss was seductive. He was seductive. He acted like he understood her, but what did he know about her life? What did he understand about her love for dogs and Seattle rain and strong coffee and good Columbia Valley wines? Not much. And yet, here she had been fantasizing about … well, she wasn't really sure what the brief fantasy had been, but at least it had been brief. She could be proud of that.

"I'm sorry about this afternoon," she said. She tried to look contrite. Was it working?

Dan looked confused. "Sorry about what? I was the one who was late for lunch."

"No, I mean I'm sorry about not being more grateful

for the roses, for pouting. I should have been happy about the job. I don't know where my head was."

Dan nodded, probably pleased about being let off the hook for missing their lunch date. Her contrition was a relief. "You're probably tired," he said. "It's hard playing golf every day. Even I get tired. Maybe we should take the day off tomorrow. Sit by the pool?"

"No, we need to play," she said. "I need to see if I really learned anything, or if I just looked better because we were playing a scramble."

"You mean you and Jake?"

"Yeah." She shook her head. Her and Jake. That wasn't going to be such a thing as "her and Jake" anymore. "And we won't be able to play in the sun again for months."

"Rain, rain, and more rain," Dan said. "What are we going back for?"

Beth blinked. She was actually looking forward to going back. First, there was ChiChi. She needed to bury her face in the big dog's furry back and soak up some unconditional love. Second, she was a bored with the unchanging weather in the desert. The same dry, sunny day over and over. She liked Seattle's rain. Or drizzle. Or whatever it is. On the other hand, would Seattle's rainy winter cause her to lose whatever golf skills she's picked up over the past week?

"When do your new clubs arrive?" Dan asked.

"Ten days, they said," she said. "I hope they don't rust before I get a chance to use them."

"But you'll be busy with the new job," he said. "Time flies. Before you know it, we'll be furiously planning our wedding."

That word "wedding" stopped Beth cold. Oh, that! She knew Jake wasn't part of her future, but did that mean she had now accepted as fate that she was marrying Dan?

As if to answer her unspoken question, Dan stood up

and dug in his pants pocket. Immediately, she knew what he was doing.

"Oh, no," she uttered under her breath.

Dan knelt next to her chair and held out a diamond ring. "I've waited too long to give you this. You've already said you'd marry me. But will you say it again?"

Beth looked at the ring. It was pretty. The diamond wasn't as ostentatious as it could have been, given Dan's salary. And it was set in a wide, platinum band with just enough filigree to be interesting. She looked at it sadly.

It was time.

She nodded.

"What?" Dan said, egging her on.

"Yes, I will marry you."

Dan stood up and put his hand out. She laid her palm on his, and he slipped the ring on her finger. As he sat back down, Beth glanced out toward the patio. Jake sat watching them. He twirled his Scotch on the rocks and held up the glass to toast what he'd just seen.

She quickly looked away.

Fifteen

BETH BRUSHED HER TEETH, WASHED her face, and kicked off her shoes. Barefoot, she pulled open the sliding door to her room's balcony and stepped out with the phone to her ear.

"This is Ellen," her mother answered her call.

"Hi, Mom. It's me."

Just then a motorcycle started up in the parking lot below, and Beth stepped back inside and closed the door. She sat down on the bed, staring at the mountains in the distance.

"Beth? What is that noise? Where are you?"

"Sorry, Mom. I was out on the balcony and a Harley just started up."

"Oh. Your father and I were just talking about you, wondering how the lessons are going."

"Oh, fine," Beth said. "But I'm calling to tell you I'm coming home early. I can pick ChiChi up Friday afternoon.

I got the job at Starbucks. I'm anxious to get home and get ready. I start on Monday already."

"Congratulations, dear," her mom said. "I am happy for you. Are you excited?"

"Yes, I am."

"But do you have to pick up ChiChi? Maybe she'd like to stay with me this weekend."

Beth laughed. "I know you'll miss her. But you will have plenty of babysitting opportunities once I go to work. ChiChi will probably see you more than she'll see me."

Her mother proceeded to tell her a half-dozen ChiChi stories. How she'd chased a squirrel who was now visiting her every day, sitting on the fence to chatter insults at her. How she wouldn't let Beth's father sit on the sofa, having decided it belongs to dog and mom only. And more. Beth listened patiently. She missed the furry dog enough that even her mother's long-winded tales couldn't bore her.

"Well, lots to talk about, Mom," she said, finally cutting off the narratives. "I'll see you day after tomorrow."

Beth lay back on the bed and stared at the ceiling. Telling her mother about the new job was easy. What she'd avoided telling her was the news she was less likely to take well—the formal engagement. The ring. The promise to plan a November wedding. Ellen wasn't fond of Dan in the first place, and now that she and ChiChi had bonded so, it was unlikely she was going to like him as a dog-averse son-in-law.

Beth raised her left hand and looked at the ring. It was attractive. It was tasteful, although probably expensive. She could do worse than Dan. Stable, wealthy, healthy Dan. She tried to think back to when she fell in love with him—or at least when she had convinced herself she had. But she couldn't put her finger on any kind of turning point that represented "falling" in love. Somehow the idea that she loved him had taken over her mind and body like some low-impact chronic disease that wasn't necessarily difficult or unpleasant but was impossible to purge. Did she really think it was that bad? A chronic disease? She remembered telling Jake it was like a bad habit.

She thought about her friend Deb's relationship with Jason. It wasn't always smooth, from what Deb told her. But it seemed passionate, mulit-layered, intriguing. Maybe that's how all relationships looked from the outside. Maybe on the inside, they were all either tempestuous or boring.

Would it be the same with Jake? The charge she got out of being next to him—and that kiss!—was more powerful than anything she could remember experiencing with Dan. Or had she forgotten? Had Dan once thrilled her the way Jake did? She tried to remember Dan's first kiss. It had slipped her mind.

Weary from the rollercoaster of the day's emotions, Beth scooted off the bed and pulled off her dress. She threw it over the easy chair in the corner and slipped under the covers. She reached up to switch off the lamp next to the bed and lay back on the pile of pillows. She held her hand up and looked at the gleam of the diamond in the pale light from the parking lot.

Probably, she thought, she'd feel less conflicted about marrying Dan in the morning. Perhaps a round of golf together would be just what she needed to put Jake out of her mind and remember why she agreed to marry Dan in the first place. And if that didn't work, at least back in Seattle, she'd have ChiChi and a job. Whatever happened, she'd be okay. Better than okay. She'd be just fine.

THE SUN WAS JUST ABOUT to rise above the clubhouse behind them when Dan teed off the next morning with Beth watching. The air was crisp and the mountains to the west were pink from the early, angled rays. Beth imagined this could be her first great day of golf with Dan, ever.

Of course, that was too much to expect.

She had just walked to her tee box, set her ball, and taken a practice swing when she felt Dan's heavy presence, already judging, already critical. Taking a deep breath, she tried to ignore him and lined up for her shot. Immediately Dan yelled. She turned, and he ran up to her holding his hands in the air.

"Stop. Stop!" he yelled. "Honey, stop. You are standing too far from the ball. Didn't Jake show you this?"

He stood behind her and pushed her closer to the ball.

"There. That's better. Go ahead." He backed away.

Beth took another deep breath and tried to shake off her irritation. She lowered her shoulders like Jake had told her, but her arms were stiff, her hands too tight, and the ball never left the ground. It skittered about thirty feet, not even reaching the fairway.

She picked up her tee and stomped to the cart. "I wish you'd just let me play. I am not out here to get a lesson. I just want to play golf. Okay?" She threw her club into the bag and pulled out a smaller fairway wood. She strode forward to hit her second shot.

Dan pulled the cart up beside her. "Okay. But you're never going to enjoy the game if you don't have the right basics. And your setup on the tee box is one of the basics."

She tried to block out his voice, took her swing, and hit a fairly decent shot. Not great, but not as bad as the first one.

As they worked their way to the first green, she tried to relax. She watched how Dan took his practice swings, set up to the ball, and swung the club. Perhaps if she could garner something helpful from his example, she could rescue the day.

On the green, Dan putted first. Beth watched him sink the ball from about twenty feet. "Great putt, Dan. It looks like all that practice you had this week didn't hurt," she said.

She stepped up to her ball and lined up for her putt. She stroked, and the ball just slipped past the hole. It wasn't a bad shot. Just not a one-putt.

"You looked up," Dan scolded.

She glared at him. "What?"

"You looked up at the hole before you were finished with the stroke. That will always push the ball right for a right-handed golfer. Didn't Jake teach you anything?"

Disgusted, Beth picked her ball up. She slammed the putter back in her bag and sat in the cart.

"Aren't you going to putt out?" Dan asked. "You can't keep your score if you don't putt."

She waited until he got in the cart before answering.

"I'll say it once and not again. This is not a lesson. And I don't care about keeping score. Just leave me alone and let me play. Okay?"

Dan threw his hands in the air, surrendering, and drove to the next tee box. "Okay, I just want us to have fun when we play golf together, and you'll have a lot more fun if you stop making these mistakes."

"To you, they're mistakes," she said. "To me, it's just a shot. I can't imagine what our honeymoon golf trip will be like."

"Well, you've got a year to practice," Dan said, proving how clueless he was. "But I don't think I'll pay for any more lessons from Jake."

"Would you just drop it?" They'd finished only one hole and already Beth was angry. "Drop the Jake thing? Jake and are nothing to each other. Never were. There's only room for two people in this cart. No room for Jake. No room for George. Okay?"

Dan shook his head like he didn't understand her anger. "Okay. I'm sorry. I'll drop it." He stopped the cart, grabbed his driver, and walked up to the tee. "It's just that you two just looked awfully buddy-buddy at lunch," he said quietly, as if he wasn't sure he should say it out loud.

"What do you mean? What lunch?" Beth asked. Then she remembered. She remembered Dan and his new buddies watching them from just off the patio the day she and Jake went shopping for clubs.

"You mean Sunday? It looked like you were spying on me."

"No, we just happened to walk by when you two were on the patio."

"So that's why you didn't want me to have lunch with him again."

Dan stood with his club in his hands. "What was going on between you two?"

Beth didn't know if she should waste her breath answering. He had clearly already formed his own answer.

"We became friends," she said. "That's all. And I'll never see him again, so I don't know why this continues to bug you so much."

"It bugs me because—"

She cut him off. "You said you'd drop it!"

"Okay. Yes. I will," he said, turning to line up his drive. "Let's see if we can just forget it and enjoy the beautiful day."

"Yes. Let's." But by this time, only on the second of eighteen holes, Beth knew it was a lost cause.

PULLING UP TO THE CART barn after the eighteenth hole, Dan was figuring out their scores as he drove.

"Want to know what you got?" he asked. It was the first word either of them had said to the other in more than two hours.

"No thanks. I really don't." She shook her head and got out of the cart, pulling off her glove and putting her ball back in the bag.

Dan smiled broadly and waved the scorecard at her.

"Boy that week of golf really improved my game. I'm going to have to reconsider how much I'm working when we get back. Maybe I should find a little more time for golf."

He hopped out of the cart and chatted with the attendant who came over to clean their clubs. Beth walked away, heading for the hotel.

"Hey, wait up," he said. "I'll just arrange for them to bring our bags up. What do you want to do for lunch?"

"How about nothing," she said under her breath. She straightened up and turned to him. "I'd like to just grab a sandwich at the cantina and go to my room. I have to pack, and I'm really exhausted. Then I think I'll finally have that drink at the pool. Alone."

"Okay, I'm going to take a nap. How about dinner?"

"We have a seven o'clock flight in the morning. Do you mind if I just order room service and go to bed early?"

"No," he said, his eyebrows knit with confusion. He walked up to her. "I suppose that's fine. I'm sorry our vacation is ending on such a bad note. Maybe when we get home, we can talk things over and get back on track."

So, he did notice. He may not have minded their total lack of communication over sixteen holes, but now he finally seemed to realize they had a problem.

"Yes," she said. "We will have to do that."

Sixteen

BETH CHANGED INTO HER SWIMMING suit, determined to wear it at least once on this "vacation," and headed for the pool. She doubted she'd even get in the water. All she wanted was to sit by the pool and drink until she fell asleep in the warm desert sun.

She threw her towel on a lounge chair, kicked off her flip-flops, and walked to the edge of the pool. She sat with her feet in the water. A waiter took her drink order, and Beth leaned back with her hands on the concrete behind her and turned her face to the sun. This, she thought, was what she probably should have been doing the past six days. It would have been much better preparation for taking a new job on Monday. Better than what she'd done: Falling for her golf instructor. Fighting with Dan. Wasting money on a set of custom golf clubs.

Was that what she had done? Did she fall for Jake? Or was it just a vacation infatuation? When would she know which it was? As she played with Dan that morning, Jake was constantly on her mind. But that didn't prove anything. And it had been so long since she'd had a real crush on a man, she wasn't sure how serious to take it.

The waiter delivered her drink, and Beth stood up and stretched out on her lounge chair. Three drinks later, she put the back of the seat down and let herself fall asleep, her face in the shade of a big deck umbrella, her legs warmed by the late fall rays.

It was midafternoon when Beth left the pool and started packing for the trip home. She nibbled on a sandwich and while she folded up her golf clothes, she worked on a single-serving bottle of pinot grigio she had bought in the gift shop. She was nearly finished packing—as much as she could be before brushing her teeth again in the morning.

With her wine glass in hand, she opened the slider to her balcony and stepped out. Down on the driving range below, Jake was finishing a lesson with his new customers—a couple of women. She watched as he stepped up behind one of them with his arms alongside of hers and their hands together on the club. It was just as she remembered. She shook her head, disgusted with herself, and walked back inside.

THE FLIGHT TO SEATTLE WAS full, and Beth should have been happy to have a first-class ticket. The seat was comfortable, she had a bottomless mimosa, and the novel she had brought with her was engaging. But she was sitting next to Dan, who was focusing on the view out the window. She didn't feel happy.

They had just become formally engaged after nearly a year of an informal betrothal, and overnight she had become intolerant of him. It wasn't because his behavior had changed. It was her attitude. Perhaps the ring was the cause—was she now at the point of no return? By accepting it, her mouth had committed to something her heart had not. Yet. Perhaps it would once they were back to their normal lives and the idea sank in.

The plane climbed above a cloud layer over Pasadena on the far side of the San Jacinto Mountains from Palm Springs, and Dan turned away from the view to her.

"What did you do for dinner last night?" he asked.

'Room service." Beth tried to put some warmth into her voice. All morning, her responses had been mostly monosyllabic and cold.

"Good?"

"Just a sandwich. The wine helped."

"Did you put it on the room?"

"Yes. Was that alright?" For the first time on the vacation, she wondered if she should have been paying for some things. She didn't have any money, but she had credit cards, and soon she'd be making a nice salary. "I can pay you back. I can pay you back for this whole trip. Just give me a couple of months to get caught up on bills."

"Not necessary," he said, smiling and reaching for her hand.

"Well, I'm quite sure you don't think you got your money's worth from those golf lessons," she said. She considered saying she was sorry, but she wasn't sure what she'd be apologizing for. She'd tried. She'd made progress. It just wasn't apparent when she played with Dan. And for that, he needed to apologize; she didn't.

"It doesn't matter," he said. And he returned his gaze to the clouds out the window.

BETH WAS EXHAUSTED BY THE time she retrieved her car from her apartment garage and drove to her mother's house to get ChiChi. But seeing the big dog run to her with such joy gave her a temporary shot of adrenaline. She dropped to her knees and tried to hug the wiggling malamute, who twirled in and out of her arms as if she couldn't decide where she wanted to be scratched first.

Ellen stood over them watching. "You'd think she was mistreated while you were gone."

"You're probably tired of sitting up on that old couch with Grandma, aren't you little girl?" Beth asked ChiChi in her doggie-talk voice. "That Grandma is so mean!"

Finally, the tangle of fur, legs, and tail settled down, and Beth stood up. She followed her mother to the kitchen with ChiChi at her heels.

"Coffee?" Her mother held up the carafe from the old Mr. Coffee she'd been using for years.

"Sure," Beth said. "I could use a pick-me-up."

Her mother reached in the cabinet for the coffee can and filters, and Beth changed her mind. "Could you make it decaf. I didn't get much sleep last night. I need to go to bed early."

Her mother lifted an eyebrow suspiciously. "Not much sleep?"

Beth laughed. "It wasn't what you're probably thinking. No, Dan never saw the inside of my room nor I his."

"Well, why didn't you sleep? Didn't you have fun?"

Beth considered her answer as she watched her mother measure out the coffee and fill the maker with water.

"I had fun. But Dan and I tried to play a round together yesterday, and that was anything but fun."

"Then, when was it fun?"

"The lessons were fun," Beth said, spreading her hand out and looking at her ring again. "I had a great time with Jake. He was the best part of the trip."

Her mother pointed at the ring. "You mean that wasn't the best part?"

Beth shook her head, exasperated. "I don't even know why I accepted this." She sighed and felt her body sag. "But maybe now that we're back home, things will settle back down. Maybe Dan and I can get close again."

"You know, that's what vacations are supposed to do for you—bring couples together. You get away from all the worries back home and focus on each other. I'm sorry it didn't happen."

Beth was surprised her mother was saying anything vaguely sympathetic about her relationship with Dan. She'd never liked him, but maybe the ring had changed things for her mother, too—just in the opposite direction.

"I'm afraid Dan was more focused on his two new golfing buddies than he was on me," Beth said.

"And you, my dear. What were you focused on?" Her mother looked at her with soft eyes.

"Oh, it's not important, Mom. I'm sure I'm not the first girl to fall for her golf instructor."

Her mother rounded the bar and put an arm over Beth's shoulder. "Well, you'd better figure things out before next November. If this"—she pointed at the ring again—"is a mistake, it's better to know it sooner than later."

Seventeen

GETTING HOME DIDN'T HELP, AFTER all. Settling down and getting into a regular routine still didn't bring Beth any closer to feeling sanguine—let alone happy—about her official engagement. But the new job distracted her most of the time and kept her from panicking over her sense that her relationship with Dan was crumbling a little more every time they got together.

"Not hungry?" Dan asked her at dinner a couple of weeks after she had started working at Starbucks. Beth shrugged and pushed the green beans on her plate into straight lines.

"More tired than hungry," she answered.

"Do you like the new job?" Dan asked.

"So far." Beth quit trying to eat and pushed her plastic Lean Cuisine plate across the kitchen bar. Each day at work she was being thrown into more projects, learning the Starbucks way of doing things along the way. She expected it would take a few more weeks before she felt fully comfortable there.

"I mean, what do you know about a job at first?" she said. "Really? It's not much different from my last job except that there's a lot of pomp and circumstance about 'team'—you know, 'team player,' doing it 'for the team,' and such. No one is an employee. Everyone is an 'associate.' Kind of kitschy, I think."

Dan nodded. "It takes a while to settle in, get the feel for a new culture." He'd been patient with her refusal to see him more than twice a week while she was adjusting to the new job. Beth appreciated that.

She stood up to rinse her plate off in the sink before shoving it in the near-full garbage can. Dan got up and did the same. He stretched and looked across the bar into the living room, where ChiChi had made herself comfortable on Beth's couch. After her stay at Ellen's house, the dog had decided there were new rules, and she liked them.

"Hey, dog! Get off the couch!" Dan yelled.

ChiChi lifted her head and looked blankly at him. Then she slowly laid her big jaw back down between her front paws and closed her eyes.

"Her name is ChiChi, not 'dog,'" Beth said. "And I don't think she's going to listen to you. Not after a week with Mom."

Dan shook his head, disgusted. "Oh, well, I'm sure she'll be adopted soon now that you're back to take care of it."

Beth hesitated. She hadn't broken the news to him yet—the news that she had adopted ChiChi before they left for Palm Springs. She wiped the bar down with a sponge and dried her hands on a paper towel. She took a deep breath.

"Uh. Actually, Dan," she started, sitting back down on the barstool. "I have to tell you something."

Dan turned to her with a look that indicated he knew

he wasn't going to like this.

"What?"

"I adopted ChiChi a week before we left for Palm Springs. She's my dog now."

Dan threw up his hands. "I thought we had an agreement. No more dogs."

"It was less of an agreement than a unilateral decision," Beth said, surprised she could sound so calm and rational. "I never agreed."

"Yes, you did. I'm sure you did."

"Dan," she said, "sometimes you assume people are going along with you just because they quit arguing."

"Oh, really? Like when?"

Beth swallowed. It was time to admit her ambivalence about their engagement. "Like when you decided we were getting married. You never really asked. You just assumed."

"Didn't you say yes in Palm Springs?"

"Yes, but that was long after you—"

Dan cut in. "And now you don't know?"

Beth had no answer. Dan waited for one, even though her silence probably spoke louder than her words would have. When was she going to be strong enough, brave enough, honest enough to accept her mistake and put her voice to it?

Dan waited for her answer, but she sat mute. He slammed his palms on the counter, eliciting a growl from ChiChi, and stomped to the front door. He pulled his rain jacket off the hook.

"I don't know what more to say, Beth. Why don't you think about this for a couple of days? We need to figure this out before we make any more plans."

He slipped on his jacket, and then hesitated, as if he was waiting for her to call him back. When she didn't, he gave her one last glance and opened the door.

"Goodnight," he said, and disappeared.

Beth rose from the stool and plopped down on the couch next to ChiChi. The dog moved her head over onto Beth's lap and closed her eyes again. Beth scratched her ears affectionately. "He didn't even say goodnight to you, did he?"

BETH WAS VAGUELY AWARE OF someone standing in the doorway of her office, but her mind was elsewhere. It wasn't until Deb's voice rose to a near shout before she shook herself out of her reverie and paid attention.

"What?" she said.

"Do you want to join me for lunch?"

Beth shook her head. "Nah. I'm not hungry. Go on without me."

Instead, Debra walked in and sat down in the chair in front of Beth's desk. She twisted and lowered her head to try to catch Beth's downturned eye.

"Okay. 'fess up, sister. What's going on?"

Beth shrugged. She didn't feel like talking, afraid that even opening her mouth to speak would unlock the floodgates to the tears she was holding back.

Beth continued, all business. "You don't seem like you're really here. If you want to keep this job, you've got to get into the team spirit. You've got to start acting like you want to be part of the team."

Beth lost her battle with the tears, turned her head to look out the window, and tried to wipe her eyes without Deb noticing.

"I just don't know what I'm doing here," she said. She pointed at the rain. "Look at that."

"At what? It always rains here in the winter."

"I'm quite aware of that," Beth said with a bit of unintended snark. "I've lived here all my life."

Deb said nothing for a long minute, and finally Beth looked back at her.

"I have a feeling this has something to do with that golf instructor," Deb said, a crooked smile on her face. "It's really not the weather, is it?"

Beth shook her head and smiled, embarrassed at the truth. "Yes," she said. "It's the weather."

Deb chuckled and held her eyes.

"Okay, no," Beth said.

Deb's voice softened. "Is he thinking about you?"

"I don't know." She didn't really want to talk about Jake with anyone. She was afraid it would extend his presence in her mind. Already she was frustrated by how many weeks she'd thought about him, long after she should have gotten over her schoolgirl crush.

"What do you know?" Deb wasn't giving up.

"Well." Beth hesitated, but continued. "Dan sent me an email he got from Jake thanking him for taking lessons. It had Jake's phone number attached."

"So?"

"So he and Dan didn't exactly hit it off. Dan didn't even last a day in the lessons. There was no reason for Jake to send that email to him—no reason unless he was hoping I'd get his number that way. I don't think Dan understands that or he wouldn't have forwarded it to me. But clearly, Jake is leaving it up to me to call him—if I want to. After all, I was the one who walked away that last day with nothing to say."

Deb nodded and pursed her lips. She stood, picked up Beth's cell phone from her desk, and handed it to her.

"Here," she said. "Only one way to find out."

Beth took the phone and stared at it as if she weren't quite sure how to use it. She looked up at Deb. "Right," she said. "Why don't I make a phone call and meet you down at lunch in a few?"

Beth waited until Deb was out of earshot, and still she couldn't bring herself to select Jake's number she'd taken off of his email to Dan and stored in her phone. She imagined Jake standing in the bright sunshine of mid-day on the driving range, an eager young woman hanging on his words, watching his beautiful swing. She didn't realize she'd actually dialed the number until he answered.

"Hello?"

"Jake?"

"Beth?" Did he recognize her voice, or was he guessing only she would be calling him from a 206 area code?

"Hi ... Jake." She hadn't practiced what to say, and now she stumbled for words. "Are you busy right now?"

"Uh." Jake apparently hadn't practiced what to say if she called, either. "Uh, Beth? Um." He paused again, but then his voice strengthened, and he sounded more like himself. "I'm giving a lesson. But I can take a minute. I'm surprised. What's up?"

"I have two questions for you. Okay?"

He paused. "Okay."

"Well, the first is sort of silly. Or I should say I'm a little embarrassed to ask it. But what really happened with you and George's girlfriend?"

Jake chuckled and Beth could imagine his smile as he formed his answer. "Well, it's simple. I know Dan will probably never believe it. George certainly never did. This is it: She was furious with George and thought she'd get even by coming on to me. I'll have to admit it kind of worked. At first. But once I figured out what was going on, I ran as far away from her as I could. By then, she'd lost interest in both of us. Me and George."

"Oh." Beth let that information soak in.

"Good answer?"

"As long as it's true."

Jake laughed. "Of course it is."

Beth was surprised he took that personal question so well. If it weren't true, could he have answered so easily?

"What's the second question?" he asked, trepidation back in his voice.

"Oh, this is easier," she said. "Do you like dogs?"

Eighteen

BETH WAITED FOR DAN AT a booth next to the window at a seafood restaurant on the waterfront and watched the gulls swoop up and down over the pier. She had a hard time imagining living anywhere but Seattle, where the wide bays of Puget Sound dominated the views west, the great peak of Mount Rainier punctuated the view south, and the Cascade Range lined the horizon to the east. Palm Springs had been a nice, warm, sunny break in the otherwise drizzly and gray winter, but it wasn't home.

Jake had responded enthusiastically to the pictures of ChiChi she had sent to his cellphone, and they had fallen into a routine of swapping short text messages about the weather, work, and ChiChi. Their exchanges were platonic and trivial; apparently neither of them wanted to venture into anything more personal or revelatory. But it was a start, Beth thought. It was friendship. And didn't all true loves start that way? As friends first?

She wasn't sure she wanted more than friendship with Jake, especially if they continued to live this far from each other. But even a long-distance, platonic relationship was more satisfying than her relationship with Dan these days. Dan no longer seemed as much hurt as disappointed by what had happened to them.

And now it was time to stop disappointing him and get off the fence.

Dan spotted her from the hostess desk and waved meekly. She was surprised again—like she had been in Palm Springs—at how his confident, authoritative personality seemed to evaporate around her these days. He walked across the restaurant, his worried look indicating he knew why she'd asked him there.

"You wanted to talk?" he said, standing next to the booth.

"Yeah. Join me?"

Dan shrugged off his raincoat and slid into the booth across from her. "Why do I have a bad feeling about this?" he asked.

"Look," she said. She smiled wearily. "We both know we have to do this. It's not easy, but it's time."

Dan looked out the window at the gulls and the water and the shores of West Seattle in the distance. "Is this about Jake?"

"Kind of," Beth admitted. "But not in the way you think. I'm not in love with him."

"Yet," Dan added for her. The scene outside held his stare.

"Yes. Yet," she said. "Jake helped me realize that there are others out there, men I might have more of a connection with. And maybe with Jake it will grow into something more. But, really, Dan. It's not about Jake. It's really about us."

He refused to meet her eyes. Could a man so strong

and successful in business be so ill-equipped for affairs of the heart? If he was hurt, he couldn't admit it. He couldn't fight for her. Maybe he'd never invested much of his heart in her. Maybe it was just another item on his "grown-up" checklist that he needed to complete: Get married, have kids. Anyone would do.

She slipped off the ring and held it out to him in her open palm. He glanced at it and finally looked her in the eye.

"I guess it's been obvious for some time. But that doesn't make it easy."

"I know," she agreed. "But we've spent a lot of time together, and it just isn't working. I think trying to play golf together was a great idea. It showed us that the problem wasn't just a lack of mutual interests."

"Is it the dog thing?"

"It's not that simple either. It's not one thing."

A waiter approached their booth, and Dan waved him away. "No," he said. "You're right." He returned his gaze to the window. "I guess this is it, then?"

She nodded, holding the ring in her outstretched hand. "I know you really want marriage, a family. But you have to find the right person. Not just anyone. Not just the woman you picked up by the hamburgers and baked beans at a picnic."

Dan smiled at her description, perhaps at the memory.

"So, yeah. This is it." He picked the ring out of her palm and twirled it in his fingers.

"Yeah. It is."

Neither of them said anything for a long minute. Then Beth picked up the menu lying in front of her. "But as long as you're here, how about some fish and chips?"

"So it's just for the weekend?" Deb asked Beth as they stood together at the window in Beth's office, staring out at the rain. "You're going to fly down there and back and be at work on Monday? Is that even possible?"

"It's only a two-hour flight," Beth said. "And I have to know. It's the only way to figure this out. Text messages about the weather aren't telling me what I need to know."

"Haven't you talked about this at all? No phone calls? Just texts? Seems like not much to go on."

Beth turned from the window and turned off her computer. "Exactly. I can't keep trying to figure out what I feel from 1,200 miles away. I have to walk up to him, face him, and see if there's a there there."

"So to speak," Deb said, laughing. She turned from the window too, pulled Beth's raincoat off the hook behind the door, and handed it to her.

"Well, I hope figuring it out doesn't mean you'll leave us."

"I know. I like this job. And I complain about the rain, but I would miss Seattle. It's home. Do you know there are no decent fish and chips in Palm Springs?"

Deb looked at her watch. "Well, you'd better run if you're going to catch your flight. Want me to walk you out? Make sure you don't chicken out?"

"Oh, if I needed that you'd have to come all the way to the airport with me and shove me on the plane. No, I know I have to do this. I will do this."

"Well, good luck. I'll see you Monday morning, whatever happens, right?" Deb leaned in and gave Beth a quick hug.

"Right," Beth said, walking out the door. "Close up my office for me, will you?"

It was January, so it was already dark outside as Beth pulled her rollerbag out the heavy front door of the building and jerked the hood of her coat up over her hair. Her head down, fumbling with her purse, her suitcase, and her car keys, she walked into someone.

"Oh, I'm sorry!" She pushed the fabric away from her eyes and looked up.

"Jake?"

He stood before her, flashing his big, beautiful grin. "In the flesh. Fancy meeting you here!"

"I work here! What are you doing here?"

Jake took the handle of her rollerbag and put a hand under her elbow. He led her back under the overhang at the door of the building.

"Remember that golf school I wanted to start?" he said.

Beth didn't know what to say. Seeing Jake right there in a dark, rainy afternoon in Seattle was too confusing. It made no sense.

"Well, funny thing ... " Jake paused. Out of the rain, Beth could now study his face. She had thought she'd have time on the plane to Palm Springs to plan what to say to him and how to control her emotions when she saw him. But now that he was right in front of her, she couldn't think. Now she faced a rush of feelings she wasn't ready for.

"What?" she asked. She sounded as frantic as she felt. "What's going on?"

Jake put his hands on her shoulders as if to calm her down. "Remember when I told you about that guy I played with on the tour who grew up here?"

"Yeah." She thought she did.

"Well, he and his dad own a golf course south of town. They've got a big warehouse next to the course. They want to start an indoor, year-round golf school there. I came up to check it out. Maybe I can start my golf school there."

Beth took a deep breath and tried to clear her head. Seeing him was such a shock she had trouble concentrating on what he was saying.

"But that's not all of it," he continued.

"Uh-huh?"

"I know you were unsure about how you felt about us

318

weeks ago in Palm Springs. One minute I thought we were growing close, and then you'd pull away," he said. "But I wasn't confused. I knew how I felt. I felt it that first afternoon on the driving range. Even with Dan right there."

So it was about more than a golf school, Beth realized. This was about her. About them.

"But coming here," she said. "This is a big risk. What made you so sure?"

"I've been sure for a long time—since that call when you called to ask me if I liked dogs. It took me a while to arrange things and quit my job, but I took a chance that you asked for a good reason. Am I right? Was that a test?"

Beth laughed and nodded.

"So," Jake said, "I thought as long as I'm here checking out the golf school thing, maybe I should come by and check out my intuition." He glanced at her suitcase. "But I see you're headed somewhere?"

Beth shrugged. "I was. I'll bet you'll never guess where."

He squinted as if thinking hard. "Palm Springs?"

"Good guess."

He stepped forward, his eyes focusing on her lips. She reached for the lapels of his raincoat.

"I didn't know you owned one of these," she said.

He pulled her close and pressed his lips against hers. She melted into them, just as she had in Palm Springs. His kiss was the same, but this time, she didn't quit. She could give in.

Finally, they separated, and she took a half step back, looking into his eyes, her heart pounding in her ears.

His eyes were soft. Maybe, she thought through the rush of emotion, what they had between them was stronger than she had been daring enough to hope for. And maybe she didn't have to move to Palm Springs to have it.

"Know what sealed the deal for me?" he asked.

"My golf swing?" she guessed.

"Nope," he grinned. "Guess again."

She shook her head. She had no cogent thoughts, just a craving for more of his lips.

"ChiChi," he said. "Once I saw those pictures you sent, I knew I had to meet her."

Beth was amused. "ChiChi doesn't always have that effect on people. But I had a feeling..."

His kiss told her she didn't have to say any more.

Author's Note

I STARTED WRITING THESE NOVELLAS as screenplays about a month into the Covid-19 quarantine. I had passed the time that first month watching Hallmark Channel movies—something I had never done before. I found the films calming and mind-numbing in a good way. The formula was easy enough to parse, and Hallmark's guidelines are laid out clearly on its website: no violence and no sex. From watching, it was clear that swearing, religion, and politics were off-limits as well. Once I finished the screenplays, I turned them into these novellas. I imagine the readers most likely to enjoy this book will be those who enjoy Hallmark's romantic films. But even if you've never watched one in your life, I hope you find these stories calming and fun to read.

About the Author

Marjorie Pinkerton Miller* is the romance pen name for Marj Charlier, author of nine contemporary and historical novels, two romance novels, and three romance novellas. Her first historical novel, *The Rebel Nun*, was published by Blackstone Publishing and won first-place prizes for historical fiction and overall fiction in the 2023 Colorado Independent Book Publishers Association EVVY awards. A former *Wall Street Journal* reporter, she holds degrees in journalism from Iowa State University and the University of Wisconsin-Madison, and an MBA from Regis University. She lives and works in Colorado Springs, CO, with her husband, the journalist Ben Miller.

*Pinkerton was the author's paternal grandmother's maiden name, and Miller was her mother's maiden name. Marjorie is her given name.